THE UNRAVELING

E.J. FINDORFF

Printed in the United States of America

First Printing, 2017

www.ejfindorff.com

To my hometown.

CHAPTER ONE

An intense light assaulted my eyes; however my hands failed to shield them, bound by something unseen. My torso throbbed. I forced one eye open a sliver, in order to focus on my lap while in an odd sitting position. Blood coated my clothes like a tortured prisoner of war.

A single bare bulb wore a hood, which focused the light downward. The glowing orb hung from a long wire like a microphone that dropped to the center ring in a boxing match. Beyond the light's reach, the darkness seemed endless. The room floated in the universe, having broken away from the earth. I heard metallic clicks echo in the cavernous depths and the first twinges of understanding surfaced.

The bulb illuminated a female dressed in jeans and a white T-shirt. She had a sack over her head. Her exposed hands indicated she was Caucasian. Like me, ropes bound her against a metal girder extending high into the darkness. Could this be an industrial warehouse? We faced each other; about twenty yards apart, but she had no idea of my presence. Her outline sparked something familiar, but the cobwebs had yet to clear.

My dormant cop instincts assessed the situation with limited

capacity. The beam dug into my back and it hurt to breathe. My
flanks were numb from the cold concrete. Blood felt pasty and
heavy on my face as it dripped onto my chest. Fresh wounds.
They hadn't put a bag on my head for some reason. They wanted
me to view the female – to be able to witness something. My forehead stung as if gashed, and they'd for sure bruised a rib, possibly
fractured it. Struggling to break free sent searing pain into my
chest.

My life had been calm for the five years after quitting the New
Orleans Police Department to become a private security consultant.
That wasn't as much a lateral move as it was a plummet. But, a
boring and quiet home life had dulled my senses. An attack in a mall
parking lot hadn't been on my radar. The memory came back like a
scene in a movie. Just before unlocking my car door, a van had crept
by as if looking for a spot. With my back turned, at least two men
ambushed me. Silent, quick, and efficient, they knocked me out, but
not before a vicious kick to the ribs. I didn't know how long I had
been unconscious, or if my wife Fiona had reported me missing, or
if I was even still in New Orleans. They didn't want me dead – at
least not yet.

A distant shuffling of footsteps behind the unknown female
caught my attention. My blood pressure dropped when I realized
this lady had my wife's figure. I saw her wedding band. An immediate adrenaline rush shut off every nerve ending allowing my
escape campaign to renew. However, two men materialized from the
abyss, stopping on each side of her. They ignored me.

I assumed the captors to be the same ones that ambushed me.
Their medium-sized frames moved with athletic precision, like they
were experienced in mob hits. Non-descript gray jumpsuits hung
loose, complete with gloves, ski masks and glasses. The shoes resembled the Converse brand, except without the high top. The slight
man on the right reached for the sack on my wife's head, pulling it
off like a game show model revealing a prize.

It took a moment to see her face through the whipping hair. *It
was Fiona.*

My stiff and achy body surged against the restraints, but there was no give. My legs kicked out as I yelled, "You two are dead. You hear me? Fiona!"

Her eyes opened behind rogue locks of hair. She appeared to still be asleep, hazy and confused, like she had been drugged. One of the men cleared the hair to fully reveal her face. My anger cancelled out rational thinking. He yanked her head back, exposing her throat.

Her eyes widened. "Remi?" she croaked.

"I'm here, baby." My voice didn't sound like my own. "I'll get us out of this." *Not convincing.* I looked at the man holding the gun. "What do you want?"

The man ignored me, pushing Fiona's head to the side. He aimed at her leg with a steady hand and fired. Fiona screamed, which trailed off into a convulsing sob. My mind couldn't comprehend what had transpired. I'd made split-second decisions during police firefights many times, but my body froze. A smoky, chemical smell filled the air. Her body trembled. The spent shell casing lay near her jeans, which turned dark with saturation.

The shooter's head tilted toward me, as if to ask *how's that?*

"Fiona," I pleaded, "Okay, you made your point. I'll do whatever you want."

Repeating the worst moment of my life, he shot the other leg causing Fiona to wail again. My pleas went unheeded, and I couldn't recall any police training that might help. While the second man started toward me, blood pooled under her knees.

"Tell me what you want," I demanded.

Without a response, the man casually shot her in the shoulder. My wife's body fell slack, but her face grimaced. She stared forward, hyperventilating, possibly going into shock. *This was real.* This was happening. My objections blended together in a jumble. He shot the other shoulder and Fiona's body jolted, but she had stopped struggling. He placed the barrel of the gun against her head.

"Wait. No – *no* – *no* – *no*." I pleaded nonsensical words, promising them everything until eventually, only air hissed from my lungs.

The other man stepped in front of me to block my view. My

body wiggled and twisted to no avail. When the man struck my numb face, I renewed my resolve. If this were our fate, I wouldn't go out in a screaming, frantic mess. I pretended to surrender. Through my tears, I saw that the tongue on his shoes had an embroidered *Lee Street* in cursive. He descended to one knee and held out a recording device. A deep, digitized voice came through the speaker.

You are to kill Governor Steve Sharpe by Mardi Gras Day. If you fail, or tell anyone, Lily will die, same as your wife.

"Same as my wife?" My voice came out in a weak sob.

Fiona stared forward through glossy, haunted eyes. The recorder disappeared in the man's pocket as he stood. The triggerman fired a fifth time at Fiona's head. The soundless eternity of the gun jerking, her head tilting... the blood... that one act that destroyed my life hung there, the second hand refusing to tick forward.

When I finally caught my breath, time had resumed. Fiona's body fell limp. My thought process stayed in slow gear. The visual of my lifeless wife seared every cell in my brain. I threw up on the ground between my legs, almost passing out from the agony.

Through spotty flashes in my vision, the man who killed my wife crossed the distance toward me. I writhed, and my feet failed to gain purchase. My grunts and moans mixed with my tears and runny nose. The gun impacted my head and once again, a brilliant flash of light filled my vision. One of them cut the ropes and I fell sideways onto the concrete floor. My lips couldn't form words. The two attackers dropped out of sight as I attempted to get onto all fours. Like a beaten dog, I wobbled to Fiona's side, but I had failed. *I hadn't made everything all right.*

Another blow to my head knocked me out for good.

CHAPTER TWO

A dim hospital room came into view as I lay on an incline. My head pounded. A bandage had been wrapped around my chest and ribs. An IV was stuck in my arm. I lifted my head, but it felt like molasses coated my brain. My body suddenly thrashed from a residual reaction to Fiona being shot and I lost my breath. For a few moments, I wondered if that had actually happened.

Someone appeared from the side to push down on my shoulders, and I saw it was Gracie, my ex-partner and close friend. My equilibrium faltered and the room swiveled. I had to be on morphine as my senses were out of whack.

"Remi, it's me, baby. It's okay. You're okay." Her palm found my cheek as I gazed at her. She was on the tall side, a proud Latina, lean and muscular, with cute, stochastic freckles around her nose from her Irish grandfather. She was a natural detective with street smarts from having been born and raised in a poor area of Kenner near the airport. We had worked many cases together when I was on the force.

"Fiona's dead." The memories of the warehouse rushed back. "They shot her – right in front of me." I kept from breaking down.

She handed me a tissue and took my other hand, waiting until I focused. "A taxi driver found you on the Elysian Fields neutral ground near the Quarter. Fiona was there, too. And so was a 9-millimeter pistol."

"They left the gun?"

"It's being processed right now. A shell casing was found in the tangles of her hair."

I wiped my eyes while catching my breath. "Lily. They got Lily."

"We have an Amber Alert out. I have every unit available searching for her. I have a car outside your house – at your in-laws, too. What do you remember?"

"Fiona wasn't killed where you found us. Two men abducted me at Lakeside Mall, knocked me out, and I woke up in some kind of a warehouse."

"Do you know where it was?

"No idea. It was empty, from what I saw. They killed her right in front of me."

Gracie sat on the edge of the bed, facing me. She gently wiped my runny nose with a tissue. "What'd they say?"

"Nothing. Absolutely nothing." *Except for me to kill Governor Steve Sharpe.* But some wary, internal caution warned me to say nothing, at least for now.

"So, how do you know they have Lily?" Her brow furrowed.

My eyes closed. "She was home with Fiona. If they took *her,* they got them both. And now you say she can't be found."

She leaned toward me. "That doesn't mean anything. You and your stepdaughter don't have a good relationship, right?"

I grimaced while holding back a laugh at that understatement.

"She's ignored your calls before. Rebellious teen and all. She could be ignoring her phone in a bar or something. She could be with that friend of hers you say is a bad influence." Her face conveyed hope.

I took a fresh tissue and cautiously blew my nose, trying to keep the pain at a minimum. "Maybe. So, do Fiona's parents know?"

Gracie nodded. "They know. Your front door was forced open with a battering ram. Any ideas…?"

I squinted at her for a moment. "A police battering ram?"

"Can't tell that, but these things are sold on the Internet. Anyone can have them." She accepted my silence. "We'll put together a list. What'd they look like?"

I held her stare. There was a penalty for every lucid thought. "I don't know. They were covered up. Ski masks. Glasses. Jumpsuits without markings. Thin material. They had on Lee Street tennis shoes. Average to short in height. They never said a word. Nothing." I inhaled deeply and almost screamed out with pain.

"Doctor left about a half hour ago." Gracie pointed at my head. "You got fourteen stitches. A fractured rib. Lots of cuts and scrapes. Nothing is life threatening, but they want to keep you overnight." She rolled her eyes. "Well, for a few more hours until the morning at least. The doctor will come in to give the final okay. He said it could take four to six weeks for your rib to heal. You have to take it easy."

"Don't know if I can do that." Tears fell, even while I fought to keep my composure.

Gracie's phone rang and she answered it immediately. "This is Castillo." She spoke quickly, grunting and agreeing with the caller.

"What is it?" I asked after she hung up.

"Update. We're in the initial stages of the investigation. They haven't found anything yet, but Fiona was cooking at the time. Three place settings were on the table." Gracie's eyes revealed her thoughts.

"They have her." I almost lost it again, but winced instead.

Gracie gently asked, "Lee Street shoes, huh? That's off the beaten path."

"I have to get out of here." I attempted to twist my body, but lost my breath. "Jesus."

"You're not going anywhere." She cupped my cheeks, putting her nose near mine. "*It's me.* Okay? I'm on this. Every other case I have is on hold. Until we find her, Lily is my daughter, too. Trust me."

"I do trust you – with my life. But, you can't expect me to just wait here."

"I have two uniforms standing guard outside that door," Gracie stated. "I know what you're thinking."

"What am I thinking?" I pouted.

"That you're going to ignore my investigation and find Lily on your own. Is that right?" She waited.

I exhaled with discomfort. My eyes closed. "I'm not thinking any of that. I'm going to work *with* you, but I need to get out of here."

"I've arranged for your discharge in the morning. Just tell me who's at the top of your list of enemies?"

My eyes shot to hers. "It's been five years. Lots of threats back then. You were there for some of them."

She whispered, "Think about it while I'm gone. And don't do anything stupid. You always used to tell me how hard it is to deal with desperate, frantic parents."

"I won't be that parent."

"Grieve Fiona."

"You're right." A tear traced a path down my cheek. More followed.

Gracie wiped my face with tissue, then kissed the side of my head. She wrapped her arms around my neck. "I love you like my own family, you know."

"I know."

Just as Gracie stood, the door opened. My older brother Dylan entered in sweatpants and a hooded sweatshirt as if he'd been jogging. He bypassed the guards because he just happened to be a New Orleans celebrity, an ex-Saints running back in the NFL.

His expression turned grim. "I rushed right over. I can't believe this. Any news on who did this?"

Gracie answered, almost stepping in front of me like a momma bear. "We're in the initial stages. Everyone's been mobilized. As a matter of fact, I was just leaving to join CSU at Remi's house."

"Anything I can do?"

"Nothing for me." Gracie stood in the middle of the room with her hands on her hips, daring my brother to challenge her.

Dylan moved diagonally and pulled up a chair. "Remi, I'm so, so sorry." He thought to put his hands on my forearm, but pulled away. "What happened?"

"Get out of here, Dylan. I don't want to talk to you."

"Damn it, Remi. We have to get past this. Especially in a time like this."

My voice strained, "Gracie, get him out of here, please."

"Dylan – how about you try again in a few days when he's recovered a bit. You're just going to make things worse." She gently led him by the wrist.

He hesitated, looking back and forth, but didn't argue. "Alright... For now."

I stared at the ceiling until he turned to leave. The door crept closed, offering a view of one of the uniformed guards outside. My breathing eased. At this point, a girl scout wouldn't have a problem keeping me in this room.

Before the morphine took over again, I thought back to the night before Fiona's murder when life made sense. I had just taken an UBER home from a poker game hosted by Gracie and some other cops that ended early. Despite my buzz, I had maintained a straight path as Fiona played with her tablet on the couch, pretending to ignore me. This little game never lasted long, so I immersed myself into a cushion and attempted to pull her across my lap. I kissed her reluctant lips softly, tasting the residue of sweet tea. Strands of hair got caught in my mouth while roaming down her neck. Not surprisingly, she had maneuvered off me.

"I think it's time for bed," she insisted.

"Okay, but it's not really late."

Her expression remained stone. "Don't wake Lily."

I covered my mouth with exaggeration, "Sorry. Did she have a fun night with all of her *friend*? Madison."

"She's happy with the one friend." Fiona shrugged. "Sailing with that team of kids is one thing, but they haven't become her *real friends*, you know? What she needs is social interaction with a group of friends. She needs a normal boyfriend." She got up and stood in front of me with her arms folded. Her hair whipped across her shoulders.

"Normal boyfriend? Does that mean she has a boyfriend that's not normal?"

"I just mean normal kids and a boyfriend. She just turned seventeen and only has Madison, who's a questionable influence at best."

"Madison does have a wild streak." I'd tried to roam under her nightshirt, but she backed away.

Fiona was annoyed and I was oblivious, and we had argued for a few minutes until it came to a head. My wife had finally gotten to what was bothering her. Her voice was a loud whisper. "You won't talk to me about this change in you."

"What can I tell you? That I miss investigating homicides? Sure, I do. The shit was horror movie material and I loved it. But, I almost died. *I did die.* I'm good with things the way they are."

"Are you?" She leaned forward to poke my chest with her finger. "Are you?"

"For Christ's sake, I could've gotten back on the force by now."

"Tell me you're happy."

"This isn't about my happiness. It's about our happiness."

Fiona was on the verge of crying. "Do I look happy?" She had let those words settle as she walked to the bathroom. Clinking noises with a toothbrush and running water marked the end of our night.

The next day, I had every intention to apologize and give Fiona what she wanted: an in-depth conversation. She slid her slippers into the kitchen wanting coffee, like every other morning. She found me putting the finishing touches on a nice breakfast spread.

"Morning, dawlin'." I kissed her on the forehead, checking out the Medusa of hair. "Are we okay?"

"We're always okay," she had said in a raspy voice. "But, this ain't over."

"Have some coffee." I presented her favorite mug.

She pushed down on her hair in vain. "Thanks for making breakfast. I'm going to go wake up Lily."

"I'm up," Lily yelled from her bedroom, appearing at the kitchen entrance. "I'm meeting Madison after school today, so I'll be late."

Fiona replied, "No, you're not. You're punished, remember?"

I grinned awkwardly. "Grounded? Wait, you just told me she needed a social life."

Fiona looked at her daughter, then down at her food with a pause. "She used Madison as an excuse to meet up with a boy." Fiona squinted at Lily for a quick moment. "I thought it would be better if you didn't know, considering the whole father-daughter-boyfriend dating dynamic." Fiona held my gaze.

"*Step-daughter*," Lily corrected, "I already promised Madison we'd go to the movies tonight."

"Like it or not, I'm the male role model in your life right now," I said, not commenting about how her real father abandoned her. "Lily, if you want to date someone, you have to tell us. We're not going to stop you, but we need names. Your privacy will be your own *next* year." That was enough fatherly advice.

"Great speech, *Dad*." Lily rolled her eyes.

"Thanks. Gotta go. They're waiting for me. I'm helping organize security at the Dome rally. I'm going to pick up my watch after, but I should make it home for supper."

My wife planted a nice one on my lips. She grabbed me and looked in my eyes, "We're going to continue our little discussion."

"Good. I want to," I whispered into her ear. "Make us all a nice dinner, then release Lily to the movies and we'll talk. We'll really talk."

"That's all I can hope for."

Just like that, I had left Lily and Fiona alone to argue parole for the night. In just a matter of hours, my world came crumbling down around me.

CHAPTER THREE

A young, fresh-faced doctor had come into the room and gave me the rundown on how to manage my recovery once released. She gave me an envelope with instructions on wound care, phone numbers and prescriptions, then left when I had no more questions. That visit seemed like a blur.

Without interaction, sleep came and went due to my pain medication. A digital clock next to the wall-mounted television read 7:10 am. A fog settled in behind my eyes, but the tears continued. *I'm so sorry, Fiona.*

My wife and I had met four years ago on the route of Endymion, arguably the most popular parade during Mardi Gras. Six months later we were engaged, and seven months after that, we married. With Fiona, my search ended. However, her daughter Lily hated me from the start. The three of us sat down several times to try to get to the root of the problem, but Lily never expressed why. Our relationship was a work in progress, volatile at times.

The image of Lily being discarded on the streets of New Orleans the day after Mardi Gras wouldn't go away. I felt so useless, spiraling out of control, but they had empowered me, hadn't they? They gave me a choice.

What did I know about Steve Sharpe, the governor? I remembered that his security detail had been beefed up two months earlier after an attempt on his life. The news coverage went on for weeks, without any leads. As the story went, two shots fired from a distance had missed their mark and the perpetrator may as well have been a ghost. They left no evidence. There hadn't been another attempt since, but the governor hired a security firm out of his own pocket to supplement the two troopers assigned for each of his family members. Had these been the same men that abducted me? And now they devised another plan with me as the lynch pin?

In his forties, Steve Sharpe had raised two kids with an attractive wife that taught some kind of science at Louisiana State University. He had served in the Army, being honorably discharged after a bullet destroyed his kneecap. His campaign commercials constantly reminded the voters of that. He enthusiastically battled two years as a senator. But, the one thing the voters loved more than anything else, was that Steve Sharpe had been an LSU baseball star. He had thinning blond hair, was appealingly ugly, yet charming and straight-laced, even for the conservatives in Baton Rouge. He proved to be smarter than most politicians that dared challenge him.

This was the man I needed to kill.

Gracie crept through the door dressed for winter, peering through the darkness. "You up?"

"I'm up. Anything?"

"Nothing yet," she admitted, "But, we've hit a dead end with the gun."

"I figured it would be a throw-away."

"It wasn't a throw-away. It's yours. It's a Herstal FNX-9, registered to you."

"No, I saw the gun he used. It wasn't mine." I choked, wiping my eyes with the heel of my palm.

"You're right. The first thing Jerry did was test the casing. It didn't come from your gun, but it seems after taking it from your house, they wanted you to have it back."

"Are they running the shell?"

"Of course. It's being expedited through the FBI. You know the sad state of the Homicide Department. Fucking detectives fleeing left and right. No resources. We got half a staff and more killings than ever. I know they called wanting you to return several times."

"I'm desperate enough to welcome the Feds on this." The monotone words fell from my mouth. "The doctor came and went. Said I can go."

Gracie held up a bag. "I have a change of clothes." She had ditched her own outfit from yesterday, but her hair was matted and her bloodshot eyes glowed. "You need to go the morgue and identify her body."

"I know. Help me get dressed." I eased my legs over the edge of the bed.

Without embarrassment, Gracie guided me into sweatpants and a heavy coat through tolerable pain thanks to medication. The nurse brought a wheelchair and Gracie pushed me like an old man past the horde of press camped out in the freezing parking lot. They shouted their assumptions and stupid questions for lack of information. The reporters knew Gracie and me well, having headed some of the more high profile homicide cases a decade ago.

Either, I was going to find a way to kill our governor, or Lily's body would turn up somewhere in the city – or both. It was highly likely once the job was done, the kidnappers wouldn't hold their end of the bargain. But, where would I begin to search for her? I had to return to detective mode. After five years, who would know me that well, and have the resources to pull this off? A name popped into my head and I felt the blood drain from my face.

Gracie drove a white, beat-up 1985 Trans Am with an eagle airbrushed on the hood. I'd used up my *Smoky And The Bandit* jokes long ago. She recently had the engine replaced after five hundred thousand miles. Discarded coffee cups rattled around my feet. She blasted the heat and steered carefully with a cup of coffee in her hand, weaving around a slew of potholes so as not to rattle my ribs.

She said, "CSU and I spent most of the night at your house. They got everything they need. If you're up for it after the morgue, you can look around, fill in some details."

Every pebble annoyed me, but I tried not to show it. "When's her autopsy?"

"This afternoon."

"I know what killed her."

"But, what if she swallowed something that could lead us to these men? Or maybe they used a drug that will lead somewhere. Who knows what they might find."

"I know, and you're right." I turned to the window, letting my forehead touch the cold glass. A fresh napkin appeared in my hand with a squeeze. I used it, facing away from her.

Gracie rested her hand on my thigh.

Lily materialized behind my eyelids. The day she learned that Fiona and I were to be married, her reaction had been disbelief, and then anger. The twelve-year-old sequestered herself in her room for hours before allowing me to entry.

While curled up on top of a pony-patterned blanket, I sat at the foot of her bed. "Is this about your real father not being here?"

Her shoulder-length blond hair spread across her delicate cheek. I could see where tears had dried on her skin. Her swollen red eyes stared forward. "No."

"You know I love your mother, and I love you, too. So, it hurts for me to see you this way."

"Leave me alone," she whispered, trying to curl up tighter.

"If I did anything, you need to tell me, Lily. Help me make this right."

"You can't."

I exhaled, knowing this would be an uphill battle. But, she was only twelve. Eventually, we'd get to the root of the problem. She bristled at my touching her ankle. "Your mother and I are getting married. I won't be your dad, but I will be your parent. And I'll always be here for you. I'll always protect you the best I can. I can promise you that I'll try not to let you down and I'll earn your trust."

"Noted." She sat upright, pushing her back against the head-board. "Please leave."

I stood. "Your mom doesn't deserve this. She's raised and loved you all these years since your father left. Hate me all you want, but in front of your mom, you need to suck it up and act like an adult. We can be civil to each other, right? Can we agree that we both want your mom to be happy?"

She measured me before nodding silently.

* * *

The expired bodies were kept in a brand new facility, a far cry from the temporary storage trucks used since Hurricane Katrina. There was a large wall of compartments, with doors that opened like refrigerators, allowing the loved ones to slide out for viewing. The cold air drained my broken body, and every breath took in an anti-septic smell.

The nerdy, smug pathologist presented my wife's body on a shiny metal bed that hovered waist high. His bedside manner wasn't bad, just non-existent. I had dreaded this exercise for the victim's families during my tenure as a detective. I've seen many bodies mutilated by knives and bullets. I've witnessed enough autopsies to be able to name organs, and I've had to inform numerous families about their fallen loved ones. I'm ashamed to say that my sympathy had become more-less acting. Now, I wasn't quite sure when Fiona's death would really hit me.

Her skin had turned pale and blotchy under the florescent light, contrasting with the draped sheet. The back of her head lay on the spot where the bullet had exited, but her relaxed face expressed no sign of trauma. This person resembled Fiona, but I refused to acknowledge that conclusion.

My eyes followed the line of her nose down to her lips, where I stepped back upon seeing her chest rise and fall. The wounds disap-peared and her eyes fluttered as she sat upright like the special effects from a movie. Color rushed to her face and she had an expression of sorrow, as if apologetic. This was the woman that stole my heart, the woman who forgave my stubborn ways, and stood by me as I struggled to make something that resembled a career.

I blinked and she was flat on the drawer again… lifeless.

"Oh, baby," I whispered. A short burst of emotion erupted. The muscles around my ribs flared and became weak. I looked to Gracie.

"Let's give him some privacy." She escorted the boyish doctor out of the room.

I grabbed a nearby stool and instead of smashing it against the wall, I sat near her face, touching her cheek and feeling the pain of her shattered bones and broken skin. Once I left this clinical, heartless room, I would be back with my family and the ghost of relationships future would warn me about this if I didn't open my heart. I stared through clinging tears, keeping my hands on her face, placing them on different spots of her cheeks in hopes of warming her.

"We were going to talk last night. We were finally going to talk," I barely managed to say, as if it would change things. I pressed my cheek against her face.

After a chunk of time passed, I felt Gracie's presence behind me. "Remi? Captain Trout wants you to come back to the station. A couple of Feds are there."

I wiped hard at my eyes. "The FBI? They got something?"

"Don't know, but they got Captain Trout to get a Gang Unit detective on board. It took a lot of lobbying, but Trout's officially giving me the case. They're all waiting."

I took a pain killer without the help of water. "Gang Unit?" *That made sense if I was right.*

"Detective Horner is his name."

"Don't know him. Okay, let's go." I turned to my long-time friend with unsure footing, like I was standing on a mattress.

Gracie embodied patience as I inched back to the car, holding doors open and guiding my path. Her face grimaced with mine as I dropped into the Trans Am like a pregnant woman. My arms helped pull my legs inside. I lamented my morgue visit in the passenger seat in the frigid February weather. In just eighteen days, my deadline to kill the governor by Mardi Gras Day would be here.

The stitches in my forehead itched, but I resisted scratching. Instead, I thought about Lily again. I imagined her tied up, bruised and bleeding. She might be blindfolded, cold, in a damp room.

There were other things I couldn't imagine. Her frequent declaration about my ruining her life had come true.

Gracie knew the strained relationship I had with Fiona's parents, so she had interviewed them herself. Like Lily, my in-laws impression of me had started off rocky and their glacial exterior never melted. They blamed me for the car accident that gave Fiona a concussion in the first year we dated. I had been drinking that night. And without a real career, they figured she'd end up supporting me. They couldn't possibly have imagined this outcome. They would blame me for her death and I'd have to agree with that assessment. Fiona's parents and I would not be consoling each other.

In what felt like instant time travel, we suddenly arrived at Headquarters, stepping on the Homicide Departments third floor in one of its heated conference rooms. Unlike the small and chilly interrogation room, the long and lacquered table hosted many important meetings. The worn, cushioned chairs were very comfortable if I remembered right. A fifty-five inch flat screen hung on the far wall, and a large white board took up most of the opposite wall.

Gracie sat on my right and Captain Trout took position on my left. Trout's shirt and tie combined every color in the spectrum. Detective Horner with the Gang Unit positioned himself on the right of Trout. Horner was bulky black man, with a short Mohawk. He looked like he took no bullshit from anyone. I'd accept all the help I could get. The two FBI agents sat on the opposite side, dressed in nice, dark suits. A matching cup of coffee steamed in front of each one of us.

The older agent spoke first, "I'm Special Agent West Foster and this is Agent Adam Joiner. We're sorry for your loss, Mr. Doucet."

I nodded. "Call me Remi." Agent Foster didn't look sorry at all. His wrinkles were thin and sharp, as if he'd tried many facial masks. His prominent forehead sported a tan line near the crown, probably from a hat. "You had luck with the shell casing?" I asked.

"No, that's still in line to be entered into the database," Foster said.

"We don't make it a habit of injecting ourselves into police matters," Agent Joiner assured me, "But, we feel it necessary in this case." His broad shoulders and ponytail made him resemble a dojo master.

"And why is that?" Captain Trout inquired.

Foster clasped his hands. "We have an on-going investigation involving a subject associated with another man Mr. Doucet killed five years ago. After last night's unfortunate events, Mr. Doucet's name came across our desk with the shell casing request. We'd like to run the ballistics on the bullets too, once the medical examiner is done with the autopsy."

"Okay," Gracie almost said as a question, unsure if that was a jab at our ballistics department.

I squinted at them, controlling my shallow breath. "Wait. Five years ago? Edgar Baas? The drug dealer?"

"Our last case," Gracie added.

"His real name was Egor Baskov – Russian drug trafficker." Joiner waited for our reaction.

"Okay, so I killed Egor Baskov."

"You busted up a million dollar drug deal, however…" Joiner leaned forward. "…He was part of a bigger operation – a far reaching one."

"You understand my step-daughter's missing?" I straightened in such surprise that I almost hurt myself. "If you have a chance to locate her, I need to know."

Joiner allowed my outburst with a dip of his head. "We want to run that casing and the bullets against suspected murders by this crime family first. We want to eliminate the possibility that Egor Baskov's people are retaliating."

"He has people? I would have never thought of him." I spread my hands flat on the table. "Wait a minute. There was a story a few years back about the Feds busting a Russian mob boss – Victor something."

"Victor Dudko." Joiner gave his partner a subtle glance.

"Right. The informant or witness disappeared and he got off, right?"

"Correct," Foster said. "But, we are back on his trail."

"I thought Baskov was a loner – and I killed him after he shot me. Your file on me probably says I was dead for forty-seven seconds on the table. That's the main reason why I quit."

Joiner finished his statement. "We feel it's highly unlikely the two events are related. Especially after all this time."

Gracie dropped her pen on the table. "Where the hell were you guys after this Baas or Baskov was killed? Why didn't we hear about this far reaching operation?"

Foster turned over a page from a folder as if reading a delicate scripture from the national archives. "We didn't expect your involvement. If you had kept your noses out of it, the Bureau might've taken Egor down along with the Victor Dudko, but we couldn't shit on the good press. Pardon my language. We just started over."

"Good press is the reason you didn't inform us of your own investigation?" Gracie's debate face was on.

"You didn't sever the head of the snake," Joiner said. "We're just getting the investigation back to where it was. We finally have traction again."

"Jesus," I mumbled. Fresh tears appeared. "I don't know if I can help you here."

Joiner cleared his throat. "You said in your statement that the men wore Lee Street gym shoes."

"One of them for sure. The other I didn't get a good look."

Joiner pointed his pen at Horner. "I think it's fortuitous that you have one of your Gang Unit here. Did you know that Lee Street are the shoes of choice for the Latino gang *Los Serpientes*?"

"That is correct." Horner used a soft indoor voice, contradicting his size.

I shifted, having already thought of Juan Gomez, a captain in the Los Serpientes gang, earlier. "So, they handle this operation like Navy Seals only to have their cover blown by wearing their trademark shoes?"

Foster collected his printouts, but stopped before closing the folder. "Make of it what you will. Los Serpientes have direct ties to the Mexican Cartel and you *did* put away several of their men. Juan Gomez is set to be put to death on March first."

"I know that." My body stiffened. *I forgot the date was so soon.*

Foster continued, "That's just a few days after Mardi Gras. Governor Sharpe refused the family's plea for a stay of execution. You put one of their top earners there. With no hope for a stay of execution, the timing for retaliation works, Mr. Doucet. Remi."

I stammered. "That was eight years ago. Juan Gomez threatened me during the trial, but I assumed they would have retaliated already."

Foster sighed. "Whether you decide to pursue Los Serpientes or not is the NOPD's choice. As far as the Russians, give us a week to look into anyone in Egor Baskov's drug trafficking operation that would want to retaliate against you. We know for a fact that Dudko is clean as a whistle, but we have a man on the inside, so we'll know if you start asking questions."

"That's fair," I stated for the team.

"Dudko's involvement is slim, but we can't afford another monkey wrench here. One week, Captain Trout. Detective Castillo." He glared at me. "Remi? Agreed?"

Eventually, I nodded.

Detective Horner spoke, getting everyone's attention. "I'll pull the old case file on Serpientes. See who the main players were."

"I never crossed paths with any of the *main players*." I turned to Horner. "Juan Gomez murdered that family and I sent him to prison. I don't even remember dealing with any of his foot soldiers. I don't think I can help."

Gracie spoke to Horner. "I'm lead on this, and you take your orders from me. Understand? Forget Doucet's old case file for now. You're going to start rounding up the *enemies* of Serpientes – see what they know. Rivals are bound to talk if they know anything."

"Rivals. Right. That was my plan." Horner winked at her and closed his notebook. "But, if that doesn't work out, then we'll sweat a few of Gomez's hombres and bring them in. Then, we'll talk to Gomez himself."

I shook my head. "I'll be the one to talk to him."

Horner frowned. "I know where you're coming from, but like Detective Castillo said, you don't give the orders."

"Then, I'll do it without you."

"Yeah, okay." Horner held back his real response, looking at Gracie. "We'll talk soon, yeah?"

"Yeah."

Horner left the room, but failed to take the air of frustration with him. I wiped my eyes, focusing on the Feds again. "So, in short, what you're saying is that while my step-daughter is being held captive, maybe by these Russians, I have to wait a week for your report."

Joiner held up a hand to stop Foster from speaking. He softened. "Consider us doing your legwork on this theory. We can find out much more than you ever could starting from scratch."

I threw my hands up. "Fine."

Foster kept even. "But, in cases like this, they should contact you. Be sure to answer every unknown or restricted call, even the ones you might normally ignore."

"For ransom?" Gracie asked.

"Or blackmail," I said. "Or part of their vengeance is making me suffer. I'll address the media. Get Lily's face out there. If we're lucky, someone will come forward. You never know."

Trout cleared his throat. "We have a press conference scheduled in an hour. Remi, you okay to give a statement?"

"I'll give a statement, but I won't answer questions. And I need to take a look around my house." I lost my breath. "Honestly, I'm fading."

Gracie's hand found mine under the table. She squeezed. Until I found my sea legs, I'd need to keep my special mission to myself. Those men wanted the governor dead *before* Juan Gomez was to get the lethal injection. Perhaps the Feds had a point with Egor Baskov being a long shot. The reality was that Los Serpientes might have a death penalty sympathizer in the Lieutenant Governor, and there was only one sure way to get him into power that quickly.

CHAPTER FOUR

My brother Dylan stood beside me while I rested in a chair during the press conference, but all I wanted to do was lie down. Gracie convinced me we'd get better coverage using his celebrity. I couldn't argue that point. He was an ex-NFL football player, now running for Congress. We made a short, but sincere plea to every local news station for witnesses to come forward. Gracie capped off the press conference answering general questions.

Fiona's murder, Lily's recovery and vengeance gave me the will to continue on, despite the relentless stabbing in my chest. My Accord had been processed by CSU and towed to the city impound lot from the mall, so Gracie drove me home to do a quick once-over of the abduction scene. From there, I would spend the night at her house.

As Gracie turned onto my street, I immediately saw the police tape sagging from light poles. It extended beyond both sides of my house. Two news vans with large satellites were parked on the perimeter of the tape, hoping to get a scoop. The crew hopped from each vehicle upon our arrival, bundled up for the weather. The reporters spouted orders to their camera operators, trying to jockey for position. Lily's captors could be watching the coverage.

We pulled into the driveway, stopping just short of the police tape touching her windshield. That sent the reporters into a jabbering rush. My wife's car was still on the curb, near the mailbox. A squad car assigned to be my security waited across the street, parked between my neighbor's vehicles. The two reporters charged up to the Trans Am with their microphones. I held my side with one arm, dismissing them with a *no comment* and asked if they would respect my privacy. They both complied without argument, transitioning from leaning forward with outstretched microphones to standing straight and calling down their cameramen. But they didn't leave.

Gracie broke the tape, letting it fall to the ground so I wouldn't have to duck. The orange sticker on my door stood out like biohazard warning. Gracie kept her arms hovering near me as if I'd topple over. The trampled grass on both sides of the walkway proved many people had been in and out. I hadn't been home since yesterday morning, but it felt like a week. I wasn't eager to see where my family's hell transpired.

Aware that video from any cell phone could record me, I held my expression firm as Gracie sliced the sticker with a mini pocketknife. She had the key to a padlock, which was attached to the door to keep it secured. With the padlock in her hand, the door opened with a slight push as the jamb had been splintered during the break in. A carpenter would need to fix it after I was allowed back.

I entered the warm living room to find not much disturbed, but the sofa had been taken by CSU as Gracie had warned. Apparently, they found blood on a cushion. In the kitchen, the food had been cleaned out of the pan that sat dirty on the stove. Three place settings were still on the table. The furnace clicked on, however I left my coat on to save myself the agony of removing it.

"Take your time," Gracie said, only pulling off her furry cap. "You want to talk it out while you look?"

"Sure. The two men must have followed me to the mall. I needed to pick up my watch for repair. Fiona gave it to me for Christmas and I cracked the crystal."

"I'll have Horner check the surveillance from the parking lot and surrounding stores. Maybe they catch someone following you. I would think the second team heard your kidnapping was successful, and then busted in on Fiona and Lily."

"Right. Two teams. They couldn't risk having one abduction go wrong." I absently moved a pan around the burner by the handle. The metal clanking filled the silence. "Lily had probably been watching television on the couch. Lily doesn't move quick enough and was subdued. I hope the blood wasn't hers."

"This drawer was open." Gracie pointed.

"That's our specialty utensil drawer, when Fiona wants to try a new recipe. The gun was kept in the back."

"She might've went for it, but wasn't quick enough." Gracie leaned against the counter.

"They might've grabbed Fiona from behind and swung her around before she could reach in the drawer. Another man gags her or they knock her unconscious. Either way, they take my wife and daughter as professionally as they nabbed me. My neighbors?"

"Your neighbors didn't see anything. Granted, it was dusk."

I walked to the back of the house, taking a visual inventory of each room. Nothing was taken or was out of place. Inside of Lily's room, I looked at each picture she had taped up to the sides of her mirror. She basically had one friend – her constant companion, Madison. Lily stood out from other girls, having a wide smile and Fiona's beautiful eyes. With an outburst of emotion and the physical pain that came with it, I punched the mirror. It shattered in a circular, starburst pattern. My knuckles bled onto her dresser.

"What the hell?" Gracie appeared at the door.

"Sorry." I walked past her to the bathroom.

The laceration didn't open up too bad. Gracie silently helped me clean it in the sink and wrapped my knuckles with gauze from the medicine cabinet. My appreciation grew for the care she gave me. I opened and closed my hand, giving a slight smile of thanks, then traced the hallway wall with my fingers as I returned to the front.

Back in the dining room, I had to sit and find that comfortable sweet spot to relax. Gracie said, "Jerry pulled prints, but I'm not hopeful to find a set that doesn't belong here."

"If my abductors wore gloves, then so did these guys."

"So, we'll go with the two-team theory?" Tara scratched her forehead.

"Sure. They wouldn't risk good timing with me and blowing the other half of their operation. They were in contact with each other and they waited until they could take all of us at the same time."

"I have to agree. Is it odd that they wouldn't wait for all three of you to be home?"

"Easier prey divided? Or they didn't expect me to detour to the mall and took the opportunity."

"We need to get you a new phone so we can contact you."

I felt the weight of the day on my shoulders. My lids closed. "My old phone is in the junk drawer. It has all my contacts on it. I'll get the number transferred back."

"Good." Gracie found it and put it in her pocket. "When you're ready, pack a quick bag. We need to get you to my place so you can rest. Jerry told me they'd let you back in here tomorrow night."

"Okay." I gingerly got up and took another pain killer. "The hospital called in my prescription at the Walgreens down the street."

"Good."

After grabbing some toiletries and a change of clothes, we walked outside, stirring the news people back to life. One reporter sprung out of the passenger seat like her ass was on fire; a pretty, young redhead with an eagerness that made me imagine that she had always sat in the front row in school. Her cameraman followed.

"No comment," Gracie said, carrying my gym bag for me.

The reporter raised the microphone. "Do you feel like your wife's murder and daughter's abduction are retaliation from any of the criminals you put behind bars during your tenure on the NOPD?"

I looked into the camera lens. "I do."

"No more questions." Gracie gently pulled me across the lawn to her car. My breathing became rapid and the muscles around my ribs tightened. I couldn't be productive in the field at this point.

CHAPTER FIVE

G racie lived alone, so no one else was put out about my overnight stay. I felt as if she welcomed the company. However, instead of going over my abduction, she ushered me directly to the bed. She had fixed up her spare bedroom, laying multiple pillows against the headboard so I could sleep on an incline. An expansive Mexican-patterned area rug covered most of the scratched up hardwood. The dated dresser displayed a framed painting of Jesus looking directly at me. The bed had been hers as a family heirloom, but the end table and desk was IKEA. The gold Saint's logo repeated over black curtains and the matching bedspread.

Lying down in the quiet stillness, without anything to distract my mind, the day caught up with me. Fiona's murder and Lily's kidnapping wrestled in my head. I shed tears quietly, managing the pain. Eventually, the medication kicked in and helped me drift off, although every time I moved, I awoke to find myself in a strange house without Fiona by my side.

The next morning, while staring back at framed Jesus, the smell of coffee infiltrated my nose. I incrementally shifted forward, so as to sit on the edge of the bed. It was so hard to function when my mind raced – so hard to think. Still, my stomach twisted from hunger and I had to piss.

I shuffled like an old man to the bathroom decorated with figurines – black and white spotted cows to be precise. Gracie had added several new characters to her collection since the last time I visited, one sat on the vanity near the sink. No Jesus, however. She said the bathroom was the one place our Savior didn't need to be, but had no problems with Hinduism's sacred animal. The toilet flushed and Gracie met me in the hall with a tray in her hands. I gazed at her through half-closed, stinging eyes.

"How's the ribs?"

"Sore. The doctor said I should walk, so don't give me shit." I winced while touching my side.

"You can walk later. Go lay back down in bed," Gracie commanded. "I have your breakfast right here. And you're going to eat it."

I did as instructed, easing onto the mattress. "I need a pill."

"I'm on it." Gracie placed the tray over my thighs. It contained a cup of coffee and a steaming bowl of grits, with a pat of butter on top.

If I took enough pills, maybe I could make it to the correctional facility to talk to Juan Gomez. But, how loopy would that make me? Plus, the squad that had been sitting outside my house was now parked on Gracie's curb. The babysitting cop would tattletale to Gracie and her captain.

"Here you are." Gracie placed the bottle of pills next to the coffee. "I'm going into the station and I'll be back in a few hours. You'll be okay?"

"My phone is charged?" I looked to the dresser.

Gracie put the phone next to my hip. "Yep. Here's the number for the squad outside. You're all set."

"Go, I'm okay."

Gracie left, so I figured to plan out my day. But, what could I do? Who could I contact? What was the connection to the governor?

My cell rang with Fiona's father on the caller ID. I cleared my throat. "Joe. Joe, I'm so sorry."

He waited two seconds. "Any news on my granddaughter?"

"No, but we have leads."

His voice was at a higher pitch than usual. "I contacted Deluca's Funeral Home to handle the services. I figured you wouldn't mind with everything going on."

I rubbed at my eyes. "We never really talked about where we'd want to end up."

"You weren't together long enough."

"Not nearly," I whispered.

"She would be next to us at the Metairie Cemetery."

"Right. She mentioned those plots you bought."

"You can give us that much, couldn't you? You need to focus on my granddaughter."

"We have an entire task force on this." Joe had a point, although I didn't want to give in. I probably should defer the funeral arrangements. Fiona and I had only been married three years. It was hardly a lifetime. "Okay, Joe. Just send me the info."

The call ended without warning and for a moment, I stared at the phone. This cell was the model I had when Fiona and I met. There were still many digital pictures from our early days on it, but I couldn't bring myself to look at them yet.

I shoveled down the instant grits, almost throwing up a couple of times. Every cough was agony. Even if I wanted to question Los Serpientes on their turf, they'd be able to beat me down like a child. Horner would probably make more headway, dealing with them so often.

With Gracie out of the house, I carefully stood and stretched. I eased into the colorful living room with a burnt umber theme, and put on the television. Lily could be suffering any number of atrocities while I stay here helpless and recovering. Should I piss off the Feds and look into this Egor Baskov deal? If that shell casing and bullets were to match, they had to let me know.

I opened the front door to take a peek at the squad car. The uniform behind the wheel faced forward, not even looking at the house. He seemed tired, and disinterested in the goings on of the neighborhood. I almost closed the door when I spotted the manila envelope sitting on the welcome matt.

Keeping my core upright and straight, I squatted with great effort to pick it up at the corner. It was heavier than a letter. I placed it on a nearby table, then stood out on the welcome matt waving my arm. "Hey," I called out weakly.

The cop noticed me. A young kid with freckles and steel wool hair exited the car and trotted over. "What can I do for you, Mr. Doucet?"

"You see anyone approach the house after Detective Castillo left?"

He scratched his head as if to think. "No. I mean – there were a few people walking by and jogging, but that was it. I mean – I wasn't looking at the front of the house the whole time. No, I'd say no."

The kid was nervous. I patted his arm. "Just being cautious."

"Let me know if I can do something for you." He backed away.

I brought the package to the kitchen, where I found a pair of scissors to slice it open. A white Samsung cell phone slid onto the counter. A message from the kidnappers came to mind. Lily could be on it, but what if there were prints?

Next to the kitchen sink was a pair of rubber gloves. I barely squeezed into them. Gently holding the phone, I turned it on. After the Galaxy screen came to life, I searched the settings. There were no numbers, no apps, no calls or texts. Someone placed a brand new SIM card into the phone – untraceable.

I searched for audio files and there were none. The picture gallery caught my eye. I pressed the icon and saw one video. My breathing stopped as I stared at my daughter's still image and the little triangle icon begging me to start it.

Her body filled most of the screen, sitting on rollaway bed with a bare wall behind her. Her hands were on her knees tapping nervously as she spoke. Her hair was oily and flat and she looked tired with the excessive black eye shadow smeared in different directions, but otherwise, in good shape. She wore her favorite gray Army T-shirt.

"Remi, they wanted me to make this video to show you I'm okay." Her wet eyes popped up to whomever were filming, her fingers slapped against her thighs with a life of their own. "They haven't hurt me or anything, but they won't tell me what happened to my mom. They have me in a room with this bed, and they feed me. They told me letting me go depends on you. Remi, I'm scared." Tears spilled down her cheeks as she looked up again. She squinted as if the other person communicated something to her.

The video ended.

I tried to send the file to my phone, but the device wasn't active. Instead, I watched the video until the battery went dead, examining every nuance. I searched the wall, the bed and anything on her clothes. Her Army shirt had no bloodstains. They took her jewelry. Her words and speech pattern were branded into my brain. Her drumming fingers played a beat in my head. After the last viewing, I cursed aloud. I'd need to find a charger that fit this model.

* * *

Every so often, cops I'd worked with swung by to check on me. A few times they woke me from a medicated nap and every time, I thought they had news. In these short segments of sleep, I replayed Fiona's murder, so I appreciated the interruptions. Gracie had stopped by with lunch, otherwise she called throughout the day. She hated telling me about their lack of progress, but was enthusiastic about future leads. When she finally came home after first watch, I had my bag packed, sitting in the recliner with the lights out.

She switched on a lamp and noticed the gym bag. "Going somewhere?"

"Home. I'm okay."

She took off her shoulder holster. "Horner brought in three of the Serpientes' rivals from the *Sangre Niños* for questioning." She pronounced the Spanish words correctly. "And nothing panned out. But, word has probably gotten back to them by now."

"Sangre Ninos. Blood Boys, right?" I slowly stood. "Going low-level rivals or young Serpientes isn't going to get anywhere."

"Horner's trying to meet with their captains, but that means setting up neutral meetings. He's working on it." She walked to the kitchen.

"The autopsy?" I followed.

She rooted around aimlessly in the refrigerator. "The M.E. couldn't find anything. He released Fiona's body. The bullets are going to Quantico."

"Good." I didn't have my hopes up. "Hungry?"

"Yeah, you? How you doing?" She closed the refrigerator.

"Okay. I'm used to the pain now. It doesn't shock me anymore. Can you take me to the impound lot to get my car? We can stop for food. They cleared my house, right?"

She hesitated, concerned. "Two uniforms that do side construction even fixed your door."

"That's good."

"You sure you want to leave the comforts of my Latina palace?"

"I'm sure. I putzed around your house just fine. Tomorrow and every day after will be a little easier. I appreciate what you've done for me, but I want to be alone for a while."

Gracie headed for the front door. "Being alone here is different from being alone at your house."

"I know."

She smiled near the door. "If you really want to get back home tonight, we don't have to stop for food."

"Why not? Someone bring food by my house?"

"You'll see."

CHAPTER SIX

Miguel had to treat Client Five with the utmost respect, yet he never hated anyone more. Client Five had been escorted from *the building* in the usual way, as they all were, hidden in a truck until they were a safe distance away. No client would ever be associated with this building – *never*. Client Five left the aftermath of his *session* for Miguel to clean up. Miguel vowed to kill Client Five one day.

A beam of light from the hallway illuminated the wound on Donna's face. She sat propped up against the wall between two other girls. Drugged Vanessa slumped on Donna's left and that cop's daughter sat alert on Donna's right. This girl named Lily had done well on the video, poised and composed. Miguel watched Donna's pupils shrink in the glare. She had no fight left in her brown eyes.

"Where's my mom?" Lily asked with authority. "Why can't you just tell me?"

"Don't worry about your mother," Miguel said. "Worry about yourself."

Donna's face had been slashed with a knife from her forehead, over her right eye and across her lips. The swollen laceration trickled blood, as her heart must have been pounding with fury. Her throat still had imprints from a strong set of sadistic fingers. Miguel had watched Client Five satisfy his deviancies on the video feed. Client Five left Donna disfigured, and then walked away whistling.

Evil bastard.

A month ago, Five had requested Donna to be his property. The boss complied, and Donna was not to be paired with anyone else. His type was the *girl next door*, and Donna was made to look that way with subtle make up, ponytail, and glasses. Now, with her beauty gone, she would never see the sadist again. She would never work again. She would never wake again.

"Donna." Miguel stepped up and offered his hand. "The time has come."

"No," she cried. The cop's daughter hugged the girl tight.

"Now, Donna." He folded his arms. "I'll do it here, but you don't want these girls to see that, do you?"

"*Por Favor,*" she sobbed.

"Right here, then." Miguel stepped forward, cupping his sheathed knife.

"Wait," Donna shouted with defiance. She gently pulled the other girl's arms off of her. "I've prayed for death many times," she said to the cop's daughter with a heavy Spanish accent. "God will deliver me. Adios, mi amigas." She used his hand for balance.

They walked out of the room and ironically up one floor to the *dungeon room* where Client Five had enjoyed his fun. Donna crumbled onto the tiles in the hallway, just before going in. She convulsed with her hands over face, repeating the word *no*. Miguel gently dragged her into the room and shackled her to the olive green bricked wall, allowing enough length in the chain so she could sit on a mattress stained with years of abuse, yet always covered with clean sheets.

The sobbing ended. She sat as if exhausted.

"Your *familia* is in Mexico, no?" he asked in a puff of smoke.

"Let me go… How can I hurt you?"

"Look at your precious face." Miguel maintained a slight accent. He threw an empty matchbook on the ground by her long toenails as smoke escaped his mouth. "You had a rough bout, eh?"

Her head nodded slightly, as if afraid it might crack off at the neck.

"I remember the day we took you off Bourbon Street – a seventeen year old runaway. I often wonder if your life really does pass before your eyes."

"I don't want to die," she whispered over her split lips.

Miguel's gaze diverted to his shoulder where a large, vicious tattoo fought to escape from under his tank top. These lost souls didn't deserve this outcome, having no idea that their chosen path would lead to their ruination. How many teenaged, female runaways make it out the other side of that choice unscathed? Miguel refused to engage in the same activities as the clients. He likened himself more of a caregiver.

"That man has a touch of Satan..." His voice trailed off, wanting to say more, but nothing came. Instead, he pulled out his eight inch, serrated hunting knife.

"Don't kill me," she finally said.

He put his face next to hers. "You were unlucky enough to have those eyes. That's why you weren't drugged. He likes to see the clarity, the fight. But, you *are* lucky in one respect. You will not be used to make babies, nor shall your organs be harvested and you will not grow old in this world that you have no hopes of escaping."

"I'm lucky?" Tears streamed down her cut.

Miguel put on a long sleeve sweatshirt. Her eyes locked on his and he gave her the respect of not looking away. He found it brave that she would want to look in his eyes while he ended her life, but then, he was about to give her the greatest gift of all... salvation.

He took a deep breath, almost hesitant. "I am feeling like a butcher in an *abattoir* as the French would say." Miguel leaned into her ear and whispered, "I really wish it didn't have to be this way, Donna. I wish I could let you go."

Miguel moved slowly, grabbing her once radiant brunette hair, pulling it back and exposing her neck. He placed the tip of the knife next to the jugular, pressing ever so slightly, allowing a trickle of blood.

She gasped – wide-eyed. He had heard her speak of her past

life. He imagined these scenes flashing before her eyes – *her mother and father, playing in the yard – being molested repeatedly by a neighbor – her first experience with drugs – celebrating a good grade in school – the huge argument with her mother – packing her clothes to begin her new life–*

Miguel hoped that one day she would have a gravestone with her name on it.

CHAPTER SEVEN

The rearview mirror framed Miguel's eyes as he checked for cops in this early morning hour, but no one had gotten close since he left the building. The temperature dropped below forty degrees and the frigid air in the late model Buick caused fog to waft from his unshaven face. This car was forgettable and inconspicuous, perfect for this discreet job just before dawn. The heater finally blew warm and soon he'd find a spot.

Tepid coffee dribbled down Miguel's chin, and although alone, his face soured. He drove along the section of Claiborne Avenue that ran parallel under Interstate 10, cursing the flimsy cap on the coffee cup.

He sped up, and then slowed, searching for a dark, vacant area. His rounded shoulders hunched forward as he surveyed, but even when nervous, his movements were smooth and unforced, as if in a Hollywood movie.

The night's chill invigorated him as each city block passed by. He turned off the headlights as he pulled under the I-10 into a bleak spot, directly next to one of its massive columns. An occasional vehicle rumbled overhead. It was desolate, except for a fenced-in lot to the left that was used to park city vehicles. He sat there for a minute with his weighty, cold gun in his lap to see if any homeless, gang-bangers or cops would approach after seeing the lone vehicle stop.

He put on a pair of gloves, slid his Beretta in the waistband behind his back, and popped the trunk revealing a thick roll of carpet with the girl cocooned inside, extending into his back seat. He pulled the dead weight out with a thud onto the pavement. His boss wanted Donna found by the police, otherwise, she would have been alligator food. But, on this cold night, Miguel didn't want to venture too far. He wanted someplace nearby, but secluded. The rug was a nice touch in case a bored cop had decided to search his trunk.

He dragged Stacy from behind his vehicle and dropped her next to the column. Sweat chilled his skin as body heat escaped through the collar of his coat. A horn echoed from far away, but he saw nothing. When a voice bounced off the darkness, his head swiveled. In certain sections of the city, there was a lawless attitude that hovered like an ominous cloud, and for some, killing was as normal as asking for directions.

Three black kids appeared from behind a large construction dumpster. Miguel knew the gang that ran the nearby territory and they were notorious. One was tall at about six foot two, and the other two stood inches shorter, smelling of aggression. They were dressed in ragged layers with knit wool caps and hoodies, and their hands were in their coat pockets. As the distance closed, the three youths separated from each other like stalking wolves.

"Say, yo," the tallest one squeaked with a high pitched voice, "Why you want to throw your trash out here like dat? This is my 'hood, bitch." The boy lifted his jacket to expose the handle of his gun. The other two stood in silence, like Dobermans watching a burglar. "You're Mexican ass better put that shit in that there dumpster."

"This will sound silly, given the circumstances, but I'm giving you one chance to keep on walking."

"Listen to this Rambo, motha fucka'. Who you runnin' with?"

Miguel could never imagine that he would die from a disgruntled youth putting a bullet into his chest. "I'm not in a gang. You want my money?" He reached behind his back as if to pull out his wallet and gripped the handle of his gun, instead.

"Yo, why you think we want to rob you? Cause we niggas?" The taller one took a step forward.

"Ty, I think dat's a dead body." He had a boy's voice.

Miguel shot the tall kid first. Before the other two could react, he had put a bullet in each of their chests, ending with a shot to their heads. *Live by the sword, die by the sword.* He had to leave quickly.

The toasty warm car coasted onto the apathetic street. The NOPD should thank him. No telling how many lives he saved by taking them out. Donna would be replaced and when they found the next unfortunate soul, she would be used up and thrown away like all the others.

CHAPTER EIGHT

Gracie followed me home after I had signed out my unwashed Honda Accord from the impound lot. A haunting feeling that I might get jumped again crept over me, but I shook it away. I saluted a different watch cop sitting in the squad car across the street from my house. My side pinched while easing over the curb into my driveway. The police tape was gone, but something was blocking my front door. Gracie parked behind me.

She trotted up. "Good thing its cold out." She bent down and pulled a note off the top container. "We're praying for you. The Benoit's. It's Gumbo. Told you we didn't need to stop for food. This one looks like Jambalaya. From your brother Dylan."

"Poisoned?"

Gracie made a face as she collected the meals. The keys for the new lock worked perfectly. She put the five containers in the refrigerator, but left out the gumbo. I sat like a drunk at closing time at the island in my kitchen while she warmed up the food in a pot. We ate in relative silence, commenting on how delicious the recipe was. Afterward, I assured her I'd be fine and walked her to the door.

With a brief wave, I watched her drive away. I had enough food for weeks.

While inspecting the darkened house again, I took a pill and luckily found an old charger that fit the burner phone in a snake pit of wires. The streetlight brightened around the curtains, and yet, I couldn't bring myself to turn on a light. I groaned as my ass fell into my recliner, ignoring the gaping hole where the couch had been. I watched the video on the burner again with optimism, now imagining Lily isolated, unharmed. Minutes turned to hours. Despite intentions to just rest my eyes, I drifted off.

Lily stood in front of me with her arms folded, wearing shorts and her sailing shirt. Her face was puffy and red. Fiona appeared, taking her hand and they glided backwards, out of sight. My eyes popped open and I gasped. My head filled with a foggy panic, and I sat upright with a sharp stab at my ribs that quickly dulled. The night had passed by in what felt like twenty minutes. It was dawn.

It didn't feel like morning at all. Lily should be running through the house, not speaking to me. My stepdaughter eventually warmed a tiny bit, hidden in a little gesture I happened upon. A year into the marriage, I introduced her to a sailing team she joined on Lake Ponchartrain. She reluctantly tried it out and surprisingly, loved it. Her mood changed in the months following, going from disdain to civility while in the same room. One day she heard me listening to *Satisfaction* by The Rolling Stones and later that week, I discovered she downloaded the song onto her playlist. *Huge.*

The first two years were the hardest, but Lily stopped being contentious and slipped into silence. Her makeup made her look older, as well as her clothes, dressing much like her mom. I knew the phase of hating me would end the older she got, and I had hoped she would appreciate that I made her mother happy. But with all this, she had an entire new reason to hate me.

As I popped another one of my pain pills, the doorbell startled me. The synapses in my brain struggled to connect. Through the blinds, I saw Gracie padded in a puffy parka and headgear on my doorstep, which equated to another jolting slap in the face.

I swung open the door. "You have news?"

"No. I'm sorry, Remi. We have a different situation and I need you to come with me."

"Don't tell me you found Lily's body. Don't…"

"Oh, no. God, no. I'm sorry, Remi. That was shitty of me not to start with that. But, we may have found a clue at a crime scene."

I glanced into the house as if announcing to Fiona I'd be back. Instead, still dressed in yesterday's clothes, Gracie helped me slip into my coat and we stepped outside. "So, you still not going to tell me?"

She walked while talking to me, but looked at the ground. "Several unidentified bodies have been discovered under the Claiborne overpass. A Hispanic female and three bangers. She looks Hispanic, anyway."

"The three bangers are Latino, too?"

"Black. Her throat was slit and the boys were shot. Smells of gang activity." She pulled down at her furry earflaps.

We slipped into her warm Trans Am, now with an old school spinning light attached to the roof. "You think Serpientes?"

"Don't know for sure. But, there's something else that I want you to verify." She handed me a small coffee from the cup holder and started driving.

"You're not giving me your opinion because you want mine to be unbiased." The coffee had lost its steam, but was still welcomed.

"Something like that." Gracie navigated the vacant streets in silence.

My body felt old, like it wasn't my own anymore. After parking, I couldn't exactly remember the ride over. The sun glowing behind the clouds stung my eyes, and a murky dread coated my thoughts as I realized Fiona's funeral loomed.

Four squad cars blocked the entrance under the overpass. The responding officers had formed a misshapen circle, laughing and joking with each other as they kept stragglers from wandering too close. Outside the warm car, the chilly air stung the inside of my nose. I immediately recognized Dr. Jerry and the Forensics team standing behind the police tape while tall and lanky Freddie took pictures. They were hovering over one of the dead bodies as if it was a campfire.

The roar of passing vehicles overhead actually soothed my brain, but the cold ate at my bones. Besides my private investigating, it had been over six months since I had consulted on a murder. Occasionally, the understaffed, overworked NOPD threw me a bone that they got tired of chewing on. Despite all that'd happened, investigating always stirred something within me. I even began to wonder - would Captain Trout let me get my badge back now? Was that something I wanted?

I learned that Captain Trout came from Chicago under heavy pressure to tighten the reins at Headquarters. He had a reputation as a loose cannon as a detective, but had since settled nicely into a management role. Although, he currently managed a disgruntled department reduced to half of its size.

"Take your time." Gracie ducked under the police tape.

Muscle memory told me to pull out my notepad, but I didn't have one, so I folded my arms instead. Gracie led me to the deceased girl where the Forensics team offered their condolences. We had to watch our step as tiny, colored markers indicated where evidence was to be collected. The cold triggered little tremors of shivering, which felt like electric shocks to my chest.

The team watched as I tilted my head forward to see the wounds. Gracie pulled absently at her furry cap. "At first, we figured a hooker's body was being dumped and these boys stumbled upon it and paid the price." She looked at Dr. Jerry for collaboration.

"Probably," he agreed. His long blonde hair was pulled into a ponytail, which showed the initial stages of a receding hairline and translucent red ears.

"Anything?" Gracie asked me.

I stood tall to take in the entire crime scene, waiting for Gracie's clue to clock me in the forehead. The nude girl was lying on some kind of woven rug, but still within a blood stained, red-cast plastic. Weeds struggled to grow through the cold cement like hair plugs. Litter consumed the scene. It would be difficult to prove whether the killer had discarded any of it.

The girl's face had been sliced from top to bottom, but that wasn't what killed her. No, the cut at her throat was severe enough that her jugular opened fully. The killer could have beheaded her if he wanted. It seemed bleeding her out did the trick.

I voiced my thoughts. "Nothing sticks out to me. He uses a knife to mutilate the girl, and then executes these boys with a gun. No panic."

"Maybe not his first time. Keep looking." Gracie blew her nose into a tissue while looking back at me. "She can't be more than twenty years old. I don't recognize her as a regular."

"Doesn't mean she's not new to the streets," I said. "Look at the scars on her, the healing bruises on her thighs. She was definitely abused. So, I don't know how I can help so far."

Gracie rubbed my arm. "What do you make of her jewelry?"

My eyes went from her hands and wrists to her neck and ears. The neck was bare, but she wore two tiny turquoise spiders hanging down about a half inch as if on a web. *They were Lily's earrings.* She had bought them at an art fair. They were one of a kind.

My eyes shot to Gracie's. "Oh, my God."

Jerry stepped up. "I take it the earrings are Lily's? You alright, Remi? You look faint."

"We need to find out who this girl is. Whoever killed *her* has Lily. Killing those boys has to be a mistake, and it's possible they used the same gun that killed Fiona. Those are shell casings, right?" I pointed at the markers on the ground. "We need to see if they match the other shell."

"Well will. We're going to treat this girl and this scene with top priority." Jerry nodded with a steel gaze, then took off for the team's SUV.

Gracie bit at her pen cap. "We have a big question to answer here."

"Did the killer put them on her to taunt me, or did my daughter pass them on to her undetected? Her hair is long enough to cover them. Could they have gone unnoticed by her killer?" I knew it was a warning of what could possibly happen if I didn't fulfill my end.

"Another question is; could this be one of Los Serpientes' girls that they pimp out?"

"Where's Horner?" I asked.

She shot her thumb over her shoulder. "Treme. He was here earlier and recognized one of the boys from a local gang. He's seeing if another member got away and can identify the killer."

"Good. Good." I was wide-awake. "That slash across her face means she might've pissed someone off." I glanced to the interstate overhead, then down to her earnest, dark eyes. "We need to show her picture around the usual spots to see who was handling her. Maybe Horner can do that."

Gracie appraised me. "I'm surprised you're not insisting on doing it yourself."

"I know my limitations right now and I trust your team."

I had to keep my emotions in check. There were too many cops walking around. Holding on to Gracie's arm, I knelt with a grunt to feel the edge of the rug with my fingers. "This pattern is weird. It has helicopters and soldiers on it. Look, tanks. This is very odd."

Gracie agreed. "*Unique* is more like it, expensive, and probably easy to track down."

Dr. Jerry spoke on his return. "This is true. The killer probably didn't know the value of this rug."

"Do your best here, boo." Gracie winked at him, helping me stand again.

Dr. Jerry couldn't hold back a cat and canary grin. "With any luck, we'll pull some prints from that plastic."

A uniformed officer came through with coffee and I welcomed another one.

Dr. Jerry put his hand on my shoulder. "These bastards – They're going to fuck up."

"I hope you're right." I paused, as did everyone else.

Jerry broke the silence. "See where these kids were shot? Head and chest – All of them. The killer knows how to handle a gun."

I nodded. "The Serpientes are into minor prostitution. Maybe a John did this and they used her to taunt me with the earrings."

"But, the question is still why? Why did any of this happen?" Gracie pondered.

Dr. Jerry gave Gracie one last glance, and then conferred with his female partner, a slim, plain-looking girl in a long, silver coat that I'd never met. They began the tedious task of collecting, bagging and labeling while Photo-Freddie did his thing. Once satisfied, the deceased would be sent to the coroner's for a medical exam, which probably wouldn't happen for a few days, and then Gracie wouldn't see results for weeks, even expedited. This was life on the NOPD.

After an hour, there was nothing left for us to examine. I stared at the crime scene from behind Gracie's windshield. On the surface, it appeared like overkill to have ten individuals scurrying around a dead body, but each cop had a job to do, no matter how menial. "What do you think, Gracie?" I asked.

She adjusted the heat as the car idled. "I think this girl was disposable. Los Serpientes are using her to send you a message, but what the hell is it? Have they contacted you and you're just not telling me?"

"No way." I put my chin on my fist, resting my forehead on the cold glass. "You knew those were her earrings."

"I commented on them at your crawfish boil last year."

"We need a name for that Doe." I faced her.

"If she was trafficked from Mexico, then we may never know."

"At least the Feds have resources we can take advantage of."

Gracie pulled onto the road, speeding toward Headquarters. "We have the shell casings and the bullets to pull from those boys. They'll go straight to the Quantico lab. If we don't match her to a missing person by the time we meet back up with Foster and Joiner, then we see if they can help identify her."

"Agreed." I closed my eyes.

"I'll have Horner take some uniforms to question local prostitutes. CSU won't have anything for us today, so what do you want to do?"

"I want to get set up in the conference room with all the files we have on Los Serpientes. I think I also want to see the Egor Baskov file. You think Trout will have a problem with me assisting you?"

"Honestly... he's drowning in unsolved homicides. Our numbers are so bad they don't post them anymore. As long as you don't touch evidence and stay with me, I think he'll be fine." My old partner smiled and firmly slapped my knee. We fell right back into our comfortable ways.

* * *

Two sturdy boxes sat in front of me in the conference room. So as not to mix up the paperwork, the first box with the case number scribbled on the front was positioned on the left end of the table. With this case, I had stumbled into a major drug deal while working on a homicide. In an exchange of gunfire, we ended up killing each other, only the doctors got my heart beating again. Apparently, we screwed up the Feds investigation.

The Los Serpientes evidence box on the right was a bit heavier. While investigating the mass murder of a family of five, including three teenaged boys, all decapitated, I determined this was retaliation from Los Serpientes. The father was believed to owe Juan Gomez fifty thousand dollars. Due to my persuasive pressure, a generous reward from crime stoppers, and witness protection, a Latino gang member flipped on Juan Gomez and named him as the killer. Juan Gomez's five-year-old son witnessed me taking liberties with his apprehension. He cursed me, and said that I would regret that day.

After several hours of going over old facts, I boxed up the files and had Gracie bring them back to Central Evidence. When she came back, I joined her in the squad room. Late morning in the station smelled like coffee and toner ink, hot from the printer. Calls transpired and files were filed. I felt at home in this place and yet I had hated it, especially the endless paperwork. Computers helped, but when it came to getting a guilty verdict, every detail counted – or counted against you.

I stared out the window at nothing in particular from the side of her desk, which was just one section of a long row of tables strewn together. The haphazard arrangement had always amused me, but once you're used to something it all seemed perfectly normal. I pretended to fiddle with my cell.

A picture of our Latina Jane Doe was on my screen. I flipped between her and my daughter. Could they have known each other? Crossed paths in captivity? Could Lily have slipped her the earrings under her thick mane, which meant they weren't sending me a message at all?

Unidentified victims burred under my skin. Family members were trying to get on with their lives, attempting to shop, going through the motions of work, managing dinner, and hoping for the best, all the while preparing for the police to knock on their door. This was the most important Jane Doe in my life. She could know my daughter's location, and somehow her dead body needed to tell us.

"You sure you're all right?" Gracie asked.

"We need to get this girl's face on the news. The national news. We can get our Photoshop god to take the slash off her face."

"I'll make the call." Gracie punched in a number on her desk phone. She instructed a police sketch artist and graphic designer of what we wanted. She said that Freddie, the police photographer, would be sending over several digital files and it was a rush job. She hung up and gave me a slight smile.

"My brother called a little while ago." I kept my eyes out the window.

"Yeah, I was surprised he showed at the hospital, and then with the Jambalaya. You think Dylan turned over a new leaf with every-thing that's happened? Or do you think that making up with you will help his run for Congress?"

I finally faced her. "I don't know. He's coming to the funeral. I couldn't dissuade him."

"I wish you'd tell me why you hate him."

"There's too much distance for hate. He just created a wound and picked at the scab for years."

"Ew."

"Now, there's just scar tissue, tough scar tissue."

"Thanks for that." Gracie leaned over to touch my arm.

"For what?"

"For confiding in me. When I used to ask about your brother, all I got was a shrug or a head shake."

"That's all he deserves." A bird flew by the window, grabbing my attention away from the discomfort.

"Still sucks."

I shifted my ass in the chair to relieve the annoying pain. "Horner check in?"

"He called while you were in the conference room. He's getting nowhere showing the picture around, but it's the daytime. He's going to go back out tonight. Oh, we also collected four videos from the businesses next to the watch repair place. Mayfair went over them."

"Good, but I need to check them out, too."

"Of course. You're in one video, but no one else stood out as watching you or following you."

"I'll confirm that, but I don't think they were following me. They were waiting by my car."

"Where no cameras were. Well, right now we have two uniforms going into local businesses within a three-block radius of where they found you to see if any have surveillance of the street."

Right."

"So, we wait a bit."

"You mean we wait an eternity."

Gracie threw a folder of pictures from the Claiborne crime scene onto her desk. "I'm sending Doe's prints to the Fed's as a general inquiry. Can't hurt."

"Which, contrary to popular belief, they don't hold every finger-print of every criminal, just the ones with the major offenses. But she's so young that I don't hold out hope that the Feds will find something unless she's been in jail."

Captain Trout approached. His suit was inexpensive, but clean and pressed. "You holding up?"

"You mean holding it together? I wouldn't be here if I wasn't."

"That's true." Trout scanned the room. "What do you figure?" Trout grabbed one elbow and pinched his chin in anticipation.

Gracie sighed. "Her DNA is going on file, along with her dental records. We also arranged for a picture of her face to be used with the press. Our Photoshop wizard can take the laceration off for identification. I want him to simulate her eyes being open, too. We have a very unique rug to track down. It's the best physical evidence we got right now."

"Keep me updated. Remi, if we weren't so short on manpower, you'd be in the bleachers. You're here on a short leash. Consulting only. I realize getting paid is the last thing on your mind, but keep track of your hours." Trout lifted his bottle of water in a subtle toast and left the room.

Gracie and I ate our delivered lunch as if a chore. I nibbled at my shrimp poboy, which I usually devoured in four bites. She handled her Muffaletta like a pro, taking a sip of Coke after every bite. We continued to comb over every detail of our Jane Doe when a text message popped into my phone. It was my father-in-law Joe sending the date, time, and name of the funeral home. It was tomorrow. Why so soon? Was he debating about actually telling me? Without warning, my eyes started watering and before I knew it, tears rolled. Gracie noticed that I wiped at my eyes and I checked to see if the other cops noticed.

"Oh, Remi." Gracie reached over and put her hand behind my neck. "Go ahead, let it out. I'm here for you."

"Sorry. It just hit me. That was weird." I attempted a laugh.

"You want to quit for the day?"

"No, are you kidding me?" I closed my eyes for an uncomfortable moment. My throat cleared with a powerful cough. "I've been very curious. You and Jerry getting down?"

She hesitated with eyes like saucers. "What? No comment. He's not my boyfriend."

"How can you not have a boyfriend with the way you wrap your mouth around that Muffaletta?" I shook my head, waiting for her retort.

She laughed with surprise, waved her finger at me, and easily found that groove. "Maybe if dick was as tasty as this sandwich."

"Maybe you need a guy who'll stick it in a sandwich first." I laughed low and deeply, releasing the last tear.

"I know what you're doing, trying to hide behind jokes." She touched my cheek as if I gave her a Hallmark card. "You can have a moment when you need it. No one here will think you can't do the job."

"You need to be able to rely on me."

"You're human. You are human, aren't you?" She waited for an actual answer.

I nodded.

"Okay, then. Back to business. The girl was pretty, a bit malnourished and not dressed in typical hooker attire. Let's not assume she was trafficked. What if she was taken right off Bourbon?"

"She probably isn't from the area we found her."

"And the rug?" Gracie asked.

"It seems like the rug would come from an Uptown home. Maybe she was a rich girl, working high-end clientele. Who says it has to be poor and dirty?"

"That was some cheap-ass perfume mixed in with corpse odor."

"I don't think Los Serpientes have high-end escorts."

Gracie's eyes locked on mine. She spoke slow and clear. "I hear doubt."

I waited a moment. "With Los Serpientes, I'd be dead right now."

"That isn't enough to rule them out."

"Why would the Feds waste all that time and effort to throw us off a trail we were never on?"

"Egor Baskov? They said they wanted to eliminate them as a possible."

"Baskov was Russian. He trafficked drugs. He was important to someone and I shot him five times. The last one in the head. They shot Fiona five times. And the last one…"

"Coincidence?"

"Maybe, but each shot was so… deliberate." I only ate a quarter of my poboy and threw the rest in the trash. The guilt of keeping Gracie in the dark about killing the governor and getting Lily's video weighed on me.

Gracie deflated. "There's just so much pointing to the Latino gang."

"There's nothing Mexican about that rug. What do you say about some legwork? We're not going to get any info on Doe from the M.E. until next month."

Gracie laughed. "Yeah, f'true."

I pulled up Google to start a search. "Let's track down the top dealers of this type of shit and go pay them a visit."

"Let's do it."

After sending out an email blast to my closest friends about Fiona's funeral, Gracie and I spent the rest of the afternoon in the field. We interviewed the owners and employees of two antique stores, learning much about the business of antiquities, but not much on the rug. The owner of Shiny Objects on Louisiana Street suggested The Artifact on Magazine, but it was too late to pay them a visit as they had closed.

Wiped from the day, we relaxed inside a small coffee shop next to the Shiny Objects store. My leg muscles were strained from trying to relieve the pressure on my rib cage as I walked. Even sitting didn't offer much relief, but Gracie would never hear me say it.

After a quick decaf, I made my way home to pass out with a couple of painkillers and a couple of shots of Jack. When I pulled up to my house, I noticed a Hurwitz Mintz Furniture truck parked outside my house along with a black Corvette. Dylan got out of his vehicle as I parked.

"Just in time." He opened his arms.

"What's this?" I asked.

"New sofa. Got you a nice, comfortable one." He had a proud grin. Every facet of his self was a little better than mine being taller, with bluer eyes, and straighter teeth.

I almost objected, but then knew it wouldn't matter. "You can't buy your way back into my life."

Two sloth-like furniture movers got out of their truck and opened the rear, exposing a lovely, brown sofa with deep cushions. Dylan had picked out a good one. I opened the door and told the men where to place it. I tipped them, and they left with grateful handshakes.

Dylan stood in my house for the first time in two years. "Let's test this bad boy out," he said, waving me over. "I'm not taking the virgin run."

"Looks nice." I eased onto the edge of the cushion. "There – it's defiled. Dylan – I need to rest."

"Ribs still hurt?"

"I'm fine until I move a certain way or take too deep a breath." I scooted farther onto the sofa. "I know I should thank you for this, but I can't say those words to you right now. Can you close the door on your way out."

"Want some company tonight? We'll order in supper."

The lightbulb went off over my head. "You're here because the funeral is tomorrow."

"Joe texted me earlier. I called Detective Castillo to see if you were back in the house and we argued over who would keep you company tonight. I made a sincere plea, told her I bought the sofa. She protects you like an offensive lineman. I like her."

"That's why she didn't offer to stay for dinner." I almost verbally threw him out, but another thought hit me. "With your political ambitions, you've met the governor, right?"

"I've met him. Nice guy."

"What do you know about Thomas Riley Beemer?" I asked.

"The Lieutenant Governor?" He sat down as if invited. "His family owns several car dealerships in the Baton Rouge area. He parrots the governor on the issues."

"The death penalty?" I asked, casually.

"Sharpe doesn't speak out about abolishing the death penalty, but he has been known to be soft on the prospect. Why?"

I didn't answer.

"It's nice to actually string a conversation together without fighting."

I still didn't answer, choosing to sip at my Coke.

"You want to meet the governor? I can arrange it."

I closed my eyes. "Maybe."

CHAPTER NINE

Bored in his stale office, Miguel reclined in the rickety, wooden swivel chair with his feet on the desk. The pale blue paint on the cracking, plastered wall made him feel like he was back in prison. The large space had a cheap kid's bed-set tucked into the back corner near the closet where he kept his clothes and some personal items. He spent more time there than in his own apartment.

Four large computer screens on a separate table contained numerous video feeds. The cameras could be switched to any location desirable. The building had hosted many prominent CEOs, religious leaders and political figures, because their weird deviancies and fetishes couldn't otherwise be placated. Most fumbled along in the sack, but one or two have proven to be very entertaining.

Having a woman in this regard was beneath Miguel, but he would gladly take money from those that would. His current girlfriend retained residence outside these walls – this world. She would never know what he did to survive, although she knew of his militant past. Despite the lack of presence in his stripper girlfriend's life, Cherry Treasure loved him anyway. He treated her like a lady, relatively speaking.

Miguel lacked an audience for educated conversation. He craved a discussion with someone on his philosophical level, however he found few equals amongst his peers. Most of the world's population didn't know that certain families with ungodly amounts of money controlled everything. There were sinister forces in the shadows of major organizations and corporations, such as the Red Cross, pharmaceutical labs and the Vatican. Oil was only scratching the surface in the Middle East. Certain regions in Africa had enough guns for multiple wars, but nothing for the starving people. The weapons were supplied by political manipulators, and in the end, Africans ended up paying for those weapons with their own land. Elections were rigged and politicians were put in place to steer world events, create conflict, and to make the rich richer. If the puppets went against their wishes, they were taken out. Suicide, gay affairs, and corruption could all be viewed as suspect.

He reclined in his chair, his rugged boots rested on the desk. They were tough, beat-up boots and he felt a kinship with them. This has been the only job where he could spend countless hours alone, thinking, assessing... not counting his time in prison, which he practically ran. Back in Mexico, Cuba, and South America, he thrived on combat, killing men that deserved to meet their maker, helping along the hypocrisy of America by putting dictators into power just to have them taken out when they got too big for their britches. The politics never mattered, as long as there was the thrill of combat and a paycheck.

Miguel's burner cell rang. Only certain people had the number and he despised talking to any of them. This man had become like a bear trap on his foot.

He purposely answered after the fourth ring. "Si."

"Everything went *bueno*?" his boss questioned.

"Like usual." He blew a cloud of smoke, then put out his Winston, automatically lighting another. "Your instructions were followed precisely. Did the cop see the earrings?"

"Yes. He was brought to the scene."

"Tomorrow is his wife's funeral, no?"

He pushed out a heavy breath. "I know about the *rug*."

"The rug? The one I wrapped her in?"

"I hope it was a common throwaway *rug*. Where did you get the *rug*?" He oozed contempt.

"From that first floor the local gringos call the basement."

"You had no business going in there."

"What's the problem?"

"Did you notice anything strange about the rug?"

"It was red."

"Did it have tanks on it?"

"Yeah, I think. It was all I could find." Miguel shot the phone with his finger gun.

The man's voice became strained. "That wasn't just any rug. I bought that rare, valuable rug from a distributor here in the city. Guess how many importers carry such an item."

"Don't sweat it. So you threw it away years ago and haven't seen it since."

"I used to display it in my house. Important people saw it. How can you be so smart and so stupid at the same time?" He stopped to breathe.

"Unless your name is on it, they won't trace it back to you. Did you charge it?"

"I paid cash, but Bobbi would probably remember me. This is just something else I have to take care of because of your carelessness."

Miguel knew not to apologize like a weakling, but he wasn't going to argue, either. "What can I do to make this right?"

"I have a plan. It'll take some time before they can track anything down. I'll take care of it." He blew his nose into the receiver.

"Let me talk to this Bobbi," Miguel said with finality.

"No, I got this one. Think, next time."

Miguel turned the phone off and cursed in Spanish under his breath. Forget the money, he had fought in revolutions… for noble causes and destructive ones. He escorted millions of dollars in

cocaine for the Mexican cartel. He has killed to help topple govern-
ments around the globe. Here, he was a disrespected baby-sitter
where he would never earn the true loyalty of men.

His boots deserved better.

CHAPTER TEN

My choice for us would have been cremation in old age. New Orleanians weren't buried because of ground saturation, which caused the coffins and bones to eventually creep to the surface. Most were cremated, but those who could afford it chose tombs above ground where family members can be stacked like bunk beds. Another alternative was a concrete box raised above ground and filled with dirt, so as to give the illusion of being buried. This was what my father-in-law Joe had planned for Fiona.

Gracie picked me up in her Trans Am, dressed in an appropriately stylish, black dress. I wore a navy blue Boss suit with a black tie. Despite the cold, she met me halfway up the walk. Gracie took my hands facing me, and gave me a gentle kiss on the cheek. The dense gray from the overhead clouds matched my mood, and the sharp gusts were like surges of voltage to my body.

"Any news?"

"Nothing. Horner and the team are still interviewing gang members." She squeezed my hand. "I'm going to check in with them hourly."

"How do I look?" I asked.

"You look good."

"Don't have Fiona to tell me anymore." I smiled solemnly. "And I don't even have Lily here to tell me I look like shit. She should be here. She's missing her mother's funeral."

"I know, baby." Gracie gently led me to the car. We said nothing else, and we were on our way, complete with a police escort.

We arrived early and walked in the funeral home side by side. Earth tones bathed the large room. With ample rows of seating and just enough of a religious touch, it would reach capacity today. My rib felt better, or maybe the pills had something to do with that. I could probably last a full day in the field if I didn't exert myself.

The director invited me into the next room for a private viewing. I had my moment with Fiona at the morgue, but agreed anyway. I feared that seeing her again would make me crumble. When I entered the distinguished, wood-paneled, flower-adored room, Fiona's parents were already there. They turned to face me, wiping their eyes.

The last time I saw Joe in a suit was at our wedding. He wrapped his arm around his wife and escorted her out of the room without a word. That hit me right in the heart. With no one else around, I stood near the coffin and stared my wife. The reconstruction and make up artists had done a wonderful job. Tears dropped, but I wasn't crying in the traditional sense. I stared at her for so long, she stopped looking like my Fiona.

"I'll get Lily back," I finally whispered in her ear.

When I returned to the main room, Gracie handed me a Coke as we stood near a wall hosting a landscape oil painting. Fiona's parents kept near the entrance, talking with mourners. My mother-in-law Harriet, Fiona, and Lily all looked so much alike. If you were to see a picture of them side by side, you might think it was a display of age progression. Lily looked exactly like Fiona, relative to her age, so grown up. Four days have come and gone and Mardi Gras Day was that much closer.

A tap on my shoulder barely registered. Dylan stood there barrel-chested and square-jawed. His biceps challenged his suit sleeves and I wondered which of his harem dressed him with such good taste. We stood face to face. Gracie excused herself.

"Dylan."

He appeared rested and refreshed. "No news, I imagine." He glanced at my forehead's exposed stitches. "The news makes it sound like a kidnapping gone wrong. Did they want a ransom? You know I'd give you any amount of money."

"Would you?" Had I fallen into an alternate universe?

"I would." He reached his hand out to me, but withdrew.

"Thanks for coming, but all you're doing is making me uncomfortable."

"That's the last thing I want. I'm still your brother."

"You're a better running back than brother." I felt my heart racing. "I've watched you play football in a Saints uniform every Sunday, and you know what's sad? I like that relationship more."

"I messed this up." His hand moved back and forth between our chests.

"Mom and dad are gone. You don't have to pretend anymore. We don't have to be *related* anymore."

"How many times do I have to apologize?"

"All you want."

"There's going to come a time when we might be all each other has." His eyes squeezed shut. "Shit, that came out wrong. I'm not good at this." He hesitated. "I've grown - matured."

"Then, prove it. Let me grieve in peace."

Dylan backed away to leave, however on his way to the exit, he stopped to whisper in Joe and Harriet's ear. I thought Fiona's parents hated Dylan along with me, but maybe I was wrong. Dylan disappeared into the milling visitors as Gracie gravitated once more to my side. I sipped my Coke, wanting to make a joke that there should be Jack in it, but Gracie was already worried about my state of mind.

My parents had been killed two years ago when their train derailed on its way to Chicago, otherwise they'd be at my side. Dylan hadn't argued for our parent's train settlement. An NFL star suing his brother wouldn't sit well with the public. The money set me up for the rest of my life as long as I didn't live like a rock star. It made my sporadic consulting paycheck easier deal with.

My eyes found Fiona's profile in the coffin... so beautiful. The more I struggled not to picture her in the morgue, the more the image haunted me. Juan Gomez would be put to death and I had been instructed to kill the one man that refused his stay of execution. I needed a bathroom break.

Within a few steps, I saw Lily's best friend Madison looking lost. She had obviously been crying. She was talking with members from Lily's sailing team. It was a hobby I never thought Lily would stick with, but it turned out to be a passion. Madison wasn't on the team, but these kids knew each other. She saw me and we engaged in a hug. Madison held on for dear life, heaving with stifled sobs. Lily was her best friend and I imagined her to be distraught beyond words.

Madison pushed away from me. "Anything?" She squeaked. Her normally tan skin looked ashen.

"Not yet, honey. We're doing all we can."

"I told the detective everything I know. We texted each other the day before. I couldn't help." She wiped her nose with a handkerchief.

"Just stay positive."

Someone as pretty as Lily should have a group of fan friends, but she resented cliques. She and Madison had been like twins since they were ten. Madison kissed me on the cheek and then went to pay her respects. I just got more affection from Madison than I ever did from my stepdaughter.

CHAPTER ELEVEN

The morning after my wife's funeral, I woke with a moderate hangover, but ready to get on the road. The guilt had already set in from not searching for Lily yesterday. Before I could get out of bed, I got a call from Joe. My cottonmouth required a cup of water before I could talk to Fiona's father clearly. Her parents had gotten the funeral and burial they wanted. My throbbing head couldn't handle an argument.

"Hi, Joe. Sorry, I'm not quite awake yet." I wiped at my face.

"You slept? Funny, we couldn't sleep over here." His grating voice made me want to wring his neck, but he was hurting, too.

"Well, I had some liquid help, not that your opinion of me will ever change. No news on Lily yet, if that's why you're calling."

"I wanted to catch you before you give away or throw away Fiona's things."

"Joe, I swear to God..." I glanced around the room. Her stuff was still as she had left it.

"The wife and I want to go through her personal belongings first."

"I loved her, Joe. You know I loved her."

"Doesn't mean you were good for her." An exaggerated breath

came over the other end. "Just call us when you're ready. Goodbye, Remi."

I thought back to the last time the in-laws were in my house two years ago. We had a barbeque and they only came at Fiona's urging. Dylan had even made an appearance having received an invitation from Lily. It was one of the most uncomfortable days of my life. While I pretended to prepare the food and cook, Fiona occupied her parents and Dylan spent a lot of time with Lily – too much time.

"You were pretty chummy with my brother," I had said to Lily after everyone left. "I didn't even know you had his number. When did all this happen?"

She sat on her bed in tight shorts and a tank top, concentrating on her cell. She showed too much cleavage for a girl her age. Her head popped up and her hair flew behind her back. "He gave me his number at your wedding. So?"

I hesitated to choose my words. "I just don't understand why you'd rather talk with him than me, the guy who loves your mother."

"I'm not talking about this with you right now." Her head dipped again. "Please leave."

But, I didn't leave. I stepped up to her bed and sat. "Okay, forget about me. Dylan isn't what he seems. He's... got problems. Don't let yourself get wrapped up in them."

She stood to get away from me. "Are you actually forbidding me from seeing him?"

"You're going to do what you want, but I want it on the record. Yes, I don't want you to talk with him."

"Why?"

"Because." I stood to leave. " If you knew someone your entire life that was a bad person, and then someone you cared for wanted to be friends with them, wouldn't you warn them?"

She pretended to think about it and shrugged in that condescending way that made a parent's blood boil.

"Don't see him anymore." I left the room before she could respond. Had she heeded my words? I had no idea.

CHAPTER TWELVE

According to the antique stores we had visited the day before Fiona's funeral, many treated the Afghan War rug as a piece of art, something to showcase on a wall. The Artifact was next on the list, opening at ten this morning. I parked at Headquarters and Gracie drove us down the oak-lined St. Charles Avenue toward The Artifact, situated in a high traffic area of Magazine Street. The shadows of leaves caressing the windshield offered some tranquility, at least.

Gracie let me wallow in silence for the ride. For just a moment, I imagined that getting nearly shot to death never happened, and that I never killed Egor Baskov. I rewound to the time before arresting Juan Gomez. I pretended that I hadn't joined the force and my wife was still breathing.

"Did you see the news this morning?" Gracie asked, breaking me out of my hypnotic state.

"No."

"We got Jane Doe's picture out to the networks. We have a dedicated hotline."

"Good."

"Nothing so far, obviously. But, I think the only way to get this national – on Good Morning America and shit – is to offer the truth on the earrings."

I looked at her. "Not yet. We can't spook the Serpientes into killing my daughter."

"Okay." Gracie's hands bounced off the wheel with imperfect rhythm and her eyes darted. She appeared to not know the route, but she knew every damn street in the city by heart. We eventually parked in front of The Artifact, but she didn't open the door. Instead, her hand found my elbow and paused.

She finally spoke. "I smell last night's alcohol on you."

"Stick of gum – got it."

"I know yesterday was horrible, but you were once a cop. You know what can happen at any given moment."

"Give me a break. You want a field sobriety?"

She petted my hair before lightly slapping the back of my head for the sarcasm. "I got nothing against drinking. We've hit the bottom of a bottle a couple of times, but hangovers aren't good. Being sluggish isn't good. While you're on the job with me, you need to be clear headed."

"I got it. Alcohol – lunatic – sluggish."

"It'll be so easy to fall into a hole you can't climb out of." Her eyes found her lap. "Don't go back to the bottle tonight – or tomorrow night. Promise me you'll want it instead of need it."

"Promise." I smiled as her eyes softened. I touched her hand. "I'm lucky to have someone to call me on my shit." We sat in silence for a moment. "Damn, you're a strong-willed southern woman."

"You know where I came from."

"I do. Your maw maw pole vaulted into the States from *Meh-he-co*."

Gracie gave me the stink-eye, but couldn't hold her laughter.

"Tell me the story again."

Gracie's eyes grew reminiscent. "My maw maw migrated to New Orleans and became an American citizen, living on welfare and government cheese and peanut butter." She sighed. "She married an Irishman. They raised my mother in poverty and she eventually married a Latino friend so that he wouldn't be deported.

She thought she loved him and had me just a year later." Her eyes turned wet. "My momma took a frying pan to his head when she saw my bruises. He left and I never saw him again. I come from a long line of strong women."

"That's an amazing lineage."

"End of story time. Let's go." She got out of the car.

Shops and restaurants that were popular with the more frequent tourists and locals peppered Magazine Street, just outside the Quarter. We suffered through the mild chill until reaching the shop. The bell chimed, alerting a pleasant, middle-aged woman behind the counter. The heated store was filled with antiques on tables, shelves and walls. Chandeliers of every age and size hung everywhere.

"Welcome," the lady greeted, slow as honey. She wore a tight, low-cut blouse with pushed up breasts. I easily imagined her as a heartbreaker when she was younger.

"Is Mr. Morris here, Ma'am?" I asked.

"Yeah, he's in the back, *hawt*. One moment please."

It was Sanford and Son for the new millennium. What looked like junk had some pretty hefty price tags. One small section of iron balcony was priced at three hundred bones. Makeshift aisles throughout the shop were lined with antiques and memorabilia, some of which I wouldn't look twice at if it was in an alley.

Moments later, Mr. Morris came out taking short quick steps. "Yes?"

"I'm Remi Doucet and this is Detective Gracie Castillo. We understand that you're an expert on woven rugs and Persians."

"Does Bill Gates know computers?" He pushed his glasses back up to his face. "What would you like to know?"

I handed him a picture of the rug and his eyes lit up. "Oh, I know this design. These rugs were available during the Russian War. It's an Afghan War Rug… very desirable, but we've never sold that kind of item here."

"Anyone you know sell them?"

"Could have been any number of shops, but there is one dealer here in New Orleans that specializes in these items. But I'm afraid I have some bad news." His grim face puckered. "This is a rather odd coincidence."

Gracie and I turned to each other, knowing we were too late.

* * *

We drove Uptown to the address of Bobbi's International Luxury, which had been reduced to a charred shell the day before, just like Mr. Morris said. They set the fire the day of Fiona's funeral, when I could have made it here in time. The windows and doors had been boarded up with *do not enter* signs posted. Although the structure was still intact, we weren't getting inside anytime soon. Gracie had made a call to the senior inspector of the Fire Prevention Division, who said the fire had been set with accelerant, most likely gasoline.

The seventy-six-year-old owner, Sonje Bobbi, had died from a blow to the head, not being burned alive. There were no computers, and all handwritten records that had survived Katrina were not so lucky against the fire. The inspector also told Gracie that the Second District caught the case.

I called a friend in blue that I had just spoken with briefly at Fiona's funeral. "Captain Rigsby, please."

"Who may I say is calling?" the polite female voice asked.

"It's Remi Doucet."

"Former Detective Doucet?"

"Yes."

"My condolences, detective. One moment, please."

Five seconds later, Rigsby came on the line. "Where y'at, Remi? Any news on your daughter?"

"No news, but I'm assisting Detective Castillo and the investigation may involve a certain arsonist that burned down Bobbi's."

"Witnesses say two Latino gangbangers were fleeing the scene as the building lit up."

"Did you catch them?"

"No. That's being looked into, but I have other problems right now."

"What's going on – if you don't mind me asking?"

Rigsby moaned through the phone. "We had a guy commit suicide in the cell yesterday."

"What?"

"The cause of death hasn't been released yet, but it will be soon. Surprised you haven't heard the whispers. Our boys pulled over a driver that ran a red about a mile away from Bobbi's, as a matter of fact. He hung himself with his own shirt."

"Hung himself? Really?" I bit my tongue, as there had been many *mysterious* deaths in jail cells over the years. "Who is he?"

"No identification. He never said more than *yes* and *no* in custody. Didn't ask for a lawyer. Didn't speak another language. He just stared at us like he was drugged. Thought he was retarded for a while. A few of the boys think he might've been the arsonist, but we have two separate witnesses that gave the same description of two Hispanics."

"If you collar them, can you let me know?"

"Sure thing. Take of yourself, Remi."

"Thanks, Cap." I hung up the phone and faced Gracie. "Rigsby said witnesses saw two Latino gangbangers fleeing the fire yesterday."

"Serpientes, it would seem." Gracie started for the car.

"They also pulled over a guy who ran a red light and when he couldn't produce identification and wouldn't say anything, they took him in."

"Wait, unrelated to the fire?"

"Yeah, unrelated as far as they know."

"What about him?" She opened her door, but waited there.

"He hung himself in his cell."

"Yikes. So, our Latino arsonists are still on the loose?" She asked, and then slid into the driver's side.

"Yep," I answered once inside the car. A dull pain had crept into my chest, so I took a pill without water. "Why would they kill this girl and wrap her in evidence that we can trace, only to have to cover their tracks?"

"Someone fucked up," Gracie spouted, putting the heat on full blast. Her cell rang, interrupting our train of thought. She answered, nodding and agreeing before ending the call. "The Feds want to meet us this afternoon."

"All they're going to tell us is Egor Baskov's people wasn't involved and to stay away from him."

Gracie rubbed my shoulder. "Let's not assume anything."

CHAPTER THIRTEEN

The warm conference room and this constant state of draining anxiety had me ready to doze off against my will. Agents Foster and Joiner waited silently for everyone to gather. Our first meeting replayed in my mind in choppy clips, but things had settled and I was more focused. Gracie and Captain Trout also attended. Detective Horner, I learned, was trying to track down the Hispanic arsonists.

We had made a round of shaking hands. Agent Foster's bulbous knuckles barely squeezed and the younger, enthusiastic Joiner was the opposite, almost crushing my fingers. I couldn't take my eyes off several folders stacked near them.

"You're looking much better today, Mr. Doucet," Joiner said. "Got your color back."

"Remi, please. Not a hundred percent yet, but getting there."

"Let's get to the matter at hand, shall we?" Foster asked.

"Let's." I leaned forward on the table, hands clasped.

"We've determined that Baskov's trafficking ring and your wife's murder are unrelated. Sorry, to be so blunt."

The table sat silent.

I finally spoke. "You mean you came all the way over here to tell us one sentence? Who was Baskov working for?"

"Victor Dudko," Joiner began.

"Joiner." Foster merely gave his partner a look to shut up.

Joiner continued, with a bit of flush to his face. "But, that doesn't matter to you, does it? Turns out the casing from your wife's murder matches casings recovered from a cartel shooting near South Padre Island, just over the Texas border."

I cocked my head. "That gun is now here in New Orleans?"

"With the Serpientes, I would assume." Joiner paused. "The second set of casings from the Claiborne overpass murders don't match anything in the database, but the female victim was Hispanic, yes?"

"Yes," Holly said, "And the bullets from the three boys?"

"They either hit bone or fragmented. Too damaged to tell. You'll notice we brought files from our Violent Gang Task Force."

I held up my hand. "So, you don't know the second set of casings weren't from the Russians."

"Correct." Foster placed pictures of Juan Gomez and several other members of Los Serpientes on the table. "But, there's nothing to indicate Russian mob about those four deceased. That was gangbanger territory. Los Seripientes run through those neighborhoods. You collared the nephew of a cartel boss. As you know, Los Serpientes mule in millions of dollars of drugs into the city and have direct cartel affiliations."

Trout scooted his chair closer to the table to see the pictures.

"George..." He pronounced it '*hor-hey*.' "...Torres." Foster pointed down at a man with a thin face and neck tattoos. "He did six months for attempted murder. Before coming to New Orleans, he kidnapped an American woman in Mexico for ransom. He got away with sixty-six thousand dollars, and his victim was released unharmed."

"We'll pick George Torres up," Trout offered.

I absently looked at George's picture. "I'm a bit of a high-risk, low reward, wouldn't you think?"

"Not with your brother who can pay millions."

"They'd be wasting their time."

"The money might be secondary, Mr. Doucet. They get to retaliate, plus they get a pay-out." Foster collected the pictures and placed them back into the file. He pushed the folder toward me.

"You're completely pulling out?" I asked.

"The Bureau's Violent Gang Task Force is at your service should you want it. Just give them a call. Ask for Agent Stan Brock at the Lakefront field office. We appreciate your patience, Mr. Doucet."

I stared at the file.

Foster stood. "We'll leave you to it. Good luck, Mr. Doucet."

The agents left after another round of handshakes. This time, I braced myself for Joiner's grip.

Trout handed the file to Gracie. "Get on finding George Torres. Take some uniforms. Remi, I can't have you involved in this."

"I'm okay, Captain."

"No. You can go over the file with Castillo here, but you are not to do any field work. You're going to be a witness if this goes to trial. Whatever we find needs to stick. We can't have any lawyer claiming you tampered with evidence because you went out on the call."

I sucked in a breath and threw my pen on the table, knowing where to fight my battles.

Satisfied with my submission, Trout left. When Gracie and I were alone, we spoke freely. Gracie said, "It's really concerning why no one has contacted you yet."

"What if the Feds just wanted to throw us off Egor Baskov's trail? Who is this Victor Dudko that Joiner made the mistake of mentioning? His people are Russian drug traffickers, right? Possibly, human traffickers."

She stared at me. "Like, they're purposely pointing us at a red herring?"

"Here are the realities: Los Serpientes would kill *me* and leave Fiona a widow. They didn't. The Russians would kill everyone I love and leave *me* alive to suffer. That's what's happening."

"We found out a lot today. Let's work the case with the facts we have, okay?"

"Right." I stood. "Excuse me a second, I have to make a call."

I found my way outside Headquarters, to the scenic courtyard with benches and a monument in honor of Louis J. Sirgo, an officer killed in the 1973 Howard Johnsons sniper incident. I scrolled the contacts on my cell for an old acquaintance and dialed.

"Hey, Bobby Lee. How's my favorite warden?"

"Remi, long time, my friend. How's your business?" His twang brought back memories of working with the Marshall Correctional Facility on security for their work release program. Bobby Lee Roads and I had the same sense of humor.

"Slow, like everything down here. How's the misses? Still a slot jockey?"

He laughed and blew out air. "Hell, yeah. Wish they'd ban her ass. Although the other day she came home with five thousand dollars."

"No shit. Well, that can go toward your girl's college tuition, right?"

"Shit." He drew out the word. "Now, she needs to hit ten more of those jackpots to break even. Ah, it makes her happy. What can I help you with, Remi?"

"I need to see an inmate. One Juan Gomez."

"The *brown* fella you put in here that's set to get a cocktail?" Bobby Lee referred to all nationalities as colors, except with the press, of course. "One of the NOPD already had a visit with him."

"Yeah, I don't think he asked the right questions. As you know, I'm no longer NOPD. Can you arrange a *fais do-do* without putting me on a visitor's list? Today maybe? I can be there in two hours."

"I can set up the meeting in a private room they use with the lawyers so nothing gets recorded, but your visit has to be documented."

"Thanks, Bobby Lee. I owe you one."

CHAPTER FOURTEEN

I t had been a while since I visited this place. The Marshall Correctional Facility housed almost two thousand male prisoners on a desolate plot of land just north of Denim Springs, about a hundred miles north-west of New Orleans. The dense, solid watchtowers oversaw the property in every direction. The chain link, barb-wired fence and walls of stone indicated the finality of their fate. Within those confines, only the toughest and smartest (or possibly stupidest) survived. Each man entered with nothing; with little hope of rehabilitation, but was left with their fear and aggression to fester.

I had to sign a waiver at reception and I left my gun in the car, but thanks to Bobby Lee, my visitation would happen in a normal room without video or audio. A burly, but friendly-faced guard led me to a small room where Juan Gomez already sat, his hands chained to the top of the table. The walls were a dull, powder blue and flaking. It wasn't a place meant to inspire.

We assessed each other as I took a foldout chair. Juan had aged in his eight years of hard time. In his forties now, his wavy, dark hair developed streaks of silver over his ears and his bushy mustache drooped with his frown. His eyes were sensitive as I remembered them, but being a boss in Los Serpientes, he had to be cold and calculating.

"You." Juan had no accent.

"Me."

"I told the other gringo I don't know nothing." He lowered his head enough so he could push down his moustache with the few inches of slack in the chain.

"I'd like to think we share a bond. Respect for the enemy type of thing."

He regarded me. "You pull a few strings and get a meeting in a room with no video, no guard – no witnesses. If I don't give you what you want, you going to beat me? I'm about to *die*, detective."

"Then, die with honor." My machismo needed to match his. "You're not completely cut off from the outside world. You still give orders."

"And you're smart enough to know that nothing is free is this world." He rattled the chains.

"Always looking for a deal?"

"You don't know what I want." He cracked his knuckles.

However, I did know what he wanted. "I'm sorry your son saw me arrest you."

Juan's eyes pulsed. "That is a good start."

"The FBI is trying to pin my wife's murder and step-daughter's abduction on Los Serpientes. The killers wore Lee Street tennis shoes."

He hiked an eyebrow. "What else did they wear?"

"Full gray jumpsuits. Masks. Gloves. Sunglasses."

"I see. And then they wear shoes popular with the teen members of Los Serpientes? Because we would trust the youngest members of our organization to pull off such a delicate operation."

"I know."

He hesitated with a twitch. "These Federales – they offer up one of my men – a goat?"

"George Torres. You know where he's at?"

His jaw clenched, but his hands couldn't pull away. He again, strained to wipe at his moustache. "He'll turn up dead before you find him. That is how the government operates."

"I'm going to ask you point blank – man-to-man. Did you order the hit on my wife for retaliation for putting you in here?"

He leaned forward over the table. "After eight years?"

"A dish best served cold?"

"I'm going to tell you something that I'll never admit to another soul, amigo. I'm *glad* you put me in here."

"How's that?"

His face settled. "I was born into this life. My father is a high-ranking boss just south of the border. My uncle is *his* boss. They groomed me to rise even higher, and then I had a son. I saw my death every morning I woke. I saw my son's death every night in my dreams."

"How old is your son now?"

"Thirteen. My wife and son were legal Americans."

"Were?"

"After what my son had to witness with my arrest, I told my wife to get out. She took my son and money, and with legal passports, moved to Spain to escape the clutches of my other *family*."

"That's good."

"My son will have a chance at a normal life." His eyes closed, nostrils flaring. "My life for his. I could have ordered retaliation, but I said no. It was my choice. No one would challenge that."

I nodded. "Help me give my step-daughter a chance. Does your gang have any problems with our governor, Steve Sharpe?"

His eyes narrowed. "Other than rejecting my stay of execution?"

I nodded. "There was an attempt on his life last month."

"We cannot claim responsibility for that."

"It's my turn to tell *you* something no one else knows, and I hope it dies with you."

He swallowed, slightly smiling.

I whispered, "The person who kidnapped my daughter is blackmailing me to kill Sharpe."

"Hmmm." He lifted his chin, assessing me from under his lids.

"Forget the retaliation. My theory is that with Sharpe dead, the Lieutenant Governor will swoop in and save your ass. Makes sense."

His expression turned to concern. "How did your wife meet her God?"

A long blink lingered. "They shot her in both legs, then the shoulders, and then her head."

"There is your evidence. If I was to seek revenge, it would not go down like that. Retaliation for what you did to me – for how you crippled the organization – would have been extreme. Your wife would have been decapitated as a show of power. Skinned or dismembered even. You remember why I'm here, amigo?" His gaze took us back to that day.

"We found a dead Latino girl the other day wearing my daughter's one-of-a-kind earrings. The dead girl's throat had been slit."

"The shoes – the slit throat." He laughed. "What you Americans call a *frame-up*. Our young men kill with bullets when their *little wars* dictate these actions. The squabbles of our young members are like kids at daycare while the parents take care of the real business. Our power is based in fear. What better way to strike fear into your enemies than to remove the head from the body? How else do you send a message to those with faltering loyalties?"

"Several Latino gangs have established themselves in New Orleans. I haven't heard of any beheadings."

"They would be rare in these parts. New Orleans is a destination for the product – a distribution center. These are a younger generation, more familiar with a gun than a blade." His head flipped back in ridicule. "Drive-bys, firing randomly, hurting innocents – it's embarrassing. If I had ordered your wife's murder, a bullet would have been merciful and we have no mercy. Lee Street shoes? Are you kidding me?"

"You know who might be doing this?"

"I do." He used his shoulder to scratch at his ear. "Those who do harm to others, never find themselves with just one enemy."

I almost jumped from my seat. "Who is it? Let me take care of your our enemy for you."

He hesitated just enough. "Talk to the governor for me. Perhaps we will talk again."

"I see." I scooted back.

"Just try. If not, then come back and watch me die. Respect for your enemies, yes? Don't worry, detective. I *do* have contact with the outside world, and there are ways to exact revenge on *our* enemies without bloodshed. If you don't get to do it..." He eyed me with a cocked head and a sly smile. "Guard," he yelled.

I left the correctional facility on wobbly legs. Gomez insinuated that we had a mutual enemy. What was really behind this devious plan that included placing all suspicion on Los Serpientes? I took two pain pills, as the two-hour drive home racing against the setting sun would be a long one.

CHAPTER FIFTEEN

My cracked rib was the best alarm clock I ever had. There wasn't as much pain as annoyance. My attention focused on Fiona's pillow while I faced her side of the bed. A coating of sweat appeared on my face and my legs began to burn. I threw the covers off and welcomed the cool air. Just when I thought the tears would come, I pushed myself to a sitting position. I needed caffeine.

I grabbed my cell to make a call as a K-Cup brewed. "Gracie, you up?"

"I'm almost out the house already."

I spoke loud into the speaker while I dressed with my phone on the bathroom sink. "Call Captain Rigsby. Tell him we want to look at the body of his suicide victim this morning."

"What? Why?" Her voice crackled through the speaker.

"He was near the scene of the fire. I'll regret it if we don't. What do you think?"

"Let me make the call so Trout doesn't suspect you're with me. I'll meet you at the M.E.'s."

I believed everything Juan Gomez had told me. These witnesses that saw two Hispanic gang members running from the burning building were manufactured. This man at the morgue either committed suicide or was killed in custody, which meant someone didn't want him to sing. But, apparently he wasn't going to say a damn thing anyway. Could it have been a true suicide because he was ordered to?

I drove to the coroner's office, a brand new facility with sparkling new equipment. This place reminded me of identifying Fiona and I felt a bit nauseous, but shook it off. Morgues were usually a place free of emotion and sympathy. They had to be a clean, cold environment where bodies waited for their final resting place.

Gracie signed us in at reception, much like a doctor's office. We were directed into the next room and presented with the body by the attendant on duty. Two other bodies lay on tables side by side, in line for autopsy. All the other unfortunates were kept in another room like a huge cooler.

Our guy wasn't the most recent death and had been previously put in storage, but the M.E. took him out at Captain Rigsby's request. The naked corpse exposed a myriad of tattoos. His hair was long and brown and he had the face of a boy – very effeminate.

"Doucet and Castillo - The Deuce and *Cas-tee-yo* – like old times." Dr. Billy Phillips danced into the room as if listening to his own theme music.

"Billy," I saluted him. We had spoken briefly at Fiona's funeral, so there was no need for him to inquire about the investigation.

"He suffocated himself." Billy stopped dancing. "Definitely the cause of death. Samples were taken from his exterior and sent to the lab. Other than that, I'd have to cut him open to tell you more and it doesn't seem like that's going to happen for a while – a long while."

"Why's that?" I asked. The tattoos were mesmerizing.

"I'm very busy, as you can see, and no one has claimed him. Detective Roberto said they have everything they need. If no family turns up, his body will be donated to a university. Tulane Medical, most likely. They'll cut him open." He spun his hands in a disco move, but stopped when noticed how serious I was.

"So, you're going to sign off on suicide?" I asked.

"That supports my findings." He wouldn't look at me, checking the hanging balance used to measure organs.

"What do you make of the tattoos?" I pointed. The two eyes on his waistline, just on the front of his hips, were especially creepy.

"Very unusual. We took pics of his front and back and a close up of his face and hands. They'll be in his file."

"We'll want to see that," Gracie said, taking her own pictures with her phone. I decided to do the same, marveling at the resolution.

The double doors swung open and the Second District detectives came in, sent by Rigsby to check up on us. They introduced themselves and we did likewise. Detective Hank Roberto was a medium build with a classic Italian look, dark complexion and wavy hair, about 40 years old. His senior, black partner, Jimmy Wingurder, had thin hair around his ears, with a long face and out-of-style moustache. His clothes hung loose, as if he had lost weight.

Windgurder took a wide stance. "Anything our guys can do to help find your wife's daughter, let us know."

Roberto agreed, "Right, we're all behind you." He gave his partner a slight glance.

I know that they didn't ask for details because without any contact from the kidnappers, they assumed she was dead. They'd never verbalize their suspicions.

"Thanks, I appreciate it."

"So, you're interested in our John Doe?" Roberto asked.

"Yeah, we're investigating a female that was wrapped in a unique rug that we believe was sold out of the location that was burned down."

"Witnesses say two Hispanics were leaving the scene. Not this guy." Windgurder said.

"But, those Latinos aren't in custody," Gracie said, "It seems like someone is covering a trail, cause now this piece of evidence is useless."

Roberto came off as defiant. "This guy didn't do it."

"Can we speak to your witnesses?" I asked.

"Really?" Windgurter's chest puffed out. "How about we send you their statements?"

"We can't interview them." I stated with annoyance.

"No, *you* can't. Detective Castillo can. Call the station. I'll give you their names."

"Wasn't anyone keeping an eye on him in the cell?" Gracie interjected.

Wingurder never lost his scowl. "Many of our guys were at your wife's funeral at the time. You know we don't monitor prisoners every minute. It was quick. The car was stolen and he had no identification. The next thing we know, he's dead."

"I do appreciate your guys coming to the funeral, detective. So, did Bobbi have any family?" I questioned.

"His daughter stands to collect the insurance and she lives in Florida. She hasn't had contact with her father in five years since he threw her out for not going to medical school. She's a teacher with a family. We don't like her for that. We're looking into Bobbi's financials, but nothing stands out."

Gracie nodded. "Then the motive is to cover up the identity of who purchased that war rug."

"War rug?" Roberto scratched his head.

She ignored him. "Los Serpientes *could* be behind this, Remi. The cartel bosses have been known to collect extravagant things."

"Mexican cartel bosses?" Wingurder did a double-take. "Didn't know we had any here."

"What do you think of the tattoos?" I asked.

"He's fuckin' crazy," Roberto countered.

"Yeah, he was an extremist," Wingurder added.

"Have you shown your pics around to tattoo artists?" I asked.

Roberto blinked hard. "Yes, we showed the tattoos to the owner of Ink Me in the Quarter. He said the ink was crude and the designs look European. Either done in prison or someone's basement."

I scratched at my ankle holster with my heel. "Any weapons found in his car?"

He stared at me. "No. No weapons." He broke eye contact to check his cell phone and then put it back.

"Anything else in his car?" I asked.

"We've been through it. No title, no registration. Stolen plates. VIN number missing."

"We'd still like to take a look if you don't mind."

Roberto eyes glossed over. "Okay."

My fists clenched. "I don't get your reluctance to answer our questions. We're not interfering with *your* investigation, we're following *ours*."

"Blue Jetta at the impound lot. Tell them it's the suicide guy's car. I'll call ahead."

I tried to imagine how I'd feel in his position, but thinking like a douche-bag didn't come naturally. "Thanks. Y'all call us if you come across anything else?"

"Certainly," Wingurder said, as we made a round of shaking hands. "Good luck with your case."

Roberto nodded as a professional courtesy, and walked back out the doors with his partner. I caught him shaking his head as if we were amateurs on their turf.

"What the hell is going on?" Gracie asked.

I arched my back while staring through her, but the sudden pain reminded me I was still healing. "I don't know. I just know this is important."

CHAPTER SIXTEEN

T he next stop of the afternoon was the Taboo Needle, a hole in the wall preferred amongst the musicians and Harley-Davidson enthusiasts. The decor was colorful, comfortable, and extremely warm. *We Will Rock You* flowed from speakers mounted in the corners. The owner made the most of its narrow space, with a small reception desk just inside the door and a long couch along the wall for a waiting area. Huge, beat to shit binders sat on a cheap, oval table near the couch, along with King Cake and coffee. Samples of the artwork were in every space available like a gallery. Drawn black curtains towards the back hid where the magic happened.

The petite blonde sitting behind the table parted her lips in a wide smile. Her teeth were whiter than most, but her left front tooth slightly overlapping the other, like her braces didn't take. Her T-shirt had been sliced into a "V" that extended so far down that a quick turn would send a boob flying out. She had trailer park good looks and appeared to be in her element.

"Ma'am," I said with charm, unzipping my coat. Gracie showed her badge.

"What can we tat for you today? A small *floor-dalee* is a great starter. We have lots of variations from traditional French royalty to the Saints."

"I'm Detective Castillo and this is my partner Remi Doucet."

"From the news." She straightened, placing both hands over her heart. "I'm so sorry about your wife and daughter. I'm Kate."

"Hi, Kate. We were hoping to talk to your tattoo expert here. Who would you recommend?"

"You need Dax, my brother. He is so into tattoos, he knows everything about them. He's written for Tattoo Magazine and always goes to conventions."

"That's our man." I slid out of my coat welcoming the heat. Gracie did the same.

"Hold on, I'll text him."

"He's not here?" I asked.

"He's in back." She continued to text until she hit send with force.

The blonde stared at her phone. It signaled a reply and she frowned. She got up, rounded the table and planted her feet, facing the back. She sported cut off jeans, presenting the kind of butt that Daisy Dukes were made for. If she suggested a tattoo, I think most heterosexual men would listen.

She projected her voice. "Detectives are *really* here. That's why I texted you."

"Give me a second," he screamed.

"He don't want me leavin' the front." She stood on her tip-toes as she yelled. "Okay." Under her shrunken shirt, I spied a butterfly carrying a snake on the small of her back.

"We're cops, so we can watch the front," I offered.

"Oh, right, duh." The little firecracker skipped to the back of the room.

Gracie frowned as I stepped up to the coffee table to grab a slice of King Cake with a mix of green and purple icing on it. "Gotta eat." I excused myself. "I'm on fumes."

Moments later, Kate returned with a tall, thick-bodied blond. A pair of glasses rested on his head and another pair hung around his neck. He had a baby face, plump, with eyes that seemed to be crossed. He wore a biker shirt that had been fashioned into a tank top and ink-stained jean shorts.

He spoke low. "Sorry, Kate here likes to joke with me about celebrities showing up for a tattoo. I thought she was kidding."

"You look dressed for summer," I commented to both of them.

"We live upstairs and Dax keeps it extra warm in here since most of the customers end up naked one way or another."

"What's this about, detectives?" He whispered. I figured he spoke like that from years of holding a conversation in close proximity.

"We'd like to show you some pictures." I handed my cell phone over, already on the first image.

He took the phone and his eyebrows arched. He swiped at the screen with a new expression for each one. "Wow," he said, scratching his head. He looked back at us, then went through the series one more time. "This is a morgue. Is this guy actually here in New Orleans?"

"What can you tell us?" Gracie asked.

"These are Russian prison tattoos."

"You know what prison?" I asked.

"Nah," he laughed boisterously, roughly inhaling between heaves. "Dat's a good one."

"Thanks. What else can you tell us?"

He continued, "This guy was a prison bitch when he was younger, if you'll pardon the expression. The tats have faded and he's what, maybe fifty?"

"About," I agreed."

"See these eyes on his waist? This guy was held down or knocked out while these tattoos were given to him. No one would voluntarily get these. These eyes on his waist signify that he was available for sex from the higher ups. You see, Russian prisoners have their own secret tattoo code, or at least they used to. Each tat means something different. It lets other prisoners know what they were in for. It's a ranking system."

"So they don't tat anymore?"

He shrugged. "I heard the tat movement shifted from status to personal beliefs, but I'm sure there's a mix going on in the rougher prisons. Time stands still in those places."

"So this guy was the bottom of the food chain?" I asked.

"Oh, yeah. See right under his real eyes? Those two dots that look like tears? He was labeled a homosexual. These guys are what they call *the lowered down*. Not all lowered down are gay, but all gays would be in the lowered down class."

"Are Russian prisons a hobby for you?" I asked.

He let another airy laugh escape, and gestured at his walls. "Look at my place. I live and breathe tattoos. You don't just appreciate the face value of a tattoo. I like the history of them, the stories behind them. Russian prison tattoos are very fascinating."

"What about these crosses around his back?" Gracie asked.

"Years he was sentenced probably. Most times they're church domes. Some tattoos are open for interpretation."

"Why would they allow tattoos in prison if it was a means to communicate?" I wondered.

"They don't allow it… wink-wink, but they always find a way. What they do is shave the soles of their boots and melt them, then mix it in their own piss for the ink. They make their own needles, too, with anything available. I read one of the things they recovered in a search was a sharpened guitar string. Wild, huh?"

"Anything in the tattoos that would indicate Russian Mafia?"

"I doubt it. They wouldn't want him as a player. Doesn't mean they couldn't get him to do stuff for them, though. He probably did everything he was told. I can't believe this guy was here in New Orleans."

"Can you tell what crimes he's committed?" Gracie asked.

He looked at the pictures again carefully. "Arson, maybe? I'm taking the fire around these bones literally, though. It could mean something else, but considering his status, arson is pretty cowardly."

"Thanks," I said, taking the phone back. "You've been very helpful. We may be back sometime in the future with more questions."

"No problem. Can you do me one favor? I'd love you to email me copies of those."

"We'll see after the case is over." I smiled, put my coat back on, and we began to walk out.

The firecracker Kate called out to me. "Detective Remi… Good luck. I'm praying for you." She leaned on her elbows. Her arms squeezed her chest together, pushing her cleavage outward. If she had a tail, it would be wagging.

"Thank you." I turned and closed the door behind us. We got into Gracie's car and put the heater on full blast while we sat pensive. Gracie spoke first. "What now, boss-man?"

"I had a meeting with Juan Gomez."

"Without telling me?"

"When my theory goes against everyone else's, I find it easier."

Gracie slapped her steering wheel. "It's me, damn it. And this is my case, not yours. You can fuck up evidence. You know this."

"I'm sorry, Gracie. You know I trust you with my life – and with Lily's life. I just didn't want to bring you into my thinking until I was sure."

"Are you sure?"

"I don't believe Los Serpientes is responsible."

"There's so much evidence."

"I need you on my side. So, I'm going to let you in on something I've held back."

She grew angrier, which was a scary prospect. "You kept more from me?"

"For Lily's safety – yes. That night when I said those men didn't say anything – that was a half-truth. One of them played a recording from an audio device. They said I had to kill Governor Steve Sharpe by Mardi Gras Day or Lily would die."

Gracie's jaw dropped. "*Our* governor?"

"So, you can see why Juan Gomez would have no reason to lie. Hell, he would tell me I'd better get moving if he wanted it to happen."

Gracie finally collected herself. "You can't kill the governor."

"Of course, I can't. I want to shift our investigation to Egor Baskov. To hell with the Feds."

"Jesus, where would we start?"

"I think the boss of Baskov's gang wants to put the blame on someone else, and reap all the benefits without consequences. But, the question is; what are the benefits? What does Sharpe have on him or won't do for him?"

"What if Sharpe has absolutely nothing to do with this? What if he's just a means to an end?"

I paused, letting that process. "I think I know where you're going. The Russians get rid of me and cripples Los Serpientes at the same time. In the drug trafficking world, they could be stepping on each other's toes."

Gracie nodded. "After the storm, the Latino gangs grew exponentially here. It's possible they're having some kind of gang-war. There's lots of money and drugs that move through New Orleans."

"… But, killing Sharpe is going to fall on me. I can scream blackmail all day, but I'll still go down for the murder, and Serpientes will deny everything."

Gracie stared in the distance, verbalizing her thoughts. "What would Russian drug traffickers have to gain by the governor's death?"

"Any number of political ramifications." I finally slipped on my seatbelt. "Maybe we should see if Sharpe has any connections to any ports along the river."

"I'm sure he does." Gracie drove toward Headquarters, making me feel much better to have an ally.

CHAPTER SEVENTEEN

The day's tour ended without much progress on the *why's*, but we were content that we had a direction. Our closed case files didn't offer much on Egor Baskov, and any information we could use was locked up tight with the Feds. With eight days left until Mardi Gras, we tossed around the option of confronting Joiner and Foster again, but shelved it for the day. I hoped for a new video of Lily, just to show me she was hanging in there.

I arrived home hungry for a hot supper and heated up Dylan's jambalaya, which was the last item left. The evening news showed the Claiborne Jane Doe again. They took ten seconds to also mention that Lily was still missing. Coincidently, the third segment featured Steve Sharpe commenting about the state budget. I imagined stepping up to him like Ruby had done with Ozwald and putting a bullet into his heart.

After the news and eating a small bowl of delicious Jambalaya, I called Dylan.

"Remi – you must have news to be calling me."

"No, I'm just eating your Jambalaya."

"Really. I thought you might think it's poisoned."

I smiled, remembering I said the same thing to Gracie. "What do you make of Steve Sharpe? Personally?"

"Ah… He's got that wall."

"Wall?"

"That honorable, strong leader wall. His smile and handshake and shiny coating is all anyone ever sees, except maybe his inner circle. He's got that wall up and I have no idea what kind of man he is. He's a nice guy. I can tell you that much. Seems like he loves his family… why?"

"I might need to meet with him." I massage the back of my neck.

"My people can arrange that. As a matter of fact, Sharpe's riding as king in Rex on Mardi Gras Day. No one knows yet, so don't go blabbing. You know how secret that organization is. They're going to announce it a few days."

Riding on a float in Rex on Fat Tuesday would be an open invitation for a sniper attack. "Will he have a glass enclosure?"

"Like the Pope? Doubt it. He told me he's going to ride with extra security."

I winced at the thought. "Thanks for that and the jambalaya. Gotta run."

"Anytime, brother."

The darkness acted as a comforting companion while sitting on the couch. The lights were off and so was the television, a rarity in this home. I missed Lily's voice, sarcastic as it was. She would never tell me what I had done to make her hate me. It had to have been a misunderstanding. Had she overheard a conversation and misconstrued its meaning? My cell chimed with a text message and an attachment. Every muscle tightened at once. An unrestricted number flashed. No doubt from another burner, figuring I wouldn't try to track it.

The attachment was another lowres video of my stepdaughter. It started the same as the first video, except she had on a different shirt. She looked clean, but her hair was unkempt and her face was free of makeup. Again, she spoke with nervous hands.

"I'm still okay, Remi. They're letting make this video to show you I'm being treated okay. I get showers. I basically sit in this room. I'm not scared anymore. I'm tired of being scared. Do whatever it is they want you to and then they'll let mom and me go." Lily looked at the person recording, then back into the camera. "You get us out of this, and I'll forgive you."

The video ended. *Forgive me?* She definitely thought I did something bad. Lily didn't know her mother was dead. I played it over and over until memorized. I compared the two videos, watching them one after the other, trying different things. I listened to it with my eyes closed. I watched without the audio. Nothing clicked. I would take it to show Gracie in the morning.

I stared at dead shadows of gray and black around my living room. Feeling guilty for my fight with Fiona would be stupid. Every man and wife, parent and child, brother and sister, had arguments. Fiona and I loved each other and our fights were a part of that love. Those were great moments, they were family moments, and they should be included as loving moments.

My ribs ached from a long day, even lying on an incline on the sofa. A vodka rocks sat within arm's reach, growing lighter and warmer. I told myself I couldn't get a full night's sleep without it.

CHAPTER EIGHTEEN

A dog's distant barking forced my nightmare to end. I threw my arm over my face as the sun beat against the living room curtains. The inclined sleeping position started to warp my spine. Getting up like an old man, I stood flat-footed in front of my refrigerator for two minutes before excavating the bottle of vodka.

The alcohol sat on the coffee table demanding attention, making my mouth water, my stomach shrink, the anticipation building. Do weak people drink, or do people drink in moments of weakness? Seven more days. *Make the right choice for Lily.*

Gracie's name lit up my cell. "I'm up." I hid my anxiety, keeping my voice steady.

"I thought about it all last night. Let's tell the Feds we like the Russians."

"Welcome aboard, boo."

"If the arsonist is Russian, the Feds can track him down."

I ran my fingers through my hair. "Plus, I'd never forgive myself if we risk Lily's rescue by holding back something from their investigation."

"I'll set up an informal meeting."

"Okay. I want to take a look at the Russian mime's car in the meantime."

She laughed, repeating, "Russian mime."

"I have a meeting with Doc Margie after lunch. The police shrink will have to clear me if I want to get my badge back."

"You want your badge? That's great."

"I'll call you later today."

I hung up. The vodka went back in the freezer, unopened. My ass found the sofa and I took a deep breath. The silent house screamed in my ears, if that made sense. I had to figure out if being a detective again was a good idea. Lily would still be my responsibility when I get her back. Of course, I'd adopt her, if she'd have me; if she didn't blame me for Fiona's murder. My brother Dylan popped into my head for second, but I swatted it dead like a fly.

With my little nest egg, I could give serious consideration to absolute retirement. But, then it wouldn't be long before Lily was off to college and then what? I leaned forward with my head in hands, still smelling Fiona's faint scent in the air.

These fuzzy minutes brought Fiona to me as if a hologram. She walked towards me in her black Brees jersey with an Abita Amber, taking a swig out of it first. I tried not to blink, but the tears wouldn't allow it. Fiona's voice spoke as a whisper. *I was looking forward to our talk.*

After the moment passed, I fixed myself a single serving of coffee with milk and sugar, a reminder of my new solitary life. Being a detective could be the only thing left in my life. How many years would pass before I found myself an alcoholic, ending my existence with a bullet in my head? My thoughts lately have been so dark and random that sometimes they scared me.

I took a tiny sip of my Italian brew. A few of Jane Doe's photos on my coffee table caught my attention. I examined them again in case I missed that one important detail. But, real life didn't work that way. The photos offered nothing new.

With a headache growing, I pulled several heavy-duty garbage bags from storage and brought them into the bedroom. The main closet contained all of Fiona's clothes. I had been relegated to the closet in the spare bedroom. Every outfit reminded me of different events we had shared. After standing like a statue for five minutes, I put the bags down to go check out the Russian's car. I could bag up her clothes later.

* * *

The Parking Division impound lot was a little farther down Claiborne from where we found the Jane Doe. Gracie called ahead for permission to inspect the Russian's vehicle, as it was no longer considered evidence in any investigation. I parked under the I-10 overpass near the entrance, walked past metal barricades used to direct the tow trucks, and knocked on the deep gray shed-like structure they used as an office.

The overweight, bearded worker answered wearing an LSU jacket and earmuffs. Days ago, we had a brief, friendly exchange when I picked up my car.

"Yeah, hi. I have permission to check out the Jetta of the suicide guy."

He reached inside for a clipboard. "Right. I got the call. How you been, Remi?"

"Dealing."

He exited the shed carefully as if stepping on ice, not commenting further. He escorted me to the location, about a block down past a row of cars. I thanked him and he waddled back to the relative warmth of his office.

The Jetta had been towed to an area marked for eventual sale by auction, probably to be sold to a junkyard for parts. Being under the shade of the overpass seemed so much colder without the sun helping out. People thought of New Orleans as a hot place, but when they visited in February for Mardi Gras, they learned different.

The dented door creaked open and I fell into the glacial passenger seat with a slight stab to my chest. The glove compartment was first on my list. Nothing jumped out at me – or at least nothing of value, as anything important would have already been retrieved by CSU.

I endured sustained pain while inspecting the floorboards and under the seats, building up welcomed body heat in the process. The car was filthy from dirt and debris, but without any discarded trash. Lastly, the trunk needed an inspection. There was an old set of ratchet tools and a can of air for tire leaks. I flipped over the carpet material covering the spare, and only saw a crinkled piece of paper that had fell next to the tire iron. I took off my glove and plucked it out, gently smoothing the thin receipt against my coat.

A faded *The Hardcore Store* was printed at the very top. The single item purchased was disguised with letters and numbers that didn't make sense, but ended with the word *video*. The purchase date was about a month ago. It had cost twenty-four dollars, which was paid for in cash. I recognized the business name from passing it by in the Quarter.

The receipt hadn't made it into the Second District's evidence. I had no issues with keeping it in my pocket until I could show it to Gracie. If this guy ended up being our arsonist and the receipt needed to be evidence, then we'd be screwed. But, we hadn't a reason for a chain of custody.

Being so close to my house and almost out of the donated food, I picked up some Popeye's chicken and stopped home to eat. A sleek, black Ferrari glowed out of place in my driveway. It had to be Dylan, but how did he get inside my house? I pulled my weapon out, anyway.

A familiar aroma infiltrated my nose upon entry. I switched off the safety and entered the kitchen in silence. I recognized his backside. My brother flipped a grilled cheese sandwich in a pan. There were three empty grocery bags on the floor.

"What are you doing?"

His palms hovered over the pan for a moment, spotting the gun at my side. "Don't shoot."

"Let me repeat…"

He adjusted the fire under the pan. "I figured you haven't

shopped. I thought I'd stock you up. Decided to make a sandwich and if you showed, then I could make you one, too. You want one?"

"How'd you get in here?" I put the gun down, realizing my Popeye's bag was still in the car.

He exhaled, sliding another sandwich into the pan. "Lily. She told me about the key under the brick."

"She did, did she? Well, that's going to change. How long has this been going on?"

"Recently." Dylan flipped the sandwich. "Anything new on finding her?" He looked away. "Of course, you wouldn't tell me. The only news is that she hasn't been found."

I stepped up and took a bite from the first sandwich he made, speaking as legibly as I could with a mouthful. "Why are you talking with Lily?"

"I'm her uncle, sort of. I think she figured we had a common enemy." He glanced at me with a smirk. "I talked you up… I really did. We talked about high school stuff. Boys she liked. Nothing important." He dropped a third grilled cheese in the pan.

"She didn't happen to mention why she has this life-long vendetta against me?"

He shrugged. "She thinks you're fucking your ex-partner, Gracie."

"That's ridiculous. Why?"

Dylan shrugged. "She didn't say. Maybe she misconstrued a phone conversation. But, you're always going out for drinks or poker with her."

"That'd explain a lot." I rubbed my forehead. "Of course, I'm not sleeping with her."

"None of my business."

"We've joked that she's my work-wife. I love her like a sister."

"Makes sense. You had your lives in each other's hands."

"Yeah, but why talk to you?" I finished my sandwich.

"I'm a celebrity. That's important to high school girls her age. She probably wanted to show me off to her friends."

"She only has one friend."

"Are we mending fences?"

I opened the fridge and pulled out two cans of Coke. "I think it would be a long road. But, you did figure out a secret that's been driving my crazy."

He smiled, taking the cold can. "This would make for one fine commercial – you handing me a Coke on the precipice of making up."

"More like a cliff."

"I'm going to prove I've changed."

I only nodded. We ate in silence, standing near the stove.

"I have an appointment in a half hour," I hinted.

When he realized the moment had ended, he took one last bite of the cheesy sandwich. He turned off the flame, wiped his mouth and left for the door, taking a look around before closing it. If Dylan continued in this manner, he could very well weasel his way back into my life.

I cleaned the dishes while longing to get lost inside a bottle of anything, but a drunk couldn't rescue Lily. The decision to throw out my bottle of vodka came to mind, and I opened the freezer to find it missing. *Missing.* My eyes shot to the frying pan and then the door and I almost smiled. Would I be setting myself up for another disappointment?

Full from a nice lunch, I did an Internet search of our governor and Mississippi ports while I waited for Doc Margie. To my surprise, I found something important, very easily. It looked like Governor Steve Sharpe was in charge of appointing the fifteen-member board of The Greater Port Of Baton Rouge. None of the names listed were recognizable, except for one that the feds happened to mention – *Victor Dudko*.

Interesting.

CHAPTER NINETEEN

Doc Margie arrived for the early afternoon session in casual attire: jeans and a Saints sweatshirt, something that would put a client at ease. She assessed my home, searching every wall, maybe looking for a quick conclusion to my state of mind. Her large brown eyes made her feel like a dear friend.

After some preliminary small talk, Doc Margie took position in the recliner. Her inquisitive eyes smiled at me, but she didn't comment for a moment. My hands roamed over the plush material of the new coach while waiting.

She started. "First of all, I don't report back to anyone about what is said here today. Total confidentiality."

"Got it."

"Simple question. How are you?"

"Anxious." I shrugged. "I go through the whole gamut, actually."

"Which emotion is the hardest?"

"Is guilt an emotion, or a state of mind?"

"When you witnessed your wife's murder, how did you feel at that moment?"

"Anger first. Disbelief. Panic. Sadness. All of them. I didn't think it was true. I didn't believe it was real until I saw her in the morgue."

"How long was it before you thought about your folks?"

I stared at her for a good five seconds. "Very soon after waking up in the hospital."

"Why do you think that is?"

"I wish they could have been there for me. They would have been the first call I made."

"Your brother showed up at her services?"

I nodded.

"Was there friction between you?"

"How do you know about that?"

"He was a Saint's player. You're tepid about his candidacy. Every cop knows you don't get along. The animosity is well documented."

"We were never close."

"Why do you think that is?"

"He always had his own agenda and it didn't matter who it hurt."

"Like…"

"He just treated me like shit."

"But, you were a good brother?"

"He wouldn't let me be."

"Did he treat your parents with the same disregard?"

"No."

"Did you?"

"No. I mean, I could have been there for my folks a little more than I was in the years before the accident."

She took her time in writing something in the notebook. "It can be said that each death of a loved one adds to the foundation on which you live your life."

"Look, I don't just want to tell you the right answers, but if I tell you I'm not feeling rage, you'll know I'm lying, and if I tell you I want reach into the gunman's chest and show him his beating heart, then you might not give me the check mark to return to police work. Forgive me if I'm a bit skittish."

"I don't think you'll have a problem returning, but yes, you will need my approval."

"Which makes you my new best friend." I allowed myself to grin.

"Your emotions aren't wrong, whatever they are. It's recognizing them, dealing with them and not letting them fester. I don't want to sound cliché, but bottling up your feelings is what does the most damage." She turned a page in her notepad. "You're in the process of clearing out Fiona's things?"

"What would it say about me if I packed it all up the day after she was murdered? Would you ask me if I wanted to skip my mourning period? What's the proper time to do it by society's standards, huh?"

"Do you feel that pressure?"

"Since Fiona was murdered, I've cried, I've mourned, I've hated. I've even blocked it out. And with Lily, I've held on to the fact that I'm going to get her back. In my fantasies, I dispense my own vengeance, but in reality, these men will be put to justice and I'll allow the system to work. I have to be there for Lily and killing someone would take me away from her. Lily is my foundation."

She wrote again, nodding slightly. "When you were shot up five years ago, you subsequently retired."

"I had a second chance. I ended up meeting the love of my life. It's something that probably would have never happened if I stayed a cop."

"You shot Egor Baskov five times while being shot yourself. A Hollywood type ending."

I shrugged. "Adrenaline."

"The final shot was to his head." Her eyes became slits.

"I wasn't aiming at that point. I'd been hit and didn't know how bad it was."

"It's your word against a dead man's. And there was little if no investigation into your actions and high-fives all around. You become a public figure loved by all. Great way to retire." Doc Margie scratched her nose.

"The law was on my side. I took a drug-dealing murderer off the streets and the tax payers didn't have to foot a prison bill."

"Sorry for grilling you. I'm just testing the waters. Are you more concerned with solving Fiona's murder or properly mourning?"

"Both?"

"What were your parents like?"

"Oh, here we go."

"Trust me." Doc Margie smiled without blinking. Her face was like Wonder Woman's lasso of truth. "What type of person was your father?"

"Rugged and hard-nosed. He was a construction worker. He loved being outdoors. Curious. Inquisitive. He loved puzzles and riddles."

"Do you think that's where you get your detective skills?"

"I'm sure it is. He was so proud of me when I solved one of his brainteasers. He'd give me one almost every day."

"But, not Dylan?"

"Dylan laughed at the MENSA puzzles and IQ books."

"Maybe he was jealous or upset that he couldn't figure them out."

"He seemed too conniving to be stupid."

"But, you and your father had these puzzles as a bond. And I'll bet you tried your best on every one of them."

"Sure, I wanted to make the old man proud. Ah, I know where this is going. Yes," I said with a knowing nod. "You are good. You think I'm driven by an adolescent need to make my father proud; to make up for what was lacking with Dylan."

"It's ingrained in you to find the answer. It trumps all other needs, including the need to grieve. You shouldn't beat yourself up over it." Doc Margie scribbled. "Tell me about your worst experience as a police officer."

I smiled sadly. "You sound like Fiona." And then I paused a few seconds. "I won't be cleared with the NOPD until I do this, right?"

Her eyes told me she had just won the chess match.

After three quick hours, Margie closed her notebook. "My, oh my. That went on longer that I expected. Okay, I think we've covered enough." She pulled her legs out from under her butt and massaged her calves.

"Am I cleared?"

"Not yet. My report would be a little suspect in a case like this. You just lost your wife and your stepdaughter is currently missing. If you flip out and I'm on the witness stand, I can't say I cleared you after a three-hour session under this kind of stress. I'd like to have another visit. In a few days, I promise."

"*Flipped out.* Is that a psychiatric term?"

I walked her to the door where she promised things would get better with time and she kissed me on the cheek as if we've been friends for years, but that was a New Orleans custom. Perhaps it *was* my father's influence that wouldn't allow me to let go of a mystery. But, could I live without solving my wife's murder? Could I spend the rest of my life wondering if Lily were dead or alive?

CHAPTER TWENTY

Vanessa wore a clean pair of jeans and new blouse because Client Five didn't get off on slutty clothes. He liked young and defiant females, like mean high schoolers or college feminists. Miguel lit another cigarette as he walked down the depressing hallway, giving a nod to Ivan, one of the five men in charge of the building's security.

Miguel opened the door to see the two girls. The cop's daughter paced the room while Vanessa sat awake on the mattress; her knees up in her chest, curled up like a scared spider. The poor girl *knew*. Her body was drugged into complacency while enduring a vicious circle with other clients, barely aware of the bruising and tearing.

Most girls didn't stay in the building for more than a week. Unless a client requested them, they are moved to other parts of the country, if not abroad. A few would stay, however. Client Five had targeted Vanessa and she was being weaned off the heroine, which they had only started giving her weeks ago. Her visceral reactions were Five's aphrodisiac. Miguel respected a strong spirit, but in those cases, it depressed him. She had threatened to mutilate herself, so that nothing would ever enter her again. He had heard that before.

Still, Miguel was morbidly amazed at what Client Five liked. The most sickening part was his insistence that his girls keep their eyes open, clear and aware. Once the day came that Miguel got to kill Client Five, he would make his eyes stay open, too.

"Tell me where my mother is." The cop's daughter demanded.

Miguel ignored her and took Vanessa by the elbow. "It's time."

"No." She stood despite the slack protest.

Miguel placed his palms on Vanessa's cheeks while the other girl crept into his peripheral vision. "Dear, if you imagine the vastness of the universe, the billions of stars and planets and the infinite space, and imagine the billions of years that have passed, then the mere acts that are perpetrated by foolish men on this insignificant rock are relative to the blink of the eye. You can see how irrelevant all of this is."

"Crock of shit." The girl named Lily folded her arms.

Vanessa's voice cracked as her throat closed up. "Then let me go and it won't mean anything, right?"

"Touché. However, most men believe their actions are more meaningful than the wonders of space and time. I'm still young enough to be one of them."

"This is meaningful?" The girl's voice gained volume. "You're a hypocrite. The way you talk, it sounds like you lost your soul. It sounds like you've given up on being a decent human being."

Miguel used his free hand to palm Lily's cheek. "I am a hypocrite and I am also a Gemini. It may seem ludicrous to believe in such things, but astrological forces determine all events in the universe, including human behavior. The moon even affects us."

"Isn't that just in your head?" The cop's daughter pushed his hand away.

"Humans are ninety percent water. The moon pulls at us same as the tides. We think the human race will always be here. That what we do is so important. With all that mankind has achieved, plotted and connived, all it would take is one asteroid to end it all, to start over from scratch. Wouldn't that be something?"

"Don't give me to him," Vanessa blurted.

Miguel's heart sank as he pulled out a blindfold and placed it on

Vanessa. Leaving Lily in the room by herself, Miguel and Vanessa walked the cold damp corridor with his large-knuckled hand resting on the small of her back. Behind her blindfold was a huge pair of Owl-like eyes set in a petite face. She had been captive in the building for nearly six months. Her chest appeared huge in comparison to her petite frame. She was a unique beauty, so she had been acquired.

They walked together as if on death row, each light above creating double shadows as they passed under. He knew the steps, sixty in all, forty steps to a staircase, up the stairs, then twenty more. It was there at the door, hearing the latch turn that her body shook violently. If these girls were pathetic enough, maybe no one would want them. It only added to the experience.

They stopped and he stroked her hair. "Here we are."

He pushed her forward into the dungeon room, where Client Five sat on a chair next to a wall with shackles bolted into the brick. If the building was considered hell, then this was its boiler room. The sadist had a mask and he had tools. His sessions hadn't started this way. Client Five had been rough, but the abuse and implements grew in time. He learned what he liked and Miguel determined that they would soon allow sanctioned serial killing. Her body jerked and contracted until she fell into ball.

Client Five gave a short nod to Miguel. She was to remain blindfolded until Client Five decided otherwise. He enjoyed the power to the point of seeming psychotic. Miguel slammed the door shut and returned to his video feed to watch the first few minutes of the session. She didn't cry as her wrists were shackled above her head. Instead, it was as if she braced herself.

Miguel hoped she would do what he suggested, telling herself that the sensations were someone else's and to let her mind flee. If she just let go, she could float away, watching her body as it got smaller and smaller until she was above the city, spreading her wings for flight. He hoped she would do that.

* * *

The wall buzzer pierced Miguel's eardrums, indicating that Client Five had been satisfied. In an emergency, the dungeon's door could be opened from using a key code on the inside, but that would break the strict rules. Miguel bookmarked a ragged copy of The Art Of War and glanced at the monitor. Client Five towered above Vanessa, blocking her from view. Being in the presence of that kind of evil triggered his anger.

Miguel returned to the specially designed dungeon room, yelling through the door. "I'm coming in." He turned the heavy-duty handle with a loud click and Client Five pushed through the door as if he needed to escape.

"Sorry." Five pulled off his bloody shirt. He was red in the face, out of breath and sweating.

Miguel saw the young lady hanging forward in the shackles. A slash opened her skin across the eyes and her pelvis was unrecognizable, leaving a trail of blood on the wall. He had stabbed her multiple times. She was gone.

"What the fuck did you do?"

"Sorry. It got outta hand." He looked back with apparent arousal upon seeing the young girl slumped in a Jesus-like pose.

"Boss is not going to put up with this kind of behavior."

"I didn't kill the other one."

"Yes, but you forced me to. I've heard of men like you." Miguel faced him.

"Men like me?"

"Men who develop a sexual fetish that escalates. You get off on these girl's deaths. What will you have to do next, once you are unsatisfied?"

"I don't have to answer to you or your men."

Miguel stepped up to the body. Her breasts had been, as best as he could determine, tampered with. So much blood had poured out of this little four-foot-ten girl. He palmed her eyes closed and said a silent prayer. It was one thing to just have sex, forced though it may be, but the torture reminded him of his prison days when men's bodies were torn apart because of loyalties.

"Don't judge me." Echoed from the hall.

"That is for your God. Expect a meeting with *el jefe*."

"Yeah, yeah, just get one of your drivers to take me out of here, please." Client Five left to change in the washroom. His clothes would be burned in the on-site incinerator and a shower would be had. Miguel contacted a man called *Yaz* to take Five out of the building in one of the trucks and drop him off at a safe location. And disposing of Vanessa would be Yaz's job also. Miguel refused to do it again and would tell the boss so. Client Five was becoming a huge liability.

CHAPTER TWENTY-ONE

That morning I arrived at Headquarters just after Gracie and waited patiently while she settled in. The meandering cops addressed me with more familiarity, having seen me the past few days. Once the small talk ceased, I fixed a cup of coffee and found my partner. Without any onlookers, I showed her the two videos of Lily. Gracie's face froze in shock. Like me, she replayed each video. Her furrowed brow morphed, intensely watching and listening with laser focus.

"Why did you wait to show me this?" Gracie's face turned hard.

"I don't know. Maybe every time I let you in, I lose a little control. I'm scared, Gracie."

She looked back at the phone, angry. "We should let the Feds analyze this."

"Anything leaks, Lily's dead." I looked around to make sure no one was close. "No one else can know."

"Okay, I'm with you," she whispered. "I promise. I hate to say it, Remi, but seeing this video must be a relief."

"I know what you mean, and yeah. They don't want me so distraught I can't function. I only have six days left."

She fell into her chair. "I've gone over this in my head. Why kill the governor? What is there to gain?"

"Guess what I found out?"

"Tell me."

"Victor Dudko – the Feds white whale – is the president on the board of the Greater Port of Baton Rouge. The governor appoints the board."

"That's a definite connection. Dudko either wants you to kill Sharpe to take over an operation or because the governor is becoming a thorn."

"That's what I'm thinking."

"The M.E. got to our Jane Doe. We won't get tox screens back for a week, but the autopsy didn't reveal anything we didn't already know. Young girl, healthy body, but she had been beaten up on several occasions."

I eased into my own squeaky chair. "Too bad. She's still a connection."

"Phillips uploaded the report, but said we can go see the body after lunch." She paused, collecting paperwork on her desk. "So, you gonna talk to Trout about coming back on?"

"I have to wait until Doc Margie clears me. That's what he'd say anyway."

"Will she?"

"She's skeptical about doing it while Lily's missing, but I think she's going to bat for me. Let's do *something* for the time being. I don't want to waste a minute."

Gracie hiked an eyebrow. "Well, I think I got something." She handed me a laser printout. "This is a statement from an anonymous stripper right after you shot Baskov. I found it in an obscure online article about the shooting."

I read the hi-lighted portions. "Says she gave Baskov a lap dance the night before. At Booty Call. The place on Bourbon."

"Maybe that was his hang out – a Russian hangout."

"It's something." I closed my eyes for a long moment.

"You okay?" Gracie's voice seemed to drift from a long way off.

"I'm good."

Finally opening my eyes, Captain Trout came out of his office, stopping at Gracie's desk. "Horner just called. They found George Torres."

"He's not dead?" I asked, remembering Juan Gomez's premonition.

"No, he's dead. He was found in a burned out car along with another man fitting your size description from Fiona's murder. Horner's searching for Hector Aragon, next up in the chain."

I leaned back. "Glad he's still at it."

Trout patted my shoulder. "Odds are, these two are your killers, probably given an order by Aragon through Juan Gomez."

"You'll let me know when Horner finds Aragon?"

"Of course. I'm impressed how you're letting us handle this. Keep that cool head, Remi." He backed away.

Gracie remained silent. Trout had pushed the same agenda as the FBI. My paranoia told me to keep everyone out of the loop until we talked with the Feds.

* * *

Early on, viewing the Y-incision was the worst part of the autopsy experience. Now, I could eat a ham sandwich during one. Whether it was the gore or facing mortality, cops can't help but imagine themselves on that slab. The Latina girl's face had been peeled back over her head. Her throat also had been pulled apart. Lily might've been the last girl she talked to.

Dr. Billy Phillips flashed Gracie and me a pleasant smile while writing notes in an open folder on the counter near the autopsy table. "The killer used a knife with a serrated edge on her throat," Dr. Phillips said, "and yet, a sharp, razor-edged utensil was used on her face."

I tried not to focus on any one particular organ in front of me. "Two different weapons? The slit throat killed her?"

"Yes. The laceration across her face indicates a left-handed attacker. The slash across her throat was by a right-handed man. Could it be the same man? Possibly. Can't tell approximate height from either wound. Abrasions on her wrists tell me she was chained or shackled, which means she could have been sitting down or on her back or even hanging from a wall."

"Raped?" Gracie asked.

"With the obvious trauma, yes, but no visible trace of semen. Sodomized, too."

"Anything else out of the ordinary?" I asked.

"Take a look at her pubic region. See how the hair growth is uneven?"

"She had a pattern shaved there."

Phillips handed me a picture. "I traced the best I could. Looks like some kind of devil with long horns."

"You got the horns right. This is the Texas Longhorns logo. The college football team."

"She's from Texas." Gracie inspected the picture. "Or a football fan," she added, a bit mawkishly.

Phillips pointed at her exposed mouth. "She once had braces. Her teeth were taken care of. I doubt if she was a poor Mexican."

"Well, this narrows down the search to a state."

Phillips gave us everything he had before moving on to his next body. It was the end of Gracie's tour, but Trout approved all the overtime involved in finding my daughter. Gracie went back to the station to search missing person's records from Texas while I took a detour to a certain porn shop from the receipt I found in the arsonist's car.

.

CHAPTER TWENTY-TWO

The closed sign hung uneven by string in the door of The Hardcore Store. I had sat in my car for two hours hoping the owner just went out on an errand. A homosexual Russian buying pornography could mean nothing, but sex is sex is sex. I needed to find the connection between all the players. I drove away disheartened, but looked forward to visiting the Booty Call strip club.

The orange glow on the horizon signaled dusk as I eased my way back to help Gracie for a while. I zoned out while following the white dashed lines on the road, minding the pulsing taillights of the BMW in front of me. The car stopped, I stopped. They accelerated, I accelerated. Gracie called me while on the way and it was answered by the car's hands-free option.

"Yeah," I shouted at the Blue Tooth screen.

She sounded serious. "You need to meet me at Storyland in City Park by the tennis courts. Some kids messing around found a dead girl inside Cinderella's pumpkin carriage. Her face has that same diagonal slash."

"I'll be there in fifteen minutes." I put more pressure on the accelerator.

"And I'll be there in twenty."

The impending hugeness of another body had my pulse racing. I drove into the sparsely lit City Park entrance by Del Gado Community College and followed the winding road through massive oak trees. During daylight hours, a miniature train ran through the park with screaming kiddies holding cotton candy or sno-balls. People could play tennis, peruse the museum, ride bikes around and get food from the concession stand.

Storyland was an area in City Park that created larger than life scenes from children's stories, such as *the three pigs* and *the woman who lived in the shoe*. At night, when it was dark and deserted, anyone could drop a body off undetected. But why take the trouble to dump her inside Storyland when she could have been left under any of the park's trees for a quicker getaway? The answer could be that my time was running out, much like Cinderella at midnight.

The vibrant moon had replaced the sun. However, it was deep-woods dark under the massive, moss-covered branches. I approached the crime scene eerily lit up by squad car searchlights. The tennis court's stadium lights were on, but Storyland had closed.

I announced myself to the City Park cops and they let me pass unmolested, knowing Gracie was on her way. Surrounding us were spooky silhouettes of Goldie Locks and the Three Bears and Winnie the Pooh. In the distance, I saw the Big Bad Wolf attempting to blow down a house. They were all imposing, yet sad in their stillness. This new victim was lying halfway out of the pumpkin carriage, feet first. I glanced at the cop standing nearest to me.

"I'm Remi Doucet. I'm working with Gracie on this one."

"I know who you are, sir. Sorry about your wife. *Really*." As if not to be believed.

"Thanks."

He pointed at two individuals in his squad car. "Those black kids were loitering out here. They said they heard a noise, checked it out, and said her legs fell out as they are now." He fidgeted as if he was uncomfortable with being the center of attention. "I figure they might've been rifling through her clothes."

I did a quick once-over. She was tiny and naked. Her head was tilted as if to show off her wound. "You don't have those kids under arrest, do you?"

"They touched the body. They said they were looking for her I.D. Give me a break - black kids from the 'hood bypassing money for a license?" His breath smelled like baloney.

"Who called it in?"

"The kids." He didn't like admitting that.

I checked out his beer belly. "They call it in... And they hung around?"

"Yes, but that doesn't mean they're not trying to cover their tracks. Throw off suspicion."

"Are you *that* racist?"

"I'm a realist. You know what? As a civilian, you can wait over there behind the tape."

"I'm working with Detective Gracie Castillo, under the supervision of Captain Trout at Homicide. Do you want to make the call, or me?"

"Yeah, yeah." He didn't antagonize me any further.

"Earn your balls before you use them." I stopped looking at him. "Why don't *you* leave *my* crime scene?"

Gracie squeezed between us, appearing like magician minus the cloud of smoke. "He said you can leave this crime scene."

The cop scurried off as Gracie pulled out her own flashlight. If she hadn't arrived when she did, my fist might've found that man's teeth.

"Hate that guy." She softly patted my back, and then looked at the girl. "Ooohhhh-weee. From the lack of blood, she wasn't killed here. See anything that stands out?"

"Let me see." I checked for Lily's jewelry on her fingers, ear, and wrists. Then it hit me. I put on a latex glove to straighten out her twisted and bunched shirt. "She's dressed in my daughter's Army T-shirt from the video." My voice cracked.

Gracie squeezed my wrist. "They think they're intimidating you, but they're leaving clues."

"We need priority on this."

"CSU is on their way. Maybe Trout can have this one done overnight."

As if on queue, a white SUV pulled up to the tape. Dr. Jerry's team had been called specifically, since they were familiar with the killer's M.O. We made a round of greetings, but Gracie pulled Jerry away from the group. I watched as she spoke in his ear. Jerry nodded, touching her arm with familiarity.

Jerry took over the crime scene, spouting orders for collecting the body. For the next hour, we helped CSU and spoke with two detectives from the Third District, hoping they had found some witnesses, but there were none.

Gracie and I walked the crime scene again as the victim was placed into the coroner's vehicle. We checked the numbered markers sitting in the grass next to footprints and discarded items. Gracie broke my concentration. "We're meeting the Feds day after tomorrow. Lunch at Port Of Call."

"Day after tomorrow?"

"Both agents are in Virginia right now. They get back that morning."

"Anything on the Texas girl?"

"No, but I just started the search when this call came in. Anything happen at the porn shop?"

"Closed."

We walked back to our cars when Gracie stopped short. "It's only 7:30. Let's go check out Booty Call."

My eyes popped open. "Right. Let's do it."

Her voice lost its edge. "Besides, I got some things to talk about, and a beer might help."

"Once again, you're scaring me."

* * *

Fatigue forced unwanted yawns, but the thought of poking around Booty Call in hopes of finding a Russian connection energized me. If the Feds had the same idea, they might be watching the place. We'd find out soon enough.

The FBI's reputation for misinformation remained in the fore-front of my thinking. When we meet, I had to determine what to call bullshit on. Whether or not they believed Los Serpientes killed Fiona was immaterial. They could have orchestrated the frame up as easily as the Russians.

The streets were filled with bumper-to-bumper vehicles. We each had to park by a hydrant, so Gracie and I got separated on the one-way streets. I had to walk nearly a block, but we met up at the entrance. Dance music filtered into the crisp night air, calling Gracie and me into the bar, situated near the Canal end of Bourbon Street.

Gracie started the questioning with a handsome bartender wearing a white collared shirt and black bow tie. His name was Len Yazmovich. Russian name. Good start. He looked like he strutted right off a catwalk. However, he played dumb and we moved on.

We showed Baskov's picture to each employee with the same response – no one recognized him. It had been five years; could we blame them? However, as Gracie continued questioning, I kept noticing the first bartender Yazmovich watching us, until he eventually made a phone call.

After the last dead end, we located an open, yet somewhat sticky table in the rear, just far enough from the blasting speakers to hear ourselves talk.

My partner quickly and self-consciously checked her makeup in a compact mirror. When the busty waitress appeared wearing a two-piece bikini, I ordered a bottle of Abita Amber and Gracie selected the same. We didn't trust the cleanliness of their glassware.

"It's been a while since we were out together, socially." Gracie wiped her palms together. I wondered, was she nervous?

"How have we never hit a strip club together?" I wondered aloud.

"These places just make me sad."

The waitress set down our drinks and I fought against emptying the bottle on the first go. Instead, I took a swig and put it down on the napkin. Gracie did the same.

"We need to bring our theory to Trout." Gracie softened.

"Except for the governor thing. We need an ally. I think we can trust him."

"He won't risk his career for us."

"The squad likes him. That means something."

"I couldn't do this without you," I admitted. "I just don't know how much I trust the Feds. If they make the connection with the arsonist, we'll see if they're really being honest. See how they react." I took another pull of my beer and stared at Gracie, waiting for a revelation that never came. "So, you said you wanted to talk about something in particular."

"Right. There's something I have to tell you and I thought a cold beer might help – for you and for me. We found something that may be hard to hear." She spoke above a Billy Idol song.

"Pile it on."

"I just learned this earlier, before going out to City Park. They found something going through Lily's credit card statement."

"You're looking into her credit card statements?"

"Lily's and Fiona's. You know it's standard procedure, and I was sure we weren't going to find anything, so why get you upset?"

"I'm not upset. But you found something?"

"It seems there was a charge last month to the Stay Motel on Lily's card."

"The Stay Motel? On Rampart? That doesn't make sense."

"Remi, people go to that motel to shoot drugs, screw prostitutes, and basically, not be seen." She paused. "Did she have a boyfriend you wouldn't approve of?"

I shook my head. "No, no. Maybe." Fiona had mentioned some random loser Lily was seeing. The way things have been going for her – the way she's changed – I wouldn't doubt it."

"I've noticed the change, too. She's gotten so... Dark." Her brown eyes bored into mine as if sensing I was holding something back.

"Even if she was with a guy, it wouldn't be in that shitty place. She'd consider that place... Nasty. And it was only once, right? There's another explanation."

"It might've been the one time they didn't have cash. Do you pay her card?"

"No. She pays it. And why wouldn't the guy pay for the room? There could be another reason. We'll go down there tomorrow and interview the staff. This person could know something, or be related to the kidnapping."

"Sure. That's plausible, but Remi…"

"I know." My voice lowered. "Look, for now – for tonight, go with me on this. Things will make sense tomorrow."

Gracie put her hand on mine. "As cops, we come to expect the worst in people. We get jaded. We drink. Hell, we kill ourselves. How many times have you come home after work… missing a little more of your innocence… a little more of your optimism?" Gracie took another long look at her half empty bottle and sighed, "I'm not much for pep talks."

"I know what you're sayin'." I wiped my bloodshot eyes. "I have five days now before they expect me to – *you know*. I just want to shoot out of this chair and do something."

"Nothing to do, baby. We'll check The Hardcore Store and the motel tomorrow and send those agents a picture of the arsonist. See where that takes us. You've kept your head – that's why you're here with me. Don't fly off the handle now."

"I'm doing my best, but sitting still is the hardest thing to do." I finished my Abita. "But, I'm actually feeling optimistic about talking with the Feds." I drummed my fingers on the edge of the table, just as Lily had done in the video.

"Hold on to that. We have an early morning. One beer's enough for me. Don't have more than two." Gracie held up fingers to emphasis her point. She looked across the room and flagged the waitress for a check, but I pulled down her hand.

"You're going to Jerry's, aren't you?"

"Yeah, so?"

"Good. Good for you guys. I'll take care of the check."

"You sure?" Gracie stood with wide eyes. "Woo. It looks as if people are already gearing up for Mardi Gras."

"Drive safe."

She nodded, kissed me on the cheek, and patted my shoulder as she left. I didn't want to go home to an empty house. While the rotating girls avoided the obvious cop, I sat in a corner, alone, hovering over a sweaty beer. Yazmovich continued to gaze in my direction.

CHAPTER TWENTY-THREE

The morning's solitude attacked while I stared at the ceiling in my bed. Ignoring the pull of the black hole of despair, I showered, shaved, and wiped the crust from my puffy eyes. My deadline forever loomed.

Gracie pulled up to my house, revving the engine on the Trans Am.

"I'll drive." I showed my keys.

"Nope. Get in. I'm the detective."

I didn't argue. Perhaps I used my brooding, melancholy attitude to hide my nerves, but Gracie knew better. A couple of bagels on the dash steamed up her windshield. The cup holder contained an extra coffee, which I appreciated.

"How late did you stay?" she asked.

"Just for another beer. That first bartender – Yazmovich. Russian?" I asked.

"Probably. He did something?"

"No, but he seemed nervous. He got under my skin."

"Well, I do trust your gut. Maybe we can revisit him."

The Stay Motel was a two-story, three-sided box like a horseshoe with parking on the outside and in the center. Every door, every stairway, every wall was a decaying beige holding no promise of a wholesome experience. We parked by the front office and my mind wanted to shut down. Two unshaven, disheveled guys, one black and one white, crossed in front of the car, staring at us '*po-po.*' A fifty-something year old white woman in stripper garb stood in one of the doorways, smoking. A huge cloud rose as if she was smoldering compost.

Jesus, Lily.

The front office smelled like mold and weed. "Morning, sir," Gracie began, "I'm Detective Castillo. What's your name?"

"Jackson," the elderly black man stated. "Daryl Jackson."

Gracie placed a picture of Lily on the worn counter. "Do you recognize this woman?"

He put on a pair of glasses and reared back while squinting. "We don't get many of these here. Attractive, I mean. Yeah, put a hat and glasses on her. Could be."

"How many times was she here?"

"Several times that I know of. They come here to hide, but just the opposite happened. Stupid fools."

"They? She wasn't alone?" I asked.

"Nope. A man with her."

"What'd he look like?"

"White. They keep disguising themselves, you understand. Hats and glasses. She always come in here to pay. Never him." He stared at me for a long moment, shuffling papers on the counter. "The man was on the tall side, well built. Not skinny, you understand. Don't know how old, only that he wasn't old, you understand. I watch 'em 'cause nice lookin' white folks don't have to come here for cheatin', but looks like them did."

"You can't be sure of that." I leaned in.

The man scratched at his face. "Not the answer you wanted, son?"

"Why do you think something was going on between them?" I asked, forcing myself calm.

"I can see most of the lot from here. Dey kissed in the car. Dey kissed at the door. The kind of kissin' relatives don't do, you understand?"

"You remember what kind of car the man had?" Gracie asked.

"They always came in her car, an old blue Civic, but one time dey came separate. He come in a fancy dark car... maybe silver, fancy, like a Jaguar or Porsche. Parked it on the side of an SUV right over there, so I couldn't see it real good. He must'nt a cared about it too much, parking it in this lot, you understand. Folks around here looked at it like it was a *bait car* and left it alone. Ironic, eh?"

"Damn." I turned around and barreled out of the office.

Gracie caught up to me. "Are you okay?"

"Lily was having sex? I mean, I figured it could be happening, but like this?"

"This guy could be one of the kidnappers, getting in close."

"That doesn't make sense to me. If she was seeing him, then he wouldn't need to abduct her in a violent manner. He could have just brought her in his car."

"I say we don't rule it out."

I inhaled several deep breaths. "Considering the kind of car he drove and the disguise, he must be married and have money. He's not going to come forward. Let's go to Headquarters and get Trout on board. My deadline is looming and I don't want to find another dead girl." I got in the car and put my sunglasses on. Gracie didn't like that I disagreed with her assessment.

With Carnival season in full swing, most of the districts assigned their men to parade patrol, which included Headquarters. A few of the remaining cops nursed coffee while others took calls at their desks. The office looked like ghost town. Late morning in February and the station was colder inside than out.

I sat at a temporary desk with a decade-old computer and checked my personal emails, weeding out the spam. A search of

The Hardcore Store brought up a website of videos and sexual paraphernalia. Hours weren't listed.

Gracie returned from the bathroom as Trout came out of his office. He walked behind me. "Doc Margie told me your intentions. Ready to come back?" He stopped to look at my screen.

"Chomping at the bit. Look at this." I presented the receipt from the Jetta. "I found it in the arsonist's car."

Trout responded, "You show this to Rigsby's detectives?"

"They said their case was done."

"Yeah," Gracie backed me up, "they probably didn't think buying a porno meant anything."

Trout stared at me for a good few seconds before speaking again. "I've been wondering why you haven't been buried chest deep in the Los Serpientes. You don't think they did it."

"Los Serpientes *didn't* do it. We just can't prove anything."

Gracie looked at me. "Can I tell him about our Jane Doe?"

"Yeah."

"You know how Lily's earrings were on the first victim? Last night's girl had Lily's tee-shirt on. This isn't how Los Serpientes operate."

Trout scratched his head, looking like he had a senior moment. "And you've kept this to yourself?"

"Who do I trust, Captain? This is my daughter we're talking about."

"Well, I'm glad you finally trust *me*." He shook the receipt. "I know the owner of this place. Barry Franklin, known as Barry-Boy around the Quarter." Trout wiped at his lips. "He's very familiar with snuff films and the trafficking world. Human trafficking."

"Can we sweat him about this arsonist?" I perked up.

"I don't see why not."

"Bad guy?" Gracie asked.

"Harmless, petty stuff. Small time drugs, a short stint as a pimp, but his girls said he didn't have the stomach for it. Ironically, that porn shop keeps him on the straight and narrow. We've been trying to get him as a C.I. for years." Trout paused and looked around, dipping his head. "I connected him to a guy filming kiddie porn in

Covington. I'm ashamed to say that I had to lean on him rather hard – Dick Cheney hard – but he talked."

"Don't apologize to us, Cap."

"Get the Doc to clear you," Trout said. "I need more homicide detectives here, and I don't need a lawsuit."

"I'll be good."

"Gracie – regarding Barry-Boy, we crossed a line that one time, but under normal circumstances, he clams up under interrogation. But, he's a nervous talker. He'll talk your ear off, so it's almost as if you can't let him know what you're fishing for. Get him to volunteer the info." Trout dismissed us with a nod.

* * *

Gracie and I sat in wait for twenty minutes in front of The Hard-core Store. Nowhere on the storefront did it list hours of operation. Despite my sunglasses, I tried to avoid eye contact. She kept the conversation light, but I only gave her short, clipped answers and she took the hint. As optimistic as I felt last night, now I hit a low. It was as if I awoke every morning adrift with no anchor.

Noon hour approached. Not long after, the closed sign changed over. My legs felt stiff and my butt numb as I climbed out of the car, stopping to twist at the waist and hearing a resounding crack. It wasn't the rib. I felt a bit of discomfort, but nothing debilitating. I'd forgotten how invigorating a good stretch could be without shooting pain through my chest. Gracie walked ahead of me and opened the door, which jingled the bell.

A man turned, surprised that he'd have customers this quickly. "Lady and gentleman. Can I help you?"

His squat, bulky frame looked solid, despite approaching middle age. Thin strands of dark hair crossed over a balding head. He wore a Hawaiian shirt and cargo shorts with sandals as if refusing to acknowledge winter. His forearms were blanketed with sleeves of dark hair.

"Barry Franklin?" Gracie asked.

"Barry's my dad. Call me Barry-Boy."

"I'm Detective Castillo, this is my associate Mr. Doucet. We have a few questions," Gracie told him.

Barry-Boy cheered. "Dylan Doucet's brother. Unbelievable. I know you. You quit the force."

"I'm back."

He restrained his enthusiasm. "Sorry about your wife. The news said that Latino gang did it. Those bastards. I'm glad those two bangers got burned alive." Barry-Boy swallowed down a lump. "Love your brother. Awesome running back. I'll vote for him."

"You football freaks." Gracie absently checked out a couple of DVDs. "Nice place. You always open so late?"

"My regulars know my hours are hit and miss and ring my bell if they stop by. I live upstairs." He pointed at the roped-off, spiral staircase. "A perk of being the owner. What do you want to know?"

I handed him the receipt. "Would you be able to tell us who bought this video a month ago?"

"Mmm. Jesus. A month ago? Let me look up this code."

I turned to Gracie as Barry-Boy disappeared in the storeroom. "See anything you like?"

She cocked an eyebrow at me. "Everything."

Barry-Boy strutted back to us. "This video was Penal Prison Bitches Six. Some foreign guy bought it."

"You remember a name?"

He handed me the receipt. "Sorry. He barely spoke English from what I remember. He had a tattoo on his face."

"What was the tattoo?" I asked.

He touched his eye. "Teardrops? He had other shit, but I don't remember."

"Was he with anyone?" I asked.

"No. I know most of my customers pretty well. He wasn't local. Every now and then, strangers come in and I can't be nosey. They don't like that. My Mexican base has grown since Katrina. I've even added a little section for Latinos, but I don't categorize by region."

"I see you're more-or-less a sex store, more than just a video store."

"Market has changed with the Internet. I needed to expand to paraphernalia and party items. Sex is out of the closet. Business is steady."

"Tell me about your computer room," I said, pointing. A big sign read 'Pay Sites' on the wall.

He took us to a set of swinging doors that looked like they belonged in a saloon. "Four Macs, because they're stable and virus resistant. I subscribe to twenty adult sites catering to whatever the customer may be into. Guys pay ten dollars per hour and get their own private stall for, you know – privacy."

"Ew." Gracie made a face.

Barry-Boy finger-quoted. "*Accidents* happen. The room is sanitized after every customer." He laughed and thought to fist bump me, but decided pulled back. He continued, "These are guys that won't subscribe to the pay sites and burn what they like to a disk or flash drive to take care of business at home."

"Is there a demand for that? Porn is so available for free nowadays."

"Sure." Barry-Boy waved me off. "But the free stuff is mostly low-res and you still get the buffering, the viruses, and pop up ads that put malware on your computer. The last thing these guys want to do is take a frozen computer to Best Buy with the shit they look at, you know? The true porn connoisseur knows the really good stuff is on the pay sites in high def."

"Anybody do anything else in there besides porn?" I scratched my head. "Like their banking?"

"What they do in there is their business, as long as they don't break the things. I got a block against the child porn sites. I tell them I'll report them to the police if they do. And I do keep track of what sites are visited." He hacked a ball of phlegm into a handkerchief.

"How far back does your surveillance go?"

"Ah, the damn system went down. I got somebody coming out to look at it. When it's working, I got cameras just behind the register and at the entrance to the computer room."

"That's too bad." I shot a look to Gracie.

"Anything you need, detectives. I'm more than willing to help.

Twice, I've been robbed and I'll have to admit, the police have been good to me."

"Do you mind if we look around in the back?" Gracie asked.

"Just inventory."

"Do you mind?" Gracie strolled around the counter and into the back, but before Barry-Boy could follow, I stopped him.

"Can I talk to you?" I asked, as if I had a secret.

"Sure, detective. What's up?"

"Call me Remi, and I'm working my way back to my shield, so I'm not a cop yet." I picked up a bondage video. "You ever meet any of these girls that do this?"

"I've met a couple at the AVN awards." His head continued to swivel to every sound Gracie made.

I stared at the video cover, not saying anything. I picked up another one and studied it. My lips pursed. Barry-Boy's attention slowly drifted to my curiosity. Trout was right; he was a talker and the silence made him anxious.

He pointed. "You ever watch these?"

I hesitated, letting out a breath. I checked that Gracie wasn't coming out of the back, then shook my head. "This is too weird."

"What?"

"My wife never knew this about me – no one knows this about me, but I get into some of this stuff, but I was always too scared to suggest it."

"Nothing to be ashamed of, Remi. You want that?" He gestured at the video. "It's yours."

I smiled, slightly ashamed. "I'll come back for it. Thanks, man."

Barry-Boy finally smiled, as if he had converted me to his religion. "I got some new videos in yesterday that have these lesbos that just turned eighteen. I mean they are like one day legal, man. They have the bondage, whips, chains, nipple rings being pulled."

"Shut up with that shit right now." I put my hand flat on his shoulder. "We'll talk later."

Barry-Boy nodded as he turned to see if Gracie was behind him, but she had gone upstairs. The door to his apartment creaked open and we both looked up at the ceiling.

"She's checking my apartment? You got a warrant? You got no probable cause."

"We're not looking at you for anything. My partner is really hell-bent on catching this guy and she probably thinks you're lying about knowing him. If she finds something, she'll want to use it to make you talk. Just let me handle this."

"She sounds like a dream." He swatted a tiny bug on the counter. "I know the law, Remi."

I ran my fingers over one of the DVDs. "Eighteen, huh? Listen, you're discreet, right?"

"Like a friggin' psychiatrist." A hack of phlegm. His eyes stayed on the ceiling.

I'd said enough. It was best not to push too much too soon.

After some upstairs rumbling, Gracie came down with a small box of videos. She placed the box on the counter, but held a single DVD up to the light. "Look what I just pulled from a completely functional security recording box. I got your last forty-eight hours right here."

"What?" Barry-Boy turned red with surprise. "It was working? Maybe my friend got it fixed. I had a pal take a look a few days ago, but didn't tell me anything." His eyes darted between us.

"Well, that's great. We'll just take this DVD with us."

"Oh, I'm not done." Gracie stuck her hand in the box. "This DVD says German Shepherd, this one says rape, and these three say sixteen, sixteen, and seventeen – Sixth Grade – Seventh Grade? What is this sick shit? Lord knows what else is here. Anything we should know about before we notify Sex Crimes?"

"What do you have to say about this, Barry-Boy?" I asked with a wink that Gracie couldn't see.

"I'll say you found those without a warrant. You just rendered them useless."

Gracie and I looked at each other. She raised her voice. "All we have to do is mention this to the press and you're done. We'll make sure a cop is on your doorstep all day. Your customers will love that. Do you really want to open this can of worms?"

A sheen of perspiration appeared on his face like magic. "Those videos are fakes. All actors pretending to be underage. That's why they're labeled, otherwise, if they were really illegal, I'd find a way to disguise them."

"He has a point, Gracie."

Barry-Boy pointed at me. "You know what, Remi? I believe we both need to be discrete in these types of situations."

Gracie looked confused. "Remi?"

I whispered loud enough for Barry-boy to hear, "Gracie, I don't think that's necessary. They look like old, dusty DVDs and how can we even identify who's in them? Nowadays, you can't tell the real thing from a fake, right?" I glanced at Barry-Boy who fidgeted. "We have more important things to do than to tie up our day with paperwork on something that won't even stick."

Barry-Boy smiled. "That's right, officer. The quality is terrible and these actors are amateurs. So obscure you'd never find them."

Gracie looked at me and resigned to that logic. "You skate this time." Gracie clinched her jaw, then looked me square in the eye and closed the flaps on the box. "I suppose you're right."

"He's cooperating by giving us his surveillance and letting us look around without a warrant."

"Right." Gracie left first, with her shoulders pinned back as I followed, leaving Barry-Boy with the *okay* hand gesture.

"What just happened back there?" Gracie asked, standing in front of the car with her hands on her hips.

"I've got only days to get in his confidence. He obviously didn't want us to see his security footage. And if he knows this guy, then he knows people in the underbelly – people who get into torturing women and snuff films, leaving their bodies for us to find. While you were searching his place, we had a little chat. He thinks I'm a closet perv. And that thing with the DVDs couldn't have been more perfect. If he's going to reveal anything to me, it's going to be in a slip up. He's going to be a C.I. whether he knows it or not."

CHAPTER TWENTY-FOUR

Federal Agents Adam Joiner and West Foster had been working out of the field office on Leon C. Simon Drive for four years on *Matryoska*, the five-year case named after the Russian nesting dolls. The same case former Detective Doucet and Detective Castillo had stumbled upon when Baskov was killed. Foster and Joiner had to take over for the two agents who unexpectedly resigned after the first year. The former agents had been questioned, if not grilled on their resignations, but that yielded nothing. The Bureau kept tight-lipped on the matter.

Agents Foster and Joiner spent most of their time gathering and deciphering information. Since the head of the crime family, Victor Dudko had been clean for so long, all they could do was organize the people, places and events for when he made a mistake and the case became live again.

Five years earlier, they thought they had turned a witness on Victor Dudko, but in such a cliché way, the witness had been found poisoned from take-out food. In plain terms, Dudko beat the legal system. The best way for the Fed's to save face was to keep the Matryoska case open and continue surveillance.

Over the years, Foster and Joiner had assimilated to each other;

enjoying close quarters banter and creating their own *speak*. Foster came in three years removed from the Moscow office, having spent seven years in counter-intelligence, and Joiner came straight from Quantico having a knack for diplomacy.

The day grew less chilly by the hour, but a light jacket helped Agent Foster with the occasional bite of wind. Joiner preferred to wear layers. They compared notes inside a silver Beemer outside of The Hyatt Regency Hotel. The two men remained quiet, sometimes watching passersby meander as the Superdome loomed.

"Strange that Sharpe would stay here in New Orleans," Foster said.

"It's easier for him with the Rex krewe meetings. Big deal being the king of Rex." Joiner hiked an eyebrow.

Foster took a comb out of his jacket and smoothed down his thinning gray hair. He had recently discovered the two sets of bags under his eyes and has since felt ten years older. His desire to continue doing sit-ups and push-ups waned along with his libido.

Foster finally spoke. "Mardi Gras. To-go cups. Crawfish. I don't know if I love New *Orleens*."

Joiner smiled. "After four years you still say it wrong?"

"I don't give a shit."

"Don't say it that way. We want them to like us. Just *New Or-lens*, nice and regular."

Foster had more seniority, being older and near retirement. He accepted the fact that he had been passed over for promotion year after year, transferred from one office to another, and that very soon, Joiner would be his superior.

As an amateur sociologist, Joiner picked up on a culture's habits and general behavior. He knew that different societies as a whole were quicker to anger, or more likely to forgive a transgression. The man was thick-bodied with a thicker mane of hair. When he smiled, his nose flattened into a spearhead.

Foster said, "I don't need to ingratiate myself with these Louisiana politicians. I'll pronounce words anyway I want to. Hell, I spent seven years trying to pronounce all that Russian shit properly."

"It won't hurt the cause."

"I will not say c-ment."

"It's charming. They have all these words that don't sound the way they're spelled."

"Oh, Lord. This city has claimed another one. A hippie, no less."

"Calling me hippie really shows your age, old man." Joiner chuckled and they each closed their satchel.

"It'll all sound fake coming from me – even if I remembered any of their slang. But have you thought of this, my hippie friend? Like the French, these people feel pride in correcting you."

"And like the French, touché, *mon ami.*"

They exited the car and entered the hotel, heading straight for the elevator. They rode to the top floor, and were escorted by security to Governor Steve Sharpe's room. Joiner gave a professional nod to the young man, knowing they were the visiting team. It was best to be hospitable.

They entered the suite, stopping in the middle of the swank room. "Governor Sharpe. I'm Agent Foster, this is Agent Joiner, FBI. Thanks for taking this impromptu meeting with us."

"Call me Steve. No reason to let the public know the FBI wants to interview me, right?" The governor shook their hands, deliberate and with a firm grasp. Then he looked to the third party sitting on the sofa. "Gentlemen, this is Anthony Baas, my attorney. He'll be joining us. Anthony, these are Agents Joiner and Foster." Turning back, he asked, "Can I get you gentlemen a Coke, coffee, water?"

"No, thank you." Joiner replied.

"Well, then. What can I do for you?"

Foster put on a sincere smile. "Thank you for taking the time to answer some questions, Governor. Would you mind telling us about your relationship with Victor Dudko?"

"Besides being president of the board of commissioners of the Baton Rouge port – we don't have a relationship."

"Really? You received substantial contributions from several Louisiana big hitters for the upcoming gubernatorial election, correct?"

"Sure."

Joiner flipped through his folder. "There's a common theme among them. Take Lyle Deforest of Deforest Seafood, Inc. He donated twenty grand for your first campaign and three hundred thousand for this campaign. Our financial analysts can't fathom how he pulled that kind of capital out of thin air. There is a long list of similar occurrences."

"What are you saying?"

Foster continued, "I'm saying someone gave Mr. Deforest that money to give to you. And legally, he doesn't have to disclose where he got it."

"Proves nothing other than I'm getting more money from my supporters." He glanced at his lawyer.

Foster spoke, "We believe Dudko is a major player in a trafficking ring being run out of your port. If you know anything, it's best you tell us now, before it comes out through the course of the investigation and possibly leaks to the press."

Sharpe casually made his way to a leather chair with a high back and sat down. He motioned again for the agents to sit, but they didn't move from the center of the room. "Well, I hope you can understand how this makes me feel. If it turns out to be dirty money, or related to Dudko, this could cripple my run for re-election."

"But if you do the right thing before he's exposed, you may just come off as noble and virtuous." Joiner said. "Even saintly. American people, especially New Orleanians, forgive their politicians."

Picaud's shoulders slumped. "Let me know when you prove Dudko is behind this shell game."

"So, you haven't had any dealings with Victor Dudko, other than his appointment to your board?"

"The governor has given his answer." Baas interjected.

Sharpe continued speaking anyway. "I want to help, but I don't know anything."

Foster said, "He's linked to several murders, Steve. I think you should be aware of this and conduct yourself carefully around this man. You never know what kind of favors he might expect in return."

"I don't do favors for contributions. You can check my record on that."

"You're friends with Dylan Doucet," Foster stated blandly, but with a dead stare.

"I don't know if I'd say friends. I've met him. He's running for Congress."

"How close are you and Mr. Remi Doucet?"

"His brother? Never met him," Sharpe stated. "I've seen the news, though. Horrible. Wait, Victor didn't have anything to do with that, did he?"

"Look, governor. To be blunt, our investigation is coming to a head. We suggest you go over your office and campaign with a fine tooth comb and get your facts in order."

"Is there anything else?"

"If you do suspect anything, Steve, the smallest little thing, don't hesitate to call us." Foster handed him a business card.

"Thank you." The governor put it in his shirt pocket. Spots of sweat had appeared through the fabric. "If you'll excuse me, I'm very late for a meeting."

Foster and Joiner would later comment about the spotty shirt, and the governor's clammy handshake.

CHAPTER TWENTY-FIVE

Gracie and I sat at my kitchen table with The Hardcore Store surveillance video playing on my laptop. There were long periods where we fast-forwarded through Barry-Boy's empty, dark closed shop.

"I sent the arsonist's picture to Agent Foster." Gracie said.

"Good. Guess what I heard."

"Huh?" Gracie kept her eyes on the laptop.

"Dylan donated a hundred grand to the NOPD."

"What?"

"Trout called me earlier. He gave to the Fraternal Order."

"No shit."

"I don't understand him. Growing up he didn't even want us to be brothers and now that he got his wish, he wants to hug it out."

"Now that he's got fame, wealth, all the chicks he wants, he realizes what's important?"

I shrugged wryly. "He might just miss tormenting me."

"If that's his objective, then he's a bigger shit than you make him out to be with everything going on."

"You have a point. He used to bring me down from the highs, not kick me when I'm down."

She scrutinized me. "You need to shave."

I felt my chin. "I'm going for the disheveled look for Barry-Boy. I'm supposed to be a man who's leaning on S&M while his life is in ruin."

"Then, stop combing your hair, too."

The video scrolled along. Barry-Boy's customers were normal locals, meaning strange individuals. Every now and again an adventurous tourist wandered in. Two hours into fast forwarding we stopped at a well-built man who entered the frame and stopped dead in the center of the store. He wore a trench coat cinched at the waist. His collar covered his jaw line and he had a scarf for good measure. The weather made it perfect for disguising one's self without being suspicious.

His handsome face turned to the camera.

"That's the bartender," I said, "Lenn Yaz-ovich or Yaz-something."

Gracie paused the video. "Yaz-MO-vich. Sure is. He is one good-looking white dude."

Barry-Boy shuffled from the storage room and handed Yazmovich a large grocery bag. Without much of a verbal exchange, he walked out with the item.

"Now, what is that about?" I asked.

"A bag of pornography? Unfortunately, this proves nothing." Gracie frowned. "But, you're right. Arsonist, Baskov's strip club, and Barry-Boy – boom – pieces coming together."

"Let's only tell Trout if we have to."

"Got it." Gracie continued through the rest of video.

"I think I might go back to Booty Call tonight. Alone, if you don't mind."

"Is that a good idea?"

"I don't know. I just think I can learn more in a strip club without a woman by my side. No offense."

"Okay, but you don't want to antagonize them. As long as you don't show your hand, Lily will stay safe."

I faced her. "There is absolutely nothing I can gain by accusing any of the workers. But, if I sit at a table, maybe take a lap dance, who knows what I might learn?"

"Worth a shot, I guess."

"Right now, I want to go back to Barry-Boy's. Keep looking at the footage. We can hook up later."

"Good luck."

On my way to the porn shop, I stopped at a convenience store. The more *on edge* I presented myself, the better. Having a few sips from a bottle of vodka wouldn't impair me. Plus, it would help me disguise my intentions.

After pouring out a quarter of the bottle, I found myself standing outside The Hardcore Store to begin the process of becoming one of Barry-boy's trusted customers. I ruffled my hair as Gracie suggested.

Barry-Boy gave me a cautious greeting as I entered. "Remi. Back so soon. This a professional visit?"

"Nope." I took a swig from my bottle and placed it down on the counter. "I had some time to kill. My partner's running some errands. Still not a cop, so I run my own show."

"Vodka, huh?"

"Yeah, don't smell." I smirked.

"You mind?" He glanced at the bottle.

"Go ahead."

He took a swig, closed his eyes and his entire body relaxed. "Ahhh, that's the stuff."

If it was a test, I'd passed. "Helps me get through the day."

"You must be proud of your brother," he announced out of nowhere.

"I'd rather not talk about him. But, I'm still a die-hard Saints fan. I cried when they won the Superbowl."

"Pussy." Barry-boy threw some kind of magazine at me. "Saint-sations calendar. It's yours. They got some nice broads in there."

"Thanks."

"You must watch the games from the Benson Suite or some shit, but I got season tickets and if you want, we can go to a game or two next season."

"I'd like that. I'd rather sit with the real fans."

"I really appreciated the way you controlled your partner the other day."

"Chicks." I chuckled.

"Pick out the game you want and I'll jot it down on my schedule if it's available." He patted my shoulder. "I cried after Porter intercepted Manning, too, along with every motherfucker in that bar."

* * *

I had bought two videos with barely legal bondage queens and then spent about twenty minutes discussing the Saints' future. It killed me not to mention Yazmovich. As much as I wanted to dislike Barry-Boy, underneath it all, he had a decent head on his shoulders. He was easy to underestimate, and that was to his advantage. Without pressing for anything other than small talk, I left for Headquarters.

Unexpectedly, my brother sat like a statue on one of the benches outside the station as I arrived. He stood when he noticed me, with his chest out and shoulders wide, so I couldn't avoid the confrontation. Maybe I could walk past him, but a part of me wanted to believe. I had to meet Gracie at a local dive bar up the block where she liked to work in private, so I planned to quickly excuse myself.

"Got a minute?" he asked.

"I heard about your donation."

"It's a good cause." His body slumped, with his gaze to the sidewalk. "I did something horrible. A bell that can never be un-rung."

"Right."

"I had a problem. I might still have it, but at least I recognize it and I'm dealing with it."

"You have no idea what that did to me. It's like you hated me." I tensed for an argument.

"More like jealousy." He shoved his hands in his pockets.

We locked on each other, sizing each other up much like we did just before our legendary fist fights. Except, his sorrow had me at a loss. He had never bothered, or cared enough to fake it before. My fingers dug into my palms. "What do you expect from me?"

"I want to talk… every now and then, like when we had the grilled cheese. Hell, let's talk to a marriage counselor for brothers." He sheepishly smiled.

"There might be too much to forgive and to forget."

"Maybe." He nodded. "But, if there's a chance, I want to find out. Just don't shut me out."

"You realize Lily has been kidnapped, right? I can't be worried about your feelings right now."

"Just let me be here for you."

"If I need you, I promise I'll call."

His expression brightened. "That's all I ask."

I glared at him. "As a matter of fact, maybe there is something."

"Anything."

After leaving Dylan with a little mission, I trekked a block to Sally's Bar to meet Gracie. When I walked into the shadowed hole in the wall, it took a moment to spot her sitting at a tiny table with a lone spotlight above. The place was otherwise empty. She read from a folder filled with staggered documents trying not slip out. Gracie's eyes instinctively found me as the pretty bartender waved in my direction. I nodded to her and sat by my partner.

Gracie shifted in her chair. "Anything on Barry-Boy?"

"My porn collection is growing exponentially, but no - nothing yet. Still working it. There's more to that guy, I know it."

Gracie sipped on her Coke. "Can I borrow one of those DVDs sometime?"

"What about Jerry? Not hitting the spot?" I asked, and she hit me with the folder.

"Here's something you need to know for tonight." She singled out a laser printout. "Booty Call is owned by Victor Dudko. A legitimate business helps, right?"

"Jesus."

Neither of us needed to comment further.

* * *

After a long shower, I put on my boxers and rested on my side of the bed. I still hadn't washed the sheets. It would just be another way of moving on, and I wasn't ready. Sure, Fiona would forever be with me in Lily, but the sheets were intimate. The sheets still gave me comfort. The recurring thought of Lily and an older man made my stomach turn.

I put on a pair of jeans and a nice shirt that Fiona had bought and looked to the bathroom in the hopes that she would be there fixing her hair and putting on her earrings. The memory lingered for a moment.

Dylan called when he was seconds away from pulling in my driveway, and I met him beside his shiny, detailed Aston Martin.

"Nice car." I shut the door and clicked my seat belt.

"This is my favorite. I was actually thinking of losing the Corvette," he said. "You want it?"

"No. I'm not a Corvette kind of guy."

"You know I'm so heartbroken about all this." He pulled onto the street.

"I know."

Dylan's expression turned grim as his brow flattened. "Two FBI agents questioned me about the whole thing. I couldn't help."

"Let's not talk about it."

"Okay. So, what's tonight about?" Dylan hugged a corner, barely stopping.

"Consider it like a stake-out. We're just going to act like normal patrons."

"People are going to recognize me."

I held onto the handle above my head. "That's what I'm counting on."

After a short, but quick drive, we pulled into an expensive public French Quarter garage with covered parking and an attendant. We meandered to Booty Call and entered like any other patrons, passing two large bouncers to enter the main room. Yazmovich and I spotted each other. In less than a minute of checking out the decor, a man in a suit approached, shaking Dylan's hand. I watched as that bartender made a call on his cell.

"Welcome, Mr. Doucet. Why don't I get y'all set up in the VIP section?" He had a ferret face, with a pointed nose.

I looked where he was pointing. It was just a large open space on a raised level, roped off from the main floor. "Sounds good," I said.

Two beautiful girls appeared and pulled out our chairs at a clean table. A third strikingly attractive blonde bent over and put her boobs in our faces. "I'm Cherry Treasure. What would you gentlemen be drinking? Would you like bottle service?"

"If that bottle is Abita Amber," I said.

"Same." Dylan pushed a folded up bill toward her.

Guys from other tables waved at us, and the service was sure to be excellent. I didn't particularly want people staring, but this is what I asked for.

"So, what do we do now?" Dylan's eyes were all over the place.

"We sit. We talk. We wait."

"Shouldn't we partake in the festivities? It would look weird if we don't."

The waitress handed us our beers. I let my hand fall on his shoulder. "Actually, you should. Of course, I won't."

Miss Treasure gave a practiced smile. "Let me know if I can do anything special for you. Enjoy."

"She's hospitable," I said.

"Victoria Secret hospitable," Dylan came back, eyes boggling.

I watched as she spoke with a man coming up the stairs as she descended. "You should ask her out."

"I've dated enough strippers. Time to meet a nice woman and settle down. It's been a long time since I've dated anyone regularly."

A voice projected from a few feet away. "Dylan Doucet. Welcome!" A man I recognized from the Internet held out his hand to shake. "I'm Victor Dudko, owner."

We were so engrossed in our conversation that I hadn't noticed him. Victor Dudko pulled a third chair to our table. His razor-thin lips were frozen smug smile. He had lost most of his hair, making it worth his while to shave his head. His close-set eyes were alert and the large scar on his forehead distracted me.

"This is my brother, Remi. We're enjoying your fine establishment."

"There's no way a celebrity comes in here without my staff notifying me. I like to work upstairs during my busy hours so I can drop down from time to time."

"Dylan here would like a dance." I nodded at him to agree.

Dylan rubbed his hands together. "So, who's your best girl?"

"Particular tastes vary. Try out each one. Start with Marcy right here." Victor put his arm around the legs of a slim redhead that saddled up to the table.

The fiery-haired girl took Dylan by the hand and led him into the back room.

Dudko never looked away from me. "You didn't need to bring your brother. I would have come down for you. I didn't think the Serpientes angle would stick. You were too good a detective from what I remember. The Feds – what are you doing to do?"

I'm sure my eyes opened wider than I wanted them to. "Why? At least tell me that." My jaw barely allowed me to verbalize.

"Why what? Who exactly do you suspect took your stepdaughter?" Dudko casually adjusted the clean ashtray at the center of the table.

"I have an idea."

"Well, hopefully you'll find her safe and sound, possibly by Fat Tuesday, eh?"

Every muscle coiled. "I just hope this person understands the consequences if my daughter dies."

"Do what you're supposed to, and you will be together again. Enjoy your time here, Mr. Doucet." Dudko tapped his knuckles on the table as he stood.

"How does one trust a mobster's word exactly?"

Dudko leaned in. "Americans see the common criminal as a liar. In Russia, your word means everything. If you don't have honor, you have nothing." He bowed slightly and backed away from the table.

My brother came back adjusting his pants. "Ah, she wasn't for me. It was like she was angry at my crotch. Victor left?"

I turned to him. "You need to give me Steve Sharpe's number."

CHAPTER TWENTY-SIX

Victor Dudko murdered Fiona and abducted my stepdaughter.

It took hours to get to sleep, but when I did, I dreamed about Lily again. She wasn't angry with me during slumber, as if she never had been. Dawn came so fast. In the dream, the child version of Lily had asked if I would die if a bad man shot me. I'd told her how safe it was to be a policeman and how *not dangerous* my career was, just as if she was my own daughter – as if I had raised her. In the dream, Lily had a brave face.

Just after waking, I called Gracie who told me that Dudko had a clean record, and there wasn't any new information beyond the strip club he owned. She reminded me about meeting with the Feds today.

Until then, Barry-Boy would be first on my agenda and I headed straight there. Three gay men left his store just as I arrived. The homosexual community played a big part in Barry-Boy's business, prompting a room with leather-studded bondage-wear and other paraphernalia. He commented that he had once beaten up homosexuals when he was a teen, but today, every one of them was his best friend and customer.

I strolled into the store like a regular. Barry-Boy was showing a big, black man a DVD with Chocolate in the title. He separated from the customer and greeted me, but not with his usual excitement. He barely looked in my direction.

"What's wrong, Barry-Boy?"

"You've been in here quite a bit, Remi." He picked up a cigarette butt on the floor. "Smokers," he mumbled.

"You should be glad to have a new, steady customer."

"Should I?" He finally caught my eyes.

"You don't want me here? Fine, fuck you. I don't need this shit." I turned to leave.

He stepped between the door and me. "Wait. I'm curious – that's all."

I made a huge show of being embarrassed and pulled him close. "My wife never understood what I wanted. Our sex life practically ended after the honeymoon. You know what that does to a relationship?"

"Creates distance?" His eyes rose curiously.

"Yes. I've always hid this part of my life. Maybe this takes my mind off my problems. Maybe I'm going overboard. It's like a drug."

"Remi, sorry. I had no idea." He grabbed my elbow. "Got a new one in for you, my friend," he said. He had a proud smile on his pudgy face.

"Oh, yeah? Good?" I asked.

"My distributor told me there's high demand for this one in the underground."

"Let's see."

While the other customer continued to browse, we walked into the back room, a haphazard mess of an inventory nightmare. He knocked around a few items, tossing them on top of the least cluttered surface. "It's an amateur called Shackles and Chains. Very low distribution and none of the scenes are on the pay sites. This isn't everyday porn. Every broad in this is a questionable eighteen. They use torture techniques in here that ISIS thinks are too cruel." He shook his head, handing it over to me.

"Only copy?"

"I have more on order. I wanted to watch it first. This is unbelievable. A couple of these broads I'm told, only been fuckin' for weeks. Some first time anals, too. Plus, *da pièce de résistance* – all the boobs are real. This is a must-buy for you."

"No shit?" I looked at it like an actor would an Oscar. "Sold. Wrap it up. So, how's business, anyway?" I looked around as we exited the storeroom.

Ringing up my video, he said, "Paying the rent."

I whispered. "Between you and me, this S&M stuff is good, but do you have anything stronger? Like chicks that are into real torture or pain?"

"The one right there is pretty rough, like I said."

"Well, they're basically acting, right? No real fear in their eyes?"

"Some of these actors could be scared for real, I guess. I think you got to enjoy this shit to actually do it. Between you and me, sometimes I wonder if it's all voluntary."

"Right. They might really need the money or owned." I stepped to the side so that he could ring up the video for the customer who finally made his choice. After the man left, I put a hundred dollars on the counter. "Do you know of any women who do this type of thing?"

He stared at the money. "Like a prostitute?" he whispered.

I teetered. "Eh, not really, but someone who specializes in it. Someone that wouldn't go in the hooker category."

"An adult film star?"

"Sort of. Like, do you know any of the women who don't do this voluntarily?"

He pushed the money away. "Sorry, Remi. That's not something you just walk into. These guys run in the same circles – they pass women around."

"So you do?"

His eyes stayed wide. "That's like asking a bartender if he knows any alcoholics. I stay on my side of the bar my friend. You should, too."

I shrugged, acting bashful. "Maybe, you're right. You don't

know if you can trust me and I sure as hell don't know if I can trust you."

"You're looking to participate instead of just watching?"

"Yeah, but my problem is discretion. I can't just grab a girl off the corner."

"Maybe you should plan a trip to Amsterdam. I'm not the one to guide you on this journey."

"I think you're *just* the person. Catch my drift?" I waved a second hundred in his face, putting it on top the other one.

"I do catch your drift." He pushed the money back again. "Sorry, Remi, but that's playing with fire. Can't help you. I got inventory to attend to."

I thought I lost him. "Wait, man. How about *fake* stuff. I've seen a couple faked snuff films made by actors online. Can you get a hold of these? The more real the better."

Annoyance registered in his face. "I steer clear of those. If one turns out to be real, then I'm toast. Look, I really do have stuff to take care of in the back."

"One second," I said, reaching my torso over the counter to grab his arm at the biceps, "this conversation was just between you and me. No one can know about this. You tell anyone, I'll deny it and I'll make life miserable for you."

He nodded. "Consider me a psychiatrist."

"All right. I'll check this video out. I'm sure I'll love it."

He scratched behind his ear. I had made him nervous. I wasn't sure if I'd crossed the line or planted a seed to grow. I didn't push the issue and left with a smile and a wave. He wasn't going to give anything up for an ex-cop. I think another detective would have been better off going in undercover.

* * *

Gracie and I headed for Port Of Call on the outskirts of the Quarter where she had set up a meeting with Agents Joiner and Foster. Gracie parked her Trans Am on the street, and we weaved through some young people loitering outside the place. They embodied a generation that had nothing to do with their day.

We sat in the small, dark, sunken dining area to the left of the entrance. The tables could seat four people or six squeezed, but pairs occupied most of them today. The sketchy atmosphere lent for a quiet date, or for someone drowning their sorrows.

The door of the restaurant opened, letting in a flood of light. The waitress directed the agents into the dining area where I waved them over with a quick flip of my hand. They each slid out of their jackets after a round of hand shaking.

"Mr. Doucet, you probably heard we talked to your brother. He was the Saints' running back, right?" Joiner smiled, sliding into the booth.

"Yep. This is the last time I tell you to call me Remi."

"And Gracie. We can be on a first name basis, I think."

I pointed to Foster, then Joiner. "West, and Adam – correct?"

"That's right, but we refer to each other by our last names, so feel comfortable doing that." Joiner lit up. "I'm not a football fan but this city's enthusiasm for the Saints is infectious."

"Your Captain tells us you're coming back on as detective," Foster interrupted.

I noticed Joiner's frown. He was trying to break the ice by talking football. "Sorry about the Yank," he said.

"It's okay. I'd rather bypass the small talk, too. Yes, I'm getting my shield back."

Gracie said, "I hope that doesn't have an impact on your regulations regarding our cooperation."

Joiner adjusted his ponytail. "We're not concerned with your department's policies or your standing. We're meeting here to share information, not to go play *shoot 'em up*. Not yet, anyway." He took a recording device, and placed it in the center of the table. "Hope you don't mind. We'll send you a copy."

"It's fine." The Feds wanted to run the meeting, so I started strong. "We're thinking there's a connection with Victor Dudko and the dead Russian we sent you. We also believe this dead Russian burned down Bobbi's Rugs." I pointed at the photo and police report.

"You paid a visit to Dudko's strip club. After we asked you not to." Foster glared.

"Yes." I returned his stare. "In my defense, we didn't know he owned it the first time."

"Your pictures are very interesting," Joiner glanced at Foster almost as if to say *we can trust them.* "You may not be aware that we're investigating the death of an insider we had in Dudko's circle, a fellow agent. We believe Dudko is responsible."

"I'm sorry one of your agents died." I looked between them. They didn't react.

"You must want him badly," Gracie remarked. "But, why hold back from us?"

"You know the answer to that." Foster leaned back.

Joiner continued, "We understand we pointed you toward Los Serpientes, but we knew you'd hit a dead end eventually. Now, we can help each other. We want you to talk to Governor Sharpe without letting on about our agenda. He's friendly with your brother. If he's going to reveal anything about his relationship with Dudko, it might be with you."

"So, give it to us straight, do you or do you not believe Victor Dudko is behind my wife's murder?"

"We haven't found any evidence of that." Joiner's expression flattened. "But, concerning Serpientes... The insider in our gang task force has no information regarding a kidnapping, and after all this time, there should be whispers. So, we agree with your findings."

Foster added, "We can work together, but I'm not liking the loose canon aspect of it."

"Dudko is behind it." I took a drink. "At his club, Dudko insinuated he was behind it. It was all I could do not to rip his head off right there."

"Did he say what he wanted?" Joiner asked.

"No. But, he enjoyed my anxiety during our exchange."

Joiner turned to Foster with an agreeable look. "Have you ever heard the name Andrei Federov?"

Gracie and I shook our heads. I wrote it down phonetically.

Foster continued, "Federov became boss of the Skullbones Mafia fifteen years ago. He is currently in Butryka Prison in Russia."

"He's running things in New Orleans from there?" I asked, amazed.

"More-less, yes. Years ago, Federov was trying to get one of his men the Prime Minister spot in Russia. If he had succeeded, he would have become immensely more powerful than he already is. The Russians are constantly trying to get their people into political power. Now, we have it on good information that Federov was involved with Victor Dudko in Russia. Over there he was *Viktor Dudkoverov*. Viktor with a 'K' instead of a 'C.'"

"He has no accent. Is he faking it?"

"Yes, he's become quite the American."

"Okay." I cleared my throat. "He has fake identification. His social security number has to be stolen. Why can't you just kick him out of the country?"

"Good question," Foster said. "His social security number is really his in the eyes of the law."

"This I gotta hear." Gracie rocked in her seat.

Foster continued, "Child trafficking is huge in America. When babies are born in hospitals, they're given birth certificates, social security numbers… the works. When these unreported kids enter the trafficking network, their identifications are sold to the highest bidder, typically mobsters, crime families."

"How often can that happen?" Gracie questioned. "I mean, how are the mothers not busted by family or friends?"

Joiner cleared his throat. "Any woman can tell their friends and family their kid was adopted. Of these women, some sell their baby, some are paid to be surrogates from the start, and some are already owned – doomed to be baby makers until they can't anymore."

"Poor, rural, and desperate women," I added, shaking my head.

Joiner's face darkened. "The babies wind up being sold on the black market to be used for anything from child prostitution to child slavery to being bought by a decent couple wanting to cut out the red tape."

"Unreal," I managed. "But, for Federov to really pull it off, they'd have to hold onto these documents for the person to be the right age for the birth certificate. You can't just jump from being born to being an adult. Wouldn't questions be asked?"

"You would think." Joiner nodded. "In the more established organizations, children that were trafficked or sold twenty years ago are just now having their documents put in play. It's perfect. There is absolutely no one to discredit the information. No one to recognize the real people they belong to."

"Airtight," Gracie commented.

"While checking Dudko's background, we found that he first popped onto our radar as Kyle Olenski. His birth certificate says he was born in Broken Arrow, Oklahoma. Both parents are dead. Kyle Olenski – Dudko - never went to school, never registered to vote, never had a driver's license until Dudko applied for one. Then, he petitioned the court to change his name to Victor Dudko in Wellington, Florida. Quite arrogant to change it right back, if you ask me. They match the blood type, hair color, even ethnicity if they can. Victor Dudko is quite legally here."

"Besides," Joiner added, "even if we could deport him, we wouldn't. We believe he is the link to a much bigger fish... Federov's captains."

"Did Dudko always have that scar on his forehead?" I asked.

"Something happened to him in Butryka Prison, but we haven't found out what it was. We have some intel on Dudko before he entered prison and little after, until he came here."

Joiner spoke, "Simply put, we believe Federov sent Dudko here to put someone in political power here in Louisiana. We believe it's the governor, Steve Sharpe. They don't want him doing anything illegal at this point. He's clean as a whistle and has to stay that way if he's to run for Senate or possibly the Presidency."

"Presidency? You gotta be friggin' kidding me. Even if the governor and I become chummy, I'm the last person he'd confide in." I locked eyes with Foster. "He knows I'd bust him."

"What does Dudko think about your investigation?" Gracie leaned in.

"He knows we watch him, but he feels invincible since we haven't filed any charges. Which leads us to your pictures."

At that moment, the waitress approached the table with a smile and a notepad in her hand. "Hi gentlemen, can I get you a drink to start your afternoon?"

"Nothing for us," Foster said.

"Bullshit," I countered, "this is our meeting. You're having what we're having."

"I've heard great things about this place," Joiner smiled. "I can eat."

Foster's expression soured. "We never eat during our meetings."

"Burger dressed and potato the same," I said, "And a Coke."

Both agents and Gracie ordered the same thing, then we all paused a minute before Joiner resumed the conversation. "We scanned your pics and uploaded them to our office in Moscow. Foster here actually worked in the American Embassy and pulled a few strings. We're trying to identify your arsonist, but I wouldn't hold my breath."

Foster added, "We found something else that might interest you. I know you recognize this man." He slid a picture in front of me.

"Egor Baskov," Gracie said for me.

"Where does he sit with the Skullbones?" I inquired.

"Baskov was Dudko's partner in Russia. They grew up together. You might as well have killed his brother."

"Makes you wonder why he didn't retaliate earlier," I said bitterly.

"I agree," Joiner said. "They are known for an eye for an eye. If he took your daughter, then he's going to want to use you for something. He's just waiting."

I bit my tongue. "Dudko might lead you to Federov's captains, but in the meantime you allow him to traffic sex slaves and drugs. Is it worth it? Why can't you just pick him up and turn him back over to the Russian authorities?"

Foster answered, "Because the KGB says Victor Dudko is dead

and buried and they refuse to dig up the body to prove otherwise. We told them flat out that we have their guy, but they are washing their hands of this one."

"Federov," I said.

"He's the puppet master." Joiner watched a young couple walk past the table.

"How does Dudko just walk out of a Russian prison?" I asked.

"The guards are owned by Federov and I'm sure Dudko agreed to do whatever was necessary to get out. Butyrka is a pre-trial detention center. Russia's worst. Its conditions were horrible, though it's better now. There were reports of cramming 80 prisoners in a 20 prisoner cell; all sharing one toilet and shower."

"The criminals think they got it bad here," Gracie murmured.

Joiner slid another picture across the table, "This is Federov and *old Dudko* for your files."

Gracie and I stared at a blurry picture. His head was turned slightly in mid-stroll next to Dudko near a chain link fence. Dudko's forehead scar had me thinking of the arsonist. Then it hit me. "Could Dudko have been a bitch in prison? A *lowered down?*"

Foster raised his eyebrows, obviously wondering how I knew about that sort of thing. "Maybe. And you're thinking he got out of prison and burned off the tats that would present him to other Russians as a lowered down."

Gracie added. "He can't be a boss and a lowered-down, right? Is anyone he's involved with now known mafia?"

Foster combed his hair back and patted it down. "We believe he's working with a Cuban mercenary and drug runner named Miguel Espinosa." He presented a picture of a man in crisp, green fatigues. His dark eyes were steely. He looked like a leader of men. "The Bureau doesn't have a detailed file on him. There are no ties to any affiliation here or anywhere else. Although, take that information with a grain of salt, because the KGB and Russian mafia are basically one in the same. If they wanted to protect their interests here in the states, all they have to do is play stupid."

"Honestly, guys – I didn't expect you to be so forthright with your case." I said.

Joiner fiddled with his napkin. "Two separate investigations are weaker than one that shares information. We all want the same thing. It doesn't matter who does it. And on that note, we'll ask you not to approach Dudko until after tomorrow."

"What's happening tomorrow?"

"We received solid intelligence that Dudko has arranged a large drug shipment to come into the Baton Rouge port. We're planning a raid with a select group of agents. No one in the Bureau, except our director, or in law enforcement knows about this."

"And us…" Gracie trailed off.

"You want in?"

Gracie and I looked at each other. "We're in," we both said.

Joiner slid a piece of paper across the table. "Meet us at this location at this time. Don't mention this to anyone - *anyone*."

"Well, in the spirit of honesty," I said, "we have more."

Joiner and Foster perked up.

* * *

The burgers came, gigantic and delicious. I filled the guys in on Lily's earrings and shirt left on the dead girls. They leaned more towards the Russians tormenting me than my stepdaughter getting one by on them. They both agree that other than retaliation, they didn't know their end game, as far as I was concerned.

Gracie made sure I left out no details. They didn't believe Barry Franklin held any weight in Dudko's operation, but encouraged me to continue my relationship with him. Some of their questions and statements about our *holding back* came with a tinge of annoyance.

Despite taping the meeting, they took notes between hearty bites, agreeing that Dudko would want to use the port to traffic and the upcoming raid would be his first major mistake. By the end of lunch, Foster had devoured his burger, despite his reluctance to order it. We adjourned, deciding to meet again soon, after they amended their investigation with our new info.

Outside of Port Of Call, I turned to Gracie. "You mind if I walk? By myself?"

"Really? We just got all this information and you don't want to go over it?" She looked at me like I was a nut.

"I do, but give me an hour to soak it all in. Give you that chance, too. I think the walk will do me some good."

"Okay." She squinted at me. "But, you can't walk back to the station."

"Uber."

Gracie drove off, leaving me to walk up the street with a load on my shoulders. Dudko had Fiona killed, a tit-for-tat for Egor. Dudko also had to know if he hurt Lily, that I would kill him, but I couldn't do that from prison. So, he would get his revenge with no threat of retaliation.

Before I knew it, the Mississippi River flowed beside me like a massive python. My feet followed the French Market, a nearly two-block isle of venders selling merchandise under a long narrow roof. There were three narrow walkways with tables upon tables of merchandise, from whimsical shirts to purses to jewelry. It resembled a long gazebo with no walls, allowing access from either side of the sidewalk.

I spotted a woman that had Fiona's features and for a split second, thought it could have been Lily. I stared for a moment, walking away with goose bumps. My wife's murder clung to me, like a backpack that you forget was on your shoulder, but then you made that sudden move and felt it weighing you down. I walked along the outskirts of the French Market, down Decatur towards Jackson Square. My feet turned to a little alley leading to a public restroom. I found an isolated bench, and sat with my head in my hands for fifteen minutes.

* * *

Gracie and I ended our day with mapping out everything we learned from the Feds on our big white murder board. Different colored ink, pictures and arrows filled up every space. There were quite a few question marks, and we assumed that they held *something* back – it was in their nature. We both eagerly anticipated the raid, which shocked us to be involved. Gracie stayed at her desk to catch up on paperwork for her other cases, and I headed out.

The pressure of the deadline pushed on my chest as I held the steering wheel. My muscles wanted to lock up with every movement, but I arrived home fine. I gave every room a once over before changing into comfortable clothes. The television did little to distract me, so I spent the rest of my evening on the couch with six photo albums that documented my life with Fiona.

When we had met, we found ourselves sitting next to each other at a Harrah's blackjack table. She loved to drink, gamble, and joke about herself. She captured my heart on first sight. I stopped at my favorite picture of us leaning into each other at a crawfish boil and stared at it.

The array of pictures followed a timeline of Lily's growth as a teenager. So many of the photos were taken on her sailing team. She had joined a social club that went out on Lake Pontchartrain once a week to learn about sailing and occasionally race against other teams. I was waiting for the day she'd invite me out on the boat, but that never happened. When my emotions got the best of me, I put the albums away and spent the rest of the evening going over everything I could find on The Greater Baton Rouge Port.

What the hell was Victor Dudko up to?

CHAPTER TWENTY-SEVEN

R*ussia - Twelve years earlier...*
Viktor Dudkoverov finished stuffing fifty thousand plastic-wrapped American dollars into his wall. Egor Baskov replaced the square of drywall that had been cut out. They both applied the spackle, smoothing it over with satisfaction.

"Remember when we met, my friend?" Viktor asked in English, as they had prided themselves on learning the language through American television.

Egor smiled with pride. "Yes. I saved you from a bat across your skull."

"You did."

"Your little twelve-year-old gang declared war on the South-landers. The day of the rumble, I watched you lead those children into a massacre."

Viktor wiped the white paste from his hands. He switched to Russian. "We were all children. I often wonder why I had an angel watching over me that day."

Egor shrugged, observing their work. "No angel. Just me." He patted Viktor on the shoulder and left the room.

Viktor reminisced in the luxuriant room their crimes had

bought. Since that day of the rumble, they acted as one mind. The two brazen hoods fed off each other, shoplifting and committing petty theft to survive. Viktor had been smart for his age and Egor the strong one, making them deceptive and successful, daring each other to top their previous crimes.

Over time, Egor stopped planning their paydays and let Dudko lead. By fifteen, they had gotten rich off their talents. By the time they were twenty-two, they had amassed a small fortune, even by American standards.

Their reputation had grown through the underground, and soon even the KGB enlisted their help in covert operations. The authority forgave the petty crimes because they viewed the duo as government assets, to be disposed of when they outgrew their usefulness. Dudko knew they were to be *disappeared* one day, unless accepted by one of the Russian mafia families. They waited impatiently for the day to be indoctrinated and therefore become untouchable.

However, the inner core remained beyond their reach. Dudko had dipped his hands into too many cookie jars. Alliances were sacred and the families and the cliques and the criminal element didn't trust them. They were contracted help, never to succeed in the higher echelon, forever to be paid and forgotten as criminal nomads. Dudko couldn't move up to the next level without the mob, yet it was because of his independence that he had come this far.

The day had come when a legendary gangster enlisted Dudko and Egor to murder an up-and-coming politician, a clear-cut favorite. Andrei Federov had wanted another representative in the State Duma. He promised that if Dudko and Egor pulled off the job, they would be accepted into the Skullbones and all the protection it offered.

They waited outside the politician's house, cool and relaxed, talking of the prestige this would bring. When the target arrived, Dudko slipped behind him and ordered him to his knees. Once the rush of future accolades filled Dudko's brain, he fired, enjoying the smell of gunshot residue and the sound of the body hitting the ground. He distinctly remembered the three barks of the dog next door.

Getting away from the police proved a bit harder. The sirens blared five seconds after the gunshot, and Dudko's head screamed *betrayal*. They needed to scatter; Egor drove away while Dudko ran to the empty street, having been left at their mercy. Still, all hadn't been lost as Dudko assumed he would meet up with Egor the next day after being released by the corrupted police. Surely, Federov would be their net.

It dawned on Dudko that they'd been scapegoats, named and taken into custody for the killing of a government official they had never heard of. Dudko's gated house and property were seized, and over seven hundred thousand American dollars was taken off his estate. Even tortured, Dudko never gave up Egor, but that truth would never be told. The KGB labeled him a snitch. Dudko was thrown into Butyrka prison, believing Egor had been murdered.

* * *

Dudko cowered in the corner of the common cell that contained thirty-eight prisoners in Butyrka Prison. The cell had one toilet, one sink and thirty-eight bunks. All in all, less than one cubic meter of living space per prisoner. His cellmates were dirty, pungent and vicious... And they had been told a lie.

A barbed wire tattoo meant a life sentence, snakes symbolized high-ranking gang members, a tiger signified an enforcer and a swastika wasn't a racial marking, but indicated that an inmate would eventually be killed by another prisoner. Some of these tats were worn with pride and some were forced upon the weak.

By the second day Dudko had not yet been raped, but he waited for it. He ate food that had been spit on and he only defecated in the dead of night. His cellmates believed he had given his partner up to the FSO, but trying to deny it would only make things worse. The Federal Protective Service was a law enforcement agency, a branch from the old USSR's KGB, and was assigned the task of protecting Russia's powerful political figures. Dudko's crime was punishable by death.

His nose adjusted to the aroma of rotting garbage. The anticipation of his fate ate away at his nerves as his eyes darted to each inmate, trying to determine his executioner. He almost wanted to stand in the center of the cell and drop his pants to get the rape overwith. Maybe that was the torture… the waiting.

As he had expected, the surrounding men backed away and his true sentencing was upon him. Three lean men with tattoos of stars, cathedrals, upside down spades and rings on their fingers approached. It would make no sense to fight. He told himself to relax and let it happen. Die with dignity if he must.

A large, bald man with dead eyes stepped up to Dudko, picking him up and slapping his face before letting him fall. Two other men dropped down to his side and turned him over, pulling his pants down and ripping his dirty tank top off. A wall of prisoners blocked the view from the guards, who wouldn't care otherwise.

"He's getting a swastika," the largest one said in Russian.

"And a diamond on his forehead," one suggested.

Dudko lay naked on his stomach with his eyes closed. He was going to get a mark that would make him a target until death. There would be no one lower than him. He would be at the bottom.

"Eyes on his back," the third man said.

"No," said the large one, "he's not a fag."

There was little comfort in that. Dudko waited for the pain from the prick of a needle. What he hadn't expected was to be sodomized first and tattooed after.

* * *

The prisoners had refused to acknowledge Dudko. On the third day, he again cowered in his cell. He nursed a three-inch wide, puffy mark of a snitch on his forehead from about two hours of skin jabs – it had been hard to determine with his being unconscious. He also received a swastika on the side of his neck. The skin glowed around the edges of the tat and pain echoed inside his head where he couldn't see straight. The only consolation was not being labeled for continual rape. He prepared for his own demise like a prisoner on death row.

On Dudko's eighth day of biting his nails, he learned of an unexpected meeting with Andrei Fedorov – the man responsible for his imprisonment and a legend among thieves. He was the head of the Skullbones gang, the most powerful prisoner in all of Russia. A guard escorted Viktor through a vacant corridor. He prepared for his death at the hand of Federov. He almost welcomed it.

Andrei Fedorov relaxed in a cushioned recliner, in an otherwise empty cell. Andrei was a medium build fifty-year-old with a smooth helmet of gelled brown hair with all the false warmth of a heartless criminal.

"Unfortunately, I could not stop your tattoo," Andrei said in English.

Dudko reciprocated. "With all due respect, Mister Fedorov, why would you want to?"

"Perfect English. Perfect."

"So?"

"I know the truth. This means nothing to the animals here in prison, but I know that you are still honorable."

"Yes, but I am marked for death. No one's going to trust me again."

"I know several that would."

"They mustn't be Русский."

"Yes, true Russian." Fedorov suppressed a laugh. "I need you for a mission, Viktor. More like – your calling."

"What are you talking about?"

"The hit that brought you here came from me."

"I know. You have a snitch in your organization." Dudko gauged his reaction.

"This is true, and I have yet to weed him out. I do believe, however, that you can make it up to me."

"Make it up to you? The hit was successful."

"Ah, but my replacement for him in the Duma mysteriously died after you were caught. The hit was all for nothing."

"The road to power is paved with political bricks. Since these politicians are already criminals, why not turn them, make them work for you?"

"That is not for you to worry about. I have something else for you."

"If it will get me your protection, just tell me who to kill in this hellhole."

"What would you say if I could arrange your release in exchange for your service?"

"I would be a fool not to leave this place. I would rather give you my life in service then have it taken from me."

"And your life *would* be mine. I can give you what you've been searching for, a home in my family. I want to re-establish my presence in a city in America: New Orleans, to be precise. I have a business I need you to run."

"New Orleans? Whose toes will we be stepping on?"

"There won't be a territory war. I've made an arrangement with a drug boss in Mexico whose young son is a captain in New Orleans, Juan Gomez. We will have the cooperation of several Latino gangs that have cropped up there."

"I imagine that's good if they're useful."

"I also have a man working for the governor of Louisiana. We'll get you into the Baton Rouge port on the Mississippi River. I will send you to an English-speaking tutor to rid you of your accent. I'll set you up with several of my men, transport you to New Orleans."

"You want me to be a boss? With this diamond on my head?"

"We will erase that diamond once you're in America, along with the swastika. Just wear bandages for travel." Federov pushed his recliner back and stared at the ceiling. His accommodations looked more like a hotel room than a prison cell. "I will not surround you with typical countrymen. No, this effort will remain quiet. As you are aware, our accents tend to turn off the pampered Americans."

"You have trust that I can master this American Accent?"

"Yes. Most Americans are ignorant to our crime families. It is more glamorous for them to emulate the Italians. You will make us lots of money, Dudko, and you will regain the dignity that you did not deserve to lose."

"I'm in."

"There is one man in New Orleans who will be my eyes."

"What is his name?"

"He is also an invisible man."

"A spy?"

"My eyes, as I have said. You may get comfortable with the distance and forget where you come from."

"I see. If all comes to fruition, you will have nothing to fear from me."

"You will be given a short list of powerful men. These men are my associates. They are the backbone of my power - of your power."

"Glory to the Skullbones." He felt his tattoos throb.

"In three nights, you will be taken from your cell with a dramatic show of force. The others will believe that you were killed, but you will be taken out of the prison."

"What about the guards?"

Andrei laughed heartily. "Once you speak like an American businessman, you will be taken by cargo ship to New Orleans. You will contact a man that goes by the name of Miguel. He is a Cuban, but we work with the Cubans often and I trust him."

"So, these men will do as I say?"

"They do as I say and you will operate as I say. A man named Yaz will mentor you on the operation until you are ready, so don't try to deceive him or you really will be a dead man."

"Yaz?"

"Lenn Yazmovich. Egor will also meet you there."

Dudko lost his poker face. "Egor's not dead?"

"He is to the authorities. He is completely loyal to you. You will work well together."

"You will not be sorry, Mister Fedorov. I will build your empire."

Andrei nodded, and then they sealed their deal with a shot of vodka.

CHAPTER TWENTY-EIGHT

The other side of the bed used to be my life, and now it was my past. As soon as my eyes opened, I pulled Fiona's cold pillow to me. The scent filled my nose and I stayed there for a while. In three days if I don't commit murder, I might start grieving all over again. Doc Margie scheduled a meeting. Hopefully, she can help me focus on my emotions so that I could be productive. I dragged my ass out of bed.

I stopped myself before walking past the garbage bags lying near the closet. My leg muscles managed to hold my weight while bending down for one. I opened Fiona's closet door and pulled out a stack of folded jeans, three in all, and gently pushed them into the bag until reaching the bottom. Nausea washed over me and the bag fell to my feet. It was a start.

After a shower, I ate some grits – one of the items purchased by Dylan. While rinsing out the bowl, the doorbell rang. Margie's Sentra was on the curb.

"Come on in, Doc." I closed the door behind her.

Doc Margie had me in full view. "Are you good for today's session?"

"I'm okay. Can I get you something to drink?" I motioned to the kitchen.

"I'm fine."

She sat down in the recliner. "So, let's talk."

"Yeah, let's do it before I put a gun in my mouth." I winked.

"I know that's a joke, but have you thought of suicide?"

"I'm desperate, not depressed."

"It's a standard question in determining mental health, Remi. Do you find that you're paranoid?"

"Like everyone's out to get me? Like you're out to get me?"

"Again, standard question."

"No, besides feeling like there's a voodoo doll out there with my face on it, I just feel like I'm in a hole, and it's so hard to climb out of it."

"Do you think there's hope in finding Lily?"

"Yes, otherwise, I'd be useless."

"How are things with your brother?"

"You're all over the place today." She didn't respond to my observation. I answered, "My brother? Believe it or not, he's trying to make amends. But, I'm finding it hard to let him with my situation."

"Do you believe his intentions?"

"Maybe. In your teens, you think you know everything. Then, in your twenties, you think you're so grown up, realizing how silly you were as a teenager. Now that I'm in my thirties, those twenty-something ideals and values shifted. I had no clue as to who I was in my twenties. I imagine that the forties will be the same, offering some view of my thirties that I can't grasp now. My point being, do I believe Dylan has changed? Sure, it's possible."

"Interesting." Margie tapped her pen. "Remi, where do you see yourself in five years?

I thought for a long while as I collected myself. "Lily will be a beautiful young lady. Hopefully, I'm doing something constructive with my life. Fiona wouldn't want me to curl up like dead bug on the sill. I don't think I'll ever be married again. As far as my job? I'd like to either be back on the force or maybe be a private investigator.

"That's good. Let's talk about that."

* * *

Two hours passed. Doc Margie closed her notebook with a smile of proud teacher. "I put in a call to Captain Trout the other day. Your badge is waiting for you."

It didn't register through the emotion-induced headache that had crept up on me. "What?"

"I knew you were going to be okay, so I wanted to make sure you wouldn't have to wait. You can fill out the paperwork tomorrow when you start your first shift as a homicide detective again. I'm leaving it to Captain Trout's judgment on how much he's going to involve you in the search for your daughter. I do believe he'll keep you on the sideline, so you have to be alright with that."

"Of course. Thank you." I gave her a hug before walking her to the door.

"But, it *is* mandatory that we meet every other week for three months. My condition." She stepped outside. "Take care, Remi."

"You too." I watched her take a few steps. "Doc?"

She turned. "Yeah?"

"I didn't want to admit it, but you're good at your job."

She smiled, and continued on to her car.

I popped two Ibuprofen and sat on my sofa with a my eyes closed. There was nothing to do but wait for the raid tomorrow with Agents Joiner and Foster. All my hopes for Lily were pinned on this. I couldn't go back to Booty Call. I couldn't stake out Dudko's house. I couldn't roam the Greater Port of Baton Rouge. What I could do was try to set up a lunch with Steve Sharpe. I pulled out his card, but my cell came to life first.

Go figure. It was Sharpe.

* * *

I parallel parked behind two black Lincoln Towncars directly in front of the majestic, all white, Columns Hotel, originally built in the late 1800's as one of the many mansions set along St. Charles Avenue in the Garden District.

My blood pressure dropped as the weight of the moment hit me. Was I going in that restaurant to kill Steve Sharpe? Should I just wait out here until he leaves and murder him on the street? With my Glock at my side, I eased out of the car.

The walkway led me to a set of stairs where two men dressed in thick trench coats, gloves, and dark glasses faced the street in a military stance. Four columns guarded the top of the steps, two on the left and two on the right, stretching to the second floor where a white balcony railing extended across. Three flags fluttered in the breeze above the entrance. Those columns, steps, and balcony framed the patio, which was the popular spot to eat, weather permitting.

The governor's men recognized me, one spoke into his wrist, and I passed through unmolested. The hostess directed me to the lunch area, which was bathed in tones of brown and beige, with simple iron chairs. The intimate room was half full, but Steve Sharpe's presence couldn't be avoided. He could be considered attractive, but in the beat-up sense. He waved his hand at me to join him, but not in an arrogant way.

I shook his hand. "Thanks for meeting me, Governor."

"Steve." His sleepy eyes wrinkled with an Elvis-like smile. His cropped brown hair reached for the sky and his eyebrows were plucked. "How are things?"

"Still investigating." I eased into my chair.

The waitress appeared looking chipper, a beautifully exotic, dark-skinned Indian girl. Her hair was held back in a thick ponytail. We each ordered a sweet tea.

He lost the smile. "Still no contact from the kidnappers?"

"Not a word. But, the entire department has been very supportive. And the Feds even."

"Good. Good."

"I heard you're riding as the king of Rex on Mardi Gras Day." I picked up the menu, but knew I was getting a burger.

He blew air from his lips. "You ever rode in a parade?"

"A Metairie truck parade. Had a blast."

He brightened. "Nothing like it. I wanted Rex for so long."

"Is that a good idea considering someone shot at you recently?"

He brushed it off. "Nothing has popped up on our radar since. We think a nut case had the opportunity to shoot at me from a distance. I piss off lots of unstable people. I've been out in public since. Someone wants to get me, they're going to get me. Besides, I've hired extra security and this is Rex we're talking about."

My hand brushed down my jacket, feeling the outline of my Glock. My eyes caught his as he went on about the duties of being king of Rex. I imagined him riding on that grand float with a gigantic plaster crown above him. He would be waving and throwing beads and doubloons along the route. I envisioned him stopping at the grandstand long enough for me to put a bullet between his eyes from an unseen location. My focus returned as he described the gold costume he would be wearing.

"And then there's the ball…"

I could kill him right here – a bullet to the head, or heart. The restaurant would clear out, and I'd rest my gun on the table. When the governor's men rushed in, they'd find me on my knees with my hands behind my head. I'd be arrested minutes later. This man – Steve Sharpe – would be wheeled out under a sheet saturated with his blood. His wife would be a widow, his kids fatherless with one little pull of a trigger.

And Lily would be safe. Or would that make her disposable?

"My two little girls are over the moon about this," he went on, "My oldest made the shoebox float in her second grade class, crown and all."

I smiled. "With the aluminum foil and beads stuck on with glue. Man, that takes me back."

Every New Orleans kid made a float out of a shoebox wrapped in foil, putting the lid on the end, so that it stuck up in the air. It occurred to me that I had wanted this meeting so that I *wouldn't* be able to kill him. Maybe I could have shot him from a distance when he was just a name and not a loving father. Now, he was a human being with a full life he created that I had no right to take away.

The waitress came back and we placed our order. Steve ordered a shrimp poboy and I changed my order to match his. Our giddy server's gaze lingered on the governor before she backed way.

"So, what's on your mind, Remi?" Steve sipped at his tea. "A little birdy told me it has to do with Juan Gomez."

My voice softened. "Actually, I wanted to ask you about Victor Dudko."

His face lost all humor. "That criminal?" He looked around. "I shouldn't say that outside my circle. Sorry."

"That criminal is the president of your commission of that port. You appointed him."

He thought about his words. "A mistake. A contemporary of mine recommended him and I owed a favor. He was a business owner in New Orleans and he took a residence in East Baton Rouge Parish and I thought his experience would be perfect. He had connections to Russian exporters and speaks the language."

"I'm not saying you did anything illegal. But, does he want you to?"

"I was asked the same questions by the FBI." He measured my reaction. "I'll tell you what I told the agents. Something about the way he does business – how he treats people – is vile, for lack of a better word. Some criminals are supposed to charm the money from your wallet, right?"

"Does he have it out for you?"

He stared at me for moment. "He does now, probably."

"Why?"

"Between us? Off the record. I figured he couldn't do much damage with the other board members watching over him, but he came to me with the idea to replace several members."

"With his people," I finished.

"That's what I assumed. I told him to tender his resignation from the board."

I took a breath. "Really? How'd that go?"

He shrugged. "I gave him until the Thursday after Mardi Gras to avoid the bad press during my reign as king of Rex. He told me I'd regret it, but I've been threatened before."

Bingo – motive.

At that moment, the waitress dropped off our sandwiches. "Can I get you anything else?"

"No, thanks, sweetheart." Steve put his napkin in his lap.

"I'd take his threats seriously. I believe that my daughter's abduction has something to do with him."

His expression was genuine surprise. "Bastard. How can I help?"

"I don't know. I can't put my finger on it. I don't know what I came here to find out."

"Turn over every stone." Steve reached out and put his paw on my shoulder. A large silver watch crept out from his sleeve. "Nothing is irrelevant. You stepdaughter is missing. Ask every question you can."

"You pissed off Dudko. You'd be a perfect target on that Rex float."

"Like Dudko would have me killed?" He scoffed. "As soon as I succumb, they own me."

"Doesn't make it any less real."

"I won't bow down and I won't be bought. Like I said, I can't live in a bubble."

"I could be interested in offering extra protection for you on your float."

Steve started eating his sandwich. "That – I like."

* * *

Directly after my lunch with the governor, I sat in my cold car and released the pressure valve I'd been holding. My face grew so hot, sweat dripped from my hairline. Spots grew in my vision, and instead of resisting the wave of helplessness, I embraced it. I let my body do what it wanted, but I didn't lose consciousness. After the wooziness dissipated, I gained control again.

The drive back to Headquarters let me clear my head for the upcoming raid on the Baton Rouge port. I walked onto the Homicide floor to a round of cheers as they heard about my reinstatement. Gracie led the charge, giving me an enthusiastic embrace. I kept a subdued smile for the high-fives and fist bumps, but it didn't feel right to celebrate anything just yet. Gracie changed her demeanor to match mine, but her optimism remained. We had two hours until our rendezvous with the Feds.

I filled out the proper paperwork, putting Lily down as my beneficiary. Trout presented a thick envelope containing my badge. It felt invigorating to clip the shield to my belt and have the gun registered as my official piece. It took Fiona's death to make this happen. But, being a cop would make it that much easier to bring Dudko to justice. I saluted Trout before leaving his office.

In the name of secrecy, the Feds wanted to meet in Jefferson Parish, just off the border of Orleans Parish, behind an old abandoned bank building. It was a discrete parking lot, hidden from Vets Memorial Boulevard, Metairie's main thoroughfare. With only a handful of agents, a snitch would show his hand.

An agent in tactical gear appeared from nowhere as we turned the corner of the building. He let us pass after checking into his earpiece. We arrived at the meeting area where Agents Joiner and Foster instructed several FBI recruits. The makeshift scene included a huddle of men wearing tac helmets, vests, goggles and belts with enough gadgets to make Batman proud. Han Solo came to mind when I saw the thigh holsters. A couple of the men also had rifles, which I recognized as MP-5s and M-4s. Even when one of the agents handed us Kevlar vests, Gracie and I felt extremely underdressed.

"Detectives, glad you can join us." Joiner shook my hand. "Congratulations on your reinstatement. Just in time."

"I still can't believe you want our help." Gracie shook her head.

"We work with police often." Foster stepped up. "You just haven't had a great experience with the Bureau yet."

"You sure Lily isn't being held there?" I stressed.

Joiner reassured me. "No. It's still a legitimate business with employees that have access to all the locations. It would be too risky."

Foster said, "If he's trafficking more than drugs, we're sure they're moved out as soon as they come in. So, the team will park at strategic vantage points along the river and near the entrance. We wait until the cargo is off the ship and is in route to its final destination."

"What if it doesn't go anywhere?" I asked.

Foster answered, "Then, we wait."

Joiner nodded, pointing to a map taped to the side of a van. "We've marked entry points here, here, and here." He slapped at highlighted areas.

"And the dogs? Drug sniffers?" I pointed at two German Shepherds enjoying the chill.

"Exactly."

Foster stepped up with a gym bag, placing it on the ground. "Everyone grab a throat com."

The stone-faced men stood in line to collect more gear. Foster looked at our interested faces. He explained, "This gadget wraps around the neck with two pieces on either side of the larynx to pick up vocal vibrations. It allowed for very faint whispering failing a visual hand signal."

"Do we get them?" Gracie asked.

"No."

Joiner explained, "We don't expect much resistance. However, sometimes there's one nut with a gun and itchy trigger finger, so each of us will have medical equipment—scissors, bandages, gel for sucking chest wounds, tape and things of that nature. If a team member gets injured, use their med pack, not your own."

After learning our roles and positions, Gracie and I left for Baton Rouge in her Trans Am, which drew attention from all of the agents. Was it good attention, like appreciating a classic? We didn't know.

A little over an hour later, we met up with Joiner and Foster about a half-mile away from the port along the bank of the river. We had a perfect view of the operation from the entrance road. Large domes resembling breasts sprouted up from the ground. Towering silos reached for the sky, connected by a seemingly endless pattern of grain elevators. Roads that led to the barge docking area and the railroad tracks ran fairly close to the bank.

Gracie and I accompanied Foster and Joiner in the rear of their van and waited silently for word from the team leader. We could see all the action from out the back windows. The van contained a multitude of communications equipment.

Joiner spoke to us as he adjusted his earpiece. "This port is ranked thirty-second in the world for annual tonnage. It would be so easy to sneak shipments through. We're expecting five hundred kilos of pure, uncut cocaine."

"Nice." Gracie watched the monitor intently.

Joiner listened through his earpiece. "The men established position. Holding."

Foster continued in a whisper. "Besides Dudko, this port is run by fourteen other members on the board appointed by the governor."

I swallowed hard. "Amazing that Dudko weaseled his way in here."

Joiner said, "We spoke to Governor Sharpe about Dudko's appointment. He simply said he made a mistake."

"This is our ship," Foster said, checking the boat's number on a printout. "The container will be separated from the rest of the cargo on the dock. Its serial number is DYFV436998T. I can see it from here, front and center. Probably last on, so it could be first off."

One crane reached into the sky, moving a box on a rope and pulley system. The hoist lifted the container and slowly moved across the rail until it could be lowered onto the dock. I feared losing sight of the box as if it might vanish.

"What now?" The van suddenly became claustrophobic.

Joiner said, "We can't rush in. The inspector just let this container slide through. We can't arrest anyone until the owners come get it."

"And from there, hopefully trace it back to who helped get it through customs here," I said.

"Right." Foster drank some water. "But, the inspectors are the least of our worries."

"How does Dudko get nailed for this?"

Foster sat back. "That is something we can't share with you, unfortunately. Witness protection and such things."

As more cargo containers came off the ship, a blue vehicle that resembled a scorpion, where the tail crossed over the top of the driver's box, secured our container and carried it about a quarter mile down the road. The odd forklift set it down next to a railway where several cargo containers had already been loaded.

"What if it gets loaded on the train?" Gracie asked.

"Then we follow it." Foster continued to switch from the monitors to his binoculars.

Just after the sun dropped from sight and the port sat idle, we finally saw activity. A *Best Friend Movers* truck pulled next to the railway.

"This is unusual," Foster said.

Joiner added, "Are they going to crack the container here?" He spoke into his earpiece. "Hold on my word."

When the driver exited the moving van and joined the other men at the container, Foster looked at Gracie. "Okay, you two can bring up the rear in your Trans Am. Let's move."

Gracie and I raced back to her car and all of the team's vehicles got in line, moving down the paved road leading to the gravel path near the river. Everyone parked next to each other and the van doors opened, releasing multiple agents.

I've never witnessed an FBI led raid. These bulky, heavily equipped men moved with stealth, separating with their weapons brandished. The dogs accompanied the FBI team to the rail car. Each man found cover, throwing hand signals in the air. I scanned the oblivious crew.

"FBI! Freeze!" A voice commanded.

I quickly assessed that five men were involved in moving this cargo. Every visible person stopped with raised hands, except one. The youngster reached behind his back and his hand returned with a gun. Three agents shot simultaneously. The criminal's body danced as each bullet entered until he fell to the ground. The other, older criminals watched with apathy. I guessed no one had told him to comply in this situation.

The rest of the team approached in waves, rifles aimed. We bolted from the car and ran in behind them, guns drawn, feeling like we were late to the party, but happy to be there.

"Don't shoot. *Jee-sus Christ.*" The person speaking had a deep twang.

Several of the Feds threw the men to the ground, patting them down and discarding their concealed weapons. They wrapped their wrists with a plastic tie from their belts while the dogs went nuts in front of the container. Another agent kept the men on the cargo ship at bay.

"Everyone on your knees," Foster ordered. He snagged the nearest agent. "Get the bolt-cutter."

Joiner held a manic, intense expression as he inspected the subdued work crew. "You, you, and you…" He pointed at certain agents. "…Secure the entrance. No one in or out."

Gracie and I gravitated to the moving van. The back of the vehicle had a massive lock attached. Foster approached, waving his hand at me. "It has to be the transport vehicle, but I'm curious as to why they carried the container to the train. It could be for an exchange of some sort. We'll open the truck after the container."

We turned to face the prize. Without haste, we avoided the kneeling crew to approach the crate. The anticipation had me numb, but I needed to act like I've been here before. Several men kept their weapons trained on the container door.

Joiner immediately spoke into his watch. "Dudko's not on the premises. Execute the warrant on the residence. Bring him in."

An agent broke the padlock free with a heavy-duty cutter and they opened the locking mechanism. The metal doors swung open, revealing two palates of what looked like cocaine. After several agents entered the container, they came out holding up the merchandise and laughing. The men took pictures and cracked jokes. This was the major bust we'd all been waiting for, but it seemed hollow.

As the dogs were led away, they stopped and sat quiet at the back of the moving truck, just staring at it. Gracie and I backed away as two agents shimmied to each side hugging their assault rifles at their chest. Foster gave a silent signal with his fist. Another agent ran up to the padlock and cut it open. He handed the bolt cutter to me and then disengaged the sickle-like latch, swinging it free. With a hard shove, the door of the moving truck rose.

"Oh, my God." One of the agents signaled to the team to drop their weapons.

Inside were approximately fifteen women huddled together in a dirty, sweaty mass. One of them was lying in another's lap, battered to a pulp. A wretched stink emanated from the inside. I clambered inside the truck, ignoring Foster's warning. It took a few seconds to check, but none of the faces were Lily's. I punched the wall of the truck.

"Sorry, Remi." Gracie waved for me to jump down.

I said, "They're paying for the drugs with women." Lily's face appeared on every one of them. I pointed. "This one needs immediate medical attention."

"Call for a bus," Foster commanded to an agent with wide eyes. He stared at the unconscious, bruised and bleeding girl, then looked at me. "Sometimes they take one girl and beat her in front of the others as a way to send a message."

"Real gentlemen."

Foster explained, "It looks like the girls were going into the cargo container to be taken north where they'll be distributed. Dudko's men will be waiting."

"But, it's not going to show," I said.

Foster smiled. "Oh, it will show. It'll just be empty. We'll have a team following it."

"Nice," Gracie said.

Joiner stepped up. "This truck is from Best Friend Movers in New Orleans. They let you rent the truck with two or three movers or you can rent it yourself like Budget Rent-A-Truck. I doubt there will be a destination recorded anywhere and the driver probably paid with cash and a fake license, but who knows? We could get lucky."

"Gracie and I can investigate the company."

"No. We'll take it from here."

Two agents with surgical gloves climbed into the truck to start taking out the women. They complied like zombies, not realizing they had been rescued.

Joiner stepped up. "Just got word. They have Dudko. He's being brought in."

"Wait." I ran after him, still holding the long handle of the bolt cutter. "Gracie and I want in on the questioning."

Joiner intervened. "No. We're going to question him."

"He has my daughter. I want to throw Egor's name in his face to see his reaction."

"Sorry, this is an FBI matter. An agent is dead, detective. Don't pretend to be hurt because you'd do the same. And if it's any consolation, Agent Foster is preparing a statement for the press. The Bureau is going to share this bust with you and Detective Castillo."

"You're fucking suggesting that I'd rather have good publicity over finding my daughter?" I restrained myself from taking a swing at him.

He actually rolled his eyes. "That's not what I meant."

"How are you going to explain that the detectives that made the bust are aren't allowed to be in on the interrogation?"

"Because of your daughter. You're too close to this." He pulled me close and whispered, "Dudko will be backed into a corner. He'll want to use Lily as a bargaining chip. This is our shot to get her back for you. Let us do this."

I kept eye contact, though I was relinquishing control. "I'm counting on you."

"I know." He motioned behind him. "That's a major amount of drugs, detective. Don't you think?"

"About as much as I busted Baskov with five years ago."

"Where would you think it came from?"

"Mexico, right?" We stared at each other. "Wait a minute... Juan Gomez?"

He smiled and patted my shoulder. "Like we said, we really can't talk about our informants."

"But, he's going to be killed days from now."

"Stay of execution – as of this morning." Joiner winked. "Seems someone's little lunch with the governor did some good. If Gomez's testimony can put away Dudko, he'll work out a plea in exchange for your daughter. Let us do our job."

Dudko had attempted to set up Los Serpientes for Fiona's murder, and Juan Gomez made sure there was payback in a huge way. I almost smiled at the Karma. "You'll keep me informed every step of the way?"

"Of course."

I watched him meet up with Foster. Agents were escorting the remaining crew to a van where they were handcuffed to the benches inside. The criminals wore faces of disappointment, but weren't fighting back in the least. None of them cursed or threatened anyone as if instructed to keep quiet.

The agents on the dock had the dogs sniff the remaining cargo. This time, no one knew about the raid and no one was tipped off. Gracie smiled as she found me. We watched the one man who was killed be bagged up for transport.

I gripped both handles of the cutters, absently testing its torque. "I still feel like something's not quite right."

"Remi, why don't we go back to the city and get some coffee and talk?"

"No, I'm going to go home and wait for the Feds to contact me."

Gracie walked beside me to the car. "Trout wants us back at Broad Street."

"Can't you brief him?" I threw my new tool in her back seat.

She opened the door and continued talking as we got inside of her car. She started the engine. "Your first day on the friggin' job and you walk into this kind of bust? And you want to go home?"

"You can get off my back." I faced the window.

"Oh, my God. You're actually considering killing Sharpe."

I wiped my eyes. "I'd never do that."

"Remi, what's going on?"

"I have three days to find Lily. Practically two, now. That's what I'm focused on."

"That's what *we're* focused on." Gracie put the car in drive and peeled out of the cargo loading area. "Let's go over what we know again. And then we'll give Trout the condensed version."

* * *

My partner and I rehashed the entire raid from start to finish as Captain Trout and a group of cops listened in. Trout smiled a couple of times, but otherwise stayed even. The rest of the cops hooted, clapped, and whistled until I got to the part about the human cargo. I let Gracie handle most of the details.

As if on cue, Agents Joiner and Foster came onto our floor with somber expressions, looking ragged, like they'd slept in their clothes. They sapped all the air from the room. Captain Trout stepped in front of everyone, sensing the importance of the visit.

"You must have news," Trout said.

Joiner rubbed his temples. "Good evening, Captain Trout. Sorry for the unscheduled intrusion. Can we speak in private?"

"Of course. Follow me." Trout led everyone to the conference room, but no one sat.

"Dudko's free," Foster finally said in our circle, "Our informant was killed in a prison incident earlier today."

"Juan Gomez is dead?" I couldn't comprehend it.

Foster continued, "We still have twelve men to question. We're far from done."

Gracie grabbed my arm. "Wait, you knew Gomez was their informant?"

"Yeah, just found out at the raid. He was in solitary. No one could get to him… Unless the guards…"

"It looks like his food was poisoned. We're investigating that."

I crowded Joiner. "Well, at least you're investigating. Wonderful!"

Trout pulled me back. "Settle down, Remi."

Joiner didn't appear offended. "We believe his own gang is responsible since they still work with Dudko and considered him weak for not retaliating against you."

"It's more about the money they make together." Gracie broke from the circle.

"In other words," Foster said, "we can't tie Dudko to the bust. We don't have him saying anything on any of our taps. This group is genius in how they communicate. Unless someone talks, he's claiming he didn't know what was going on."

"This is unbelievable." I found a chair. My knees wouldn't hold me up anymore.

"We're not done, yet." Foster wiped at his tie. "We'll be in touch." The agents silently left for the exit.

"So, I'm back to square one with finding my daughter?" I yelled at their backs.

Joiner stopped and turned. "We're not done with Dudko, Remi. Remember, you can't confront him. It could ruin our next course of action." They disappeared, leaving the room in silence.

CHAPTER TWENTY-NINE

I lied to my partner about going home after the Feds dropped the Dudko bombshell. The Uber driver dropped me off by Café Du Monde and I became anonymous while meandering around the Quarter, the last place I should want to be as a local. Everyone was one of those people - *those smiling people*. The streets weren't quite as busy as the weather kept revelers inside. I had always been a social drinker, but tonight I needed to take the edge off, miscalculating exactly how much edge I had to smooth. I placed my empty pint of vodka next to an overflowing trash barrel, berating myself for getting this drunk. *This isn't good, Remi. Not good.*

With my hands shoved deep in my jacket, I stumbled off a curb on Conti Street, a block away from the Eighth District station. A bit further down on Bourbon, I found myself in front of The Booty Call. No one could say this was random. I probably resembled a zombie going through the entrance. The colorful lights disarmed me a little, but I eventually got my bearings. The dancers smiled at me as my numb mind tried to make my wobbly body look sober.

"Hello," a platinum blonde's voice squeaked over the music.

"Dudko here?"

"Mr. Dudko?"

"Yeah, the fucking owner," I yelled at her.

She reared back, looking for a nearby bouncer. "Calm down, I'll find him."

I held my hands up. "I'm sorry. I'm sorry. Is Yaz-mo-vich here?"

Her eyes softened. "Yaz is upstairs. Why don't you have a seat at the bar and I'll get him for you?"

I stumbled sideways, but caught myself on a chair. "I'll do that, and you do that." Without waiting for an answer, I surged forward, thinking it best to get my ass on a stable barstool. Sitting there, my inebriated mind realized the situation I put myself in.

"What can I get you?" The humorless bartender asked.

"Water. You got water? No, how about coffee?"

"He gets nothing," a voice said from my left.

"Where's the hospitality, Yaz? I'm a customer." My head turned so fast that I saw two faces that slowly merged into one. Like magic, my body floated off the barstool. It took a second to realize two bouncers were carrying me toward the exit. "Get the fuck off me. I'm a cop."

"I'm going to enjoy this, Doucet." Yaz followed behind us.

"Yeah, it's going to take three of you pussies to get the best of me." My struggling resulted in nothing. The few patrons scattered about weren't close enough to care about the bouncers handling a drunk.

Suddenly we stopped, just before reaching the door. Dudko blocked our progress. He pointed to the ground and the bouncers let me go. I swayed between them, waiting for the perfect moment to lunge.

"No bodily harm will come to Mr. Doucet. He has to stay in good health."

The vodka almost came up. I don't know how smooth it looked, but I reached inside my jacket and pulled out my Glock, pointing it directly at Dudko's mouth. Three distinct guns being chambered were heard behind me.

Dudko smiled like I was a child. My finger almost squeezed. "Does Federov approve of this crazy plan of killing Sharpe?"

He squinted. "So, you know about Federov. Means nothing."

The gun shook. "He might like to know how you're risking his operation by kidnapping a cop's daughter."

Dudko stepped to the side. "Get out of here."

My arm dropped to my side. When I holstered, so did his crew. I was immediately sober. "You may have killed Gomez, but I'm sure you have those Latino gangs nervous. Better watch your back."

The two giants pushed me out the door and left me stumbling on Bourbon Street. No one really cared that I couldn't walk a straight line. I considered myself lucky to be standing after that stupid move. I pulled out my cell phone and summoned an Uber to take me home.

CHAPTER THIRTY

The light above the bed flicked on, waking Lily in a strange bed. It took a moment to get her bearings, but how could she forget her situation? The two girls that had originally occupied the room had never returned. They warned her of the horrors they had endured. She prayed she wouldn't be next.

She remembered the day those men kidnapped her and her mother. She had looked out of the window to see a small Best Friend Movers truck backing into the driveway, right next to her mom's car. A man wearing a cap, sunglasses, and a shirt with the logo knocked on the door. She had planned to open the door, but instead, she yelled to them that this was the wrong house.

Lily watched them go back to the truck and check a tablet. After informing her momma of their mistake, she returned to the couch where the next sound she heard was the door exploding open. She forced the memory to end there.

She sat upright for the longest time, just trying to snap out of the daze. She scooted to the edge of the stained mattress on the roll-a-way bed and wiped away her eye-crust, gagging at the putrid smell of the bucket in the corner. Her stomach created a loud rumble.

As every morning, she tried to open the door, but it wouldn't budge. Pounding against it didn't help – neither did seeing the scratch marks. There were no windows to let the sun in. The Cuban wouldn't say if her momma was in the building or even still alive, but she had to believe so.

Her tense thigh muscles burned from pacing and she leaned back against the damp, chilled wall. She took inventory of a tiny dresser in one corner and a metal bucket in the other along with toilet paper and a can of Lysol. She had to urinate, but the bucket was so degrading. Her nerves and the pressing on her bladder prompted immediate attention. She pulled down the sweatpants and squatted over the bucket. The echo of the stream bounced off the walls and she fought against crying. Today, she was successful.

Her aching knees buckled and she fell onto the cold, gritty ground that scratched her like sandpaper. She pulled up her sweatpants, relieved that her bladder was empty. A click came from the other side of the door causing her heart to pound. Was this the day she and her momma reunited? Or would Remi be on the other side? The door crept open.

No, it was the Cuban, Miguel. He wanted to talk again – and that's all he ever wanted from her. Miguel was scary, worldly, and sensitive at the same time. She was hopeful that she could figure him out and possibly turn him.

"I hope you slept well," he spoke with a charming accent. He showed no signs of aggression.

"Do you miss Cuba?" She asked.

"As much as you miss your freedom."

CHAPTER THIRTY-ONE

Miguel had left Lily with optimism that she could be let go if her stepfather achieved the mysterious goal. It was the best he could do for the young lady. He made his regular tour of the warehouse to the rear where the four-story office building sprouted up from the back half, old and beaten as all the buildings surrounding it. His own plan to defect had been set in motion, however this time he felt like his old self. If he succeeded, this would be the ultimate score. If he failed, he would go underground like no one else could.

Dudko had gotten lax with the rules. There were two new men Miguel had hosted this month. Each one close to the billionaire club, and unbeknownst to them, each man was now owned. Wealth made some men weak and stupid, or arrogant and clumsy. They paid dearly for anything from S&M and fecalphelia to sodomy with strange objects. A few liked the plush room Dudko offered with champagne and treats, but a mere madam could set that up. No, most liked the dungeon room and the pain and degradation that came with it.

He poured a little more Jack into his Coke and took a sip. The tattoo on his neck and shoulder of the grim reaper holding a candle and sickle told the Russians in Dudko's employ that he was a killer. It was the only mark on his body, but Dudko insisted that he needed it if he was going to be respected and earned a ten thousand dollar bonus for doing so. He would burn it off once he separated from Dudko, as it's meaning changed to being a cowardly killer of women.

Did the desire to bed Lily mean that his life had peaked? He felt like a fool for letting her arouse him. Older men appreciated the flesh of young women in a way that boys couldn't. Young women kept old men from dying on the inside. Feeling like a twenty year old during a seven-second orgasm was the only way to suppress the fear of impending death. Miguel only had relations with grown women, but appreciated the beauty in youth. Perhaps he should claim Lily as his own. He had earned that right.

Lily would die.

Miguel took another sip. The whiskey quelled his anxiety. The burning on his throat relaxed him. He lit another cigarette and opened his bottom desk drawer to pull out a miniature digital recording device; the same one Yaz used during the cop's abduction. It would be Miguel's salvation. He placed the recorder in his front shirt pocket and practiced turning it on at the same time. The recorder was small enough to pass undetected by the boss during their meeting this afternoon.

Babysitting paid pretty well and he had an impressive offshore account. He missed the war in the real, as well as concrete, jungle. However, at his age, it was a hell of a lot better than being a hit-man, a soldier of revolution in a war-torn village, or hired help for the Skullbones.

Miguel made a mental note not to bend over and let it slide out. Wouldn't it be bad luck to have it drop at Dudko's feet? He figured the boss was coming to the building as a show of power. The bastard even refused the safeguard of the pickup, so he could be driven onto the property in the truck, unnoticed. He would actually arrive in his own car. Stupid.

He had the arrogance that got men killed. *It's his ass if he's followed*, Miguel thought. Especially with all the Mardi Gras shit going on. Fat Tuesday was closing in and New Orleans was lousy with amateur drunks.

Miguel poured some more Jack into his drink and finished it off, mentally counting the millions that would soon be his.

CHAPTER THIRTY-TWO

The morning was a speedy blur from bed to shower to car. After a short weaving walk, I arrived at the front entrance of Headquarters with last night's buzz clouding my mind. The press yelled at me from the steps like I had the cure for cancer. In the hubbub, I spotted a CNN and MSNBC truck. The reporters clawed over each other like a ravenous pack of wolves. I dodged their questions about the bust at the port the night before and made my way inside. Word seemed to travel fast.

"Made it through the gauntlet?" Gracie smiled at me from the top of the newspaper she held. "You're all over the news."

I nodded with disinterest, but got on the Internet to scan the New Orleans website's splash page as Gracie sat on the edge of her desk reading the article. The headline read:

REINSTATED! DETECTIVE DOUCET HELPS THE FEDS BUST HUMAN TRAFFICKING AND DRUG RING.

Gracie shrugged her shoulders. "They finally mention me three paragraphs in."

"The press sucks. Everything sucks."

"Don't spiral down, now Remi. Like the Feds said, we're far

from through." Gracie slapped my shoulder, snapping my gloom. "What do you want to do?"

"Screw the Feds. C'mon, let's go interview some employees over at Best Friend Movers."

* * *

Since I was officially on the job again, Gracie let me drive. We pulled onto the curb in front of Best Friend Movers, which blended in with the other industrial buildings on the block as if they were all built at once, with the same materials, by the same contractor. It looked like the perfect scene for the zombie apocalypse with lots of neglected, decaying structures to run in and hide.

Above the rental office, the name of the company had been painted in a bold script font in purple and gold on a large piece of plywood. The days and times of operation were listed on the window portion of the recessed door. Metal tracks lined the entrance to allow a cage to slide down after hours.

I pushed on the door, but it didn't move. Gracie pointed at the closed sign.

"According to these hours, they should be open." I saw movement within the rental office, so I banged on the glass, pressing my badge against it. A female approached and opened the door.

"I'm sorry, we're closed."

"I'm Detective Doucet and this is Detective Castillo. May we come in?"

"Okay." Without much thought, the lady unlocked the door.

Gracie entered first and the door set off a bell. We stepped a few feet up to an ancient, faded pink counter. The employee took a chair at her desk near the back wall. There were no personal touches anywhere. Something about the rental office irked me, like it was a movie set. Off to our left were display boxes for moving, bubble wrap, tape and such. I took it all in as I tried to figure out why the place felt staged.

"What's your name?" I asked her.

"Nicole Jones. The FBI was already here. They took everything." She had long, straight brown hair parted down the middle like a flower child. She appeared dazed, as if she had been up for twenty-four hours.

"If you're closed, why are you here?"

"Just straightening up." She seemed to be talking to herself.

I looked at Gracie.

Ms. Jones' eyes bounced to both of us before settling on her phone. "I'm just a cashier."

"You must set up the rentals, right?" I asked.

"I was told not to make any statements to the police."

"Who told you that?" I asked.

"My boss."

"Who is…?" Gracie tried to draw her out.

"They said don't make any statements. They said you can't make me."

I spoke softly. "True. But, there's no secret with what you do here, right? What's your job?"

She nodded and pointed around the room at nothing in particular. "I take inventory. I rent the trucks. I assign the movers if the customer wants them. I send the trucks to be serviced. I clean."

Gracie smiled, waiting for her to finish. "You rented a truck out yesterday, right?"

Nicole showed no emotion. "The truck didn't come back. The FBI kept it. They took everything."

"You remember who rented it?"

She kept staring at her desk. "Not supposed to say anything."

"Is there another employee you work with?" Gracie asked. "No secret, right?"

"No. I work by myself."

Gracie kept her patience. "Then how was it rented out?"

"I can't say."

I spoke up. "You mind if we look around in the bay? Back there?"

"Employees only," she murmured.

"Is there a manager available to speak to? The owner?" I asked.

"No one's here. There aren't any appointments. We're closed." Ms. Jones straightened a few pens on the empty desk.

Gracie sighed. "Does your manager have a name? A business card?"

She looked to go into a comatose state. I placed my card down on the counter. "Tell your boss to give me a call. Nothing wrong with that, right?"

Nicole rose from her desk and took her time in approaching me from around the counter. Her sleepy, dark eyes stayed on mine as she floated up, just inches from our bodies touching. She secured my hands, and whispered in my ear.

I cocked my head at her. She backed away and disappeared through the *employee's only* door.

Gracie ran to the door, but it had locked. "What did she say?" Gracie turned to me.

"She said, 'I pray for your daughter.'"

CHAPTER THIRTY-THREE

Gracie had to make an appearance in court, leaving me to invest some time at the Hardcore Store. Barry-Boy truly thought he made a new friend. I sort of felt bad for him. The conversation stayed on the Baton Rouge bust, and the atrocities of human trafficking. I dropped a comment that having a sex slave wouldn't be the worst thing and laughed about it. His stance was very diplomatic, but I couldn't get a bead on his level of approval.

After that, Gracie and I met up at Headquarters after she had finished with her testimony.

"Where were you during lunch?" Gracie asked.

"Barry-Boy. I'm grasping at straws."

"After I testified, I made a call and found out who owns Best Friend Movers. I got Kyle Mann's name and address, so I went to see him out in Gentilly after the Courthouse." Gracie flicked the card at me while we sat at our desks. "He's a little, greasy man. He couldn't offer us anything. He didn't even know the place was raided."

"A hands-off owner or a patsy?"

"I got a sense he's in name only. Nice business model, though.

Low inventory. Keep the trucks running and he gives the two guys that come with the truck a cut."

I swiveled in my chair to face her Gracie. "We're getting close to Fat Tuesday."

"I know."

"What am I going to do, Gracie?" The tears formed.

My partner rolled her chair next to mine. "Survive, baby. Whatever happens, you're going to survive. But no one here is giving up hope."

"I know."

The day wound down. Gracie's stomach audibly rumbled. She laughed and patted her belly. "Wanna get something to eat?"

"Not really."

Despite my objections, she forced me to grab a quick bite of fried seafood near Jackson Square. Even though I didn't have an appetite, I picked off Gracie's seafood platter.

We ate in silence until Gracie posed a question. "So. Spill it. What did your brother do to you, exactly?"

I wiped my fingers with a wet nap, then rubbed at my eyes. Gracie's soft and assuring expression put me at ease, but how do you speak of something you spent your entire life suppressing? "When I was ten and he was twelve, he overheard my parents talking one night – about how I was adopted."

"Adopted? Is that true?"

I nodded. "He couldn't wait to tell me. It was like Christmas day for him. He was so excited about it. It destroyed me."

"Remi, I'm so sorry."

"I was old enough to know they loved me. I put up a front for my parents. I still loved them. Even after we were adults, I pretended to get along with Dylan, which I think was my biggest mistake."

"Why?"

I stole another catfish strip from her plate and dipped it in tartar sauce. "We were having Thanksgiving the first year I dated Fiona. The last Thanksgiving with my folks. Dylan and I only got together for the parents, you know. Our relationship was on life support at this point. Dylan came to eat and watch football. He was giving Lily so much attention that I remember it bothered me."

"You have great instincts."

"After dinner we were playing horseshoes in the backyard, but Dylan and Lily had disappeared. I went inside and found them in her room. He was in her beanbag chair with her sitting across his lap showing him pictures on her tablet. He had his arms wrapped around her waist. His face was so close to hers. She was only thirteen for Christ's sake."

"That could be innocent."

"It was. I could see Dylan plopping in the beanbag just to try it out, and Lily being a star-struck teen… Anyway, I asked Lily some sensitive questions without being too direct. Dylan's a womanizer, not a pedophile. But, that was my girlfriend's daughter and you know the shit we see on the job."

"True, but we can tell the difference between affection and – and *creepy*."

"Dylan always dated *women* - even when he was a teenager, he went after college girls. But, I just can't let go of that image."

"I don't blame you at all. Did you confront him?"

"No. He still thinks it's the adoption thing I'm holding a grudge on. I could see myself in his place, and if I was accused of other motives, I'd be so angry and hurt. Part of me feels guilty for holding that against him. But, consider the alternative." I pushed away from the table. "So, now you know."

"That must have been difficult to tell me. Thank you."

We left the restaurant and strolled in silence, mulling over our thoughts. Three black youths tap dancing caught our attention and we stopped to watch. They reminded me of the three teens shot under the Claiborne overpass. Jane Doe's face... The clues left behind, taunting me...

"You think they were ever working together?" I offered.

"Who?"

"Juan Gomez turned on Dudko after Los Serpientes was blamed for Fiona's murder. The Russians and Latinos were certainly working together – or at least using each other. Then, someone stepped on someone else's toes. Juan Gomez fingers Dudko as one last act of vengeance and Gomez ends up dead. Kind of incestuous, don't you think?"

"From partnership to enemies - sure."

I scanned the other side of the street, hitting Gracie in the arm at the sight of Victor Dudko strolling toward us without a care.

Gracie blocked my progress, facing me. "Don't confront him. Trout put a tail on him in case he leads them to Lily. You don't want any cops seeing you lose it in public."

"I'm in control." *Now, anyway.*

He looked like a vampire that could venture out during the day. The people walking by him had no idea they were brushing up against a drug lord, sex trafficker, and murderer. We stood by a lamppost, observing Dudko about a half block away and taking his time. As soon as he was near, we interrupted his path.

"Detective Castillo," Dudko said, almost pleased, "and Doucet. You going to keep your gun holstered this time?"

Gracie looked at me. "What does that mean?"

My fists clenched at my sides. "Nothing."

"Two days, Doucet." He held up two fingers triumphantly. "And just so you understand, being that you're not too hung over today, anything happens to me, my men have their instructions."

My face burned against the chill in the air. "Why not just take care of your problem yourself?"

Dudko looked at Gracie, shaking his head. "You told her."

"Does that matter?"

His vacant eyes never blinked. "If you fail, then I *will* take care of the matter myself. The question is; can you live with your choices?"

I put my face in his. "If I don't get Lily back, I'm going to kill you, just like Egor. Oh, yeah. Bullet right in the head."

"Remi." Gracie turned me away, snapping me out of my moment. In the corner of my eye, I glimpsed the cop tailing Dudko, and he was speaking into his collar. *Great.*

Dudko's eyes bulged. "You're not drunk now, detective. I'd be very careful what you say." He stepped away, looking at me as if I spit on his shiny black shoes. He walked further on and he merged easily with the crowd.

"You confronted him. When? Last night?" Gracie turned to face me.

I suppressed a laugh. "I pulled my gun on him in his club last night."

Gracie slapped her forehead, turning away.

"It's fine," I said.

She leaned in and whispered as the crowd passed around us. "I know you're under stress that I can't imagine, but your fuse is getting way too short."

"I got it under control."

"Bullshit. Antagonizing the man who has your daughter? Drawing your gun? You're turning into a desperate parent."

"Then, don't worry about me anymore. I'll handle finding Lily. Go do whatever you want."

"Do you hear yourself?" She grabbed my arm.

I pulled from her grasp, "Either you're with me or against me."

Then the last thing I ever expected happened. She spun me around and clocked my jaw with a left hook, sending me backwards a few steps. "I'm with you."

I had never heard her voice tremble with such fury.

A few people in the crowd gasped as I checked for blood. There was none, but my cheek throbbed. Gracie's hand had to hurt, but she showed no pain.

She held her badge up for the onlookers, some with their cells recording. "Keep moving." Then she peered back at me as I wiped my face a few more times. Gracie had that stern look of a mother. "I'll meet you back at the station and you better have your head on straight."

I didn't respond. She walked away as my cell rang. It was Dylan, and he wanted a meeting.

CHAPTER THIRTY-FOUR

Gracie fumed as she weaved through the strolling tourists. Her hand tingled in pain. Threatening Dudko was inevitable, but Remi staying in control for this long surprised her. She needed to take charge of the investigation. Despite his bad judgment, she refused to believe that Remi would actually try to take the governor's life.

She figured to visit Booty Call again to question the staff, knowing Dudko wouldn't be there. She stood inside the entrance, looking around at the daytime crowd and the few dancers unlucky enough to pull this shift. The lone bartender, tall and droopy-eyed, looked bored, so she approached him first.

He frowned and picked up a glass to clean. "Can I get you something?"

"Answers. I was hoping you can tell me a little something about the other bartender here… Yazmovich."

He smirked. "We don't talk."

"At all? Hard to believe."

"Believe what you will."

This time Gracie frowned. She turned and spotted a dancer coming by. She impeded the stripper's progress to question her, but she had nothing to offer. None of the next three girls did. However, before she walked out, one girl appeared from the back, clearing off a table of empty glasses. She was young, pale, and pretty.

"Excuse me." Gracie showed her badge. "I'm Detective Gracie Castillo. I just want take a moment of your time."

The girl stood up straight and they walked towards each other, meeting in the center of the room. "How can I help?"

"What's your name?"

"Cherry Treasure." She blushed, catching herself. "Terri Piper."

"Terri, how long have you worked here?"

"Two years."

"What do you know about the bartender, Yazmovich?" Gracie pointed to where he would be standing if present.

She turned hesitant. "He's a manager here. Bartends some nights to help out."

"Know him well?"

"Not really." She bit her cuticle.

"What *do* you know?" Gracie squinted, stepping closer and touching her wrist. "Terri, this man is into some very bad things. Anything would help."

She shifted, looking around the room. "He works for Best Friend Movers on the side. I do know that."

Gracie smiled on the inside. She whispered, "Listen to me. I want you pull away from me and storm off. After get a few feet, yell back at me to leave you alone."

Terri's eyes opened wide with understanding. She nodded, following Gracie's instructions exactly. The girl was great actress.

CHAPTER THIRTY-FIVE

D ylan had arrived first. We occupied a table under a heat lamp at Pat O'Brien's where only a few brave patrons braved the cold. *Big Shot* by Billy annoyed me from the speakers and I flagged down a waiter before sitting to make sure a drink would be on the way. Dylan ordered a Coke.

He huffed at me after the waiter retreated. "A cocktail? That's not going to help."

"*Et tu, Brute?*" I deflated.

"The side of your face is red. What the hell happened?" He stared at me while I wiped imaginary crumbs off the glass table. He began again. "How'd the lunch with Sharpe go?"

"He didn't tell you?"

"We're not *besties*. I heard he approved the stay of execution, but then Gomez was killed."

"Yeah, that… Wasn't good. So, why the meeting?"

The waiter placed a Coke down for Dylan and a vodka on the rocks for me. I watched him sip as we both waited for each other to say something that wouldn't set the other off. My jaw ached as the alcohol sat before me, cubes melting, begging me to drink it.

"I want to know where you're at with finding Lily. What's our next move?"

"I don't know. There is no next move."

"We went to Booty Call for a reason. You think that Victor guy has something to do with it. You want me to go back there?" His eyes darted. "Maybe I can get someone to say something."

"Too dangerous." I looked down at my drink, which I still hadn't sampled.

Dylan slapped the table, drawing my attention away from the glass. "Don't drink that. Not until we get Lily back."

"Are you trying to make up with me to advance your political career? I mean, how good would it look to the voters if you were there for me in my time of need, right?"

Just that fast, Dylan's left hook got me on the other cheek, nearly knocking me from the chair. I recovered, acting like his punch didn't affect me. "Wow. Back to our childhood ways already?"

He pushed the metal chair back, looking around, wiping his face. He spoke low. "I'm sorry, but I'm carrying a lot of shit around, too."

My body straightened up in the chair. My other cheek now stung. Acting like nothing happened, I stirred the ice cubes. The fresh taste of blood coated my tongue.

Dylan walked past me. "You won't find Lily at the bottom of that glass. Call me when you come to your senses."

"Anyone else here wants to punch me?" I offered, my arms wide in belligerent invitation.

The drink sat there temptingly under my nose, cubes cracking and settling. I pushed the glass to the center of the table and let a guttural moan spew from my lips. My brother was trying to get back in my good graces and I shit on him. *Help*, I laughed internally. He wanted to help. Maybe I *could* use him to be my eyes. And even considering that option showed my desperation.

CHAPTER THIRTY-SIX

Yaz returned to the building with a four large pizzas to feed the men and the remaining girls, the ones not intercepted in the Baton Rouge port raid. He left the pies for Miguel to distribute on the third floor. Yaz operated from the fourth floor, away from Miguel and that business. His main forte was only to acquire innocent, beautiful, yet troubled girls.

Dudko called on his cell phone just as Yaz was about to leave. "You fucked up by having the men use one of our trucks to deliver the payment," Dudko blasted.

"That wasn't on my orders." Yaz walked in small circles in the small office they allowed him. The cell grew hot against his ear. "The men are too comfortable – got careless."

"You are in charge of the men, so the blame is on you. The FBI already took everything, which is thankfully nothing."

Yaz surveyed the street outside his fourth-story window. "I will deal with the men."

"After they get out of prison? No, they are dead to me."

"Then, I will make sure Razor knows the severity of that choice. I don't see why you put this intricate plan together to have the cop take care of our business. Why risk it?" Yaz waited through a long, controlling pause.

"There is a reason," Dudko stated.

"Look at what happened at the club. He's unpredictable. Why is he such a big part of the plan?" Yaz asked in Russian. "To satisfy your revenge?"

"Until Federov says otherwise, do *not* question me."

Yaz wiped the sweat from his forehead. "I like the old rules better, where you exploit the lambs and kill the wolves that nip at your heels. It's less complicated."

"Welcome to the world of politics."

"Wait a second, someone just pulled up to the curb." Yaz viewed his uninvited guest through the window blinds. "The Hispanic woman - Doucet's partner. No one else."

"Really? Those two just accosted me on the street."

"We're closed, but Nicole is still down there. What do you want me to do?"

"Why is Nicole still there?"

Yaz waited a second. "Uh, she lives there."

"I know that, but she should have been pulled after the Feds came in."

"Consider it done."

"Doucet told that Latina cop his mission. Go down there before Nicole lets her in and get rid of her. She can't enter without a warrant. I will be there in a little while. I have a little meeting with Miguel."

"Fine." Yaz hung up the phone, put the silencer on his gun, and then called down to Nicole. "Don't let that cop in, okay?"

"I just did. I'm sorry. I'm so sorry."

"Don't say another word. Just tell her I'll be right down."

Nicole had been one of Dudko's girls from the beginning, young and pretty, but soon the rigor of drugs and forced prostitution sapped the youth from her body. When she had outlived her value, instead of killing her, they used her. Brainwashed, spirit broken, and soulless, she knew no other life other than to be subservient to her captors.

Yaz finally made it through the bay and into the rental office. "Hello?" He glanced at Nicole who watched him cross the room.

Gracie showed her badge. "Detective Castillo. I'm here to see you, actually. Lenn Yazmovich, right?"

"Right. Call me Yaz. Nicole, you can call it a night." Meaning she would return to her small bedroom attached to the bay. He turned to the cop. "I'm afraid I have a lot of work to catch up on. Maybe we can schedule something at your district house?"

"Actually, I'd like to take care of this here. And I'd like Nicole to stay for this, please."

She looked to Yaz, who gave her a nod.

"Do you mind answering a couple of questions?"

You cocky little Latina bitch. Yaz wiped his lips. "I have urgent matters to attend to. Calls to make. Perhaps I should call your superior and explain how you are harassing me?"

"No, you won't do that. What's your relationship with Barry Franklin? Barry-Boy?"

"The porno guy? I know of him. No relationship." *This whore has some nerve.*

"Really, because we have you on video taking a large bag from him in his store. What was in the bag, Yaz?"

"Videos." Yaz put his thumbs in his waistband, inches from his piece.

"Mmm. You're lying."

And you're dead. Yaz shot his thumb behind him. "Detective Castillo, if you must ask me these questions now, do you mind talking with me while I finish up in the bay? I'll even let you look around if you like."

Gracie tilted her head, hesitating a second. She looked at Nicole who was paying more attention to the floor. "Actually, right here is good. I want my backup to see me when they arrive."

Liar. "Fine." Yaz smiled and stepped around the counter. He presented a row of chairs for customers to sit on. He couldn't believe the bitch turned to take a seat. The butt of his gun came down on the Latina's neck, sending her to the floor.

"Open the door," he told Nicole. Without expression, she held the door to the bay open so Yaz could drag the cop through.

He opened the trunk of his Mercury Cougar and laid a sheet of thick plastic near the rear tires. He placed her on the plastic and checked outside one more time. While the cop lay on her side, Yaz pointed his gun at her head and fired. Hair and skin exploded as blood immediately covered her face. He then rolled the plastic over her and lifted the detective to his trunk, folding up her legs.

With that done, he ran back up to the fourth floor.

CHAPTER THIRTY-SEVEN

"Testing–testing, Dudko, you fuck." Miguel pushed the stop button on the recorder.

He had just finished watching Yaz kill that Latina cop on his monitor like some kind of reality show. Another time, he might've rushed down to help with the body, but he didn't care anymore. *Fuck him.* Let him clean up his own mess. He watched Yaz drive the cop's car away on the outside camera. Would more cops be coming? No, they would have been here already.

Miguel wiped his fingers after eating the last bite of pizza, and then downloaded the test file to his laptop. No distortion or sound issues. Dudko would arrive after the girls had their supper and were locked up for the night. He opened up another Abita Amber and sucked down half of it. Everything around him seemed like bad dream.

"How the hell did I get here?" He mumbled in Spanish.

A lifetime ago, coming off a stint of transporting several kilos of cocaine from New York to New Orleans by car, Andrei Fedorov contacted him about Dudko. He convinced Miguel of their impending success and Federov promised him wealth. Only there were too many moving parts. And those parts made a lot of noise when they broke down.

Yo no seré agarrado. Yo no seré agarrado. (I won't get caught, I won't get caught). He thought it best to get the few remaining girls their dinner early. Maybe Lily could eat in the main room with him. Her company would be welcomed.

The building currently had a handful of girls since they had been removed for the drug deal. Miguel lit a cigarette to steady himself, checking the recorder again to make sure it was still in his pocket. He left his office and staggered down the hall. Lily occupied the last room. She wasn't a slut, a runaway, or drug addict. She wasn't the kind of person he'd ever expected to see here. She was just a high school girl, probably someone's sweetheart.

Miguel paused with his fingers on the handle, hearing nothing on the other side. He opened the door, finding Lily sitting in the lotus position with her eyes closed and lips moving silently. She was meditating. *Ah, an old soul.* He watched for a moment, transfixed.

As if feeling his presence, Lily opened her eyes.

"Want another slice of pizza?" Miguel asked as he cleared his throat. Lily didn't waiver. "You hungry still?"

She nodded as Miguel hoped his smile would ease her tension.

Lily rose to her feet. The pizza's aroma mixed with the stale defecation. He guided her down the hall towards a large room with tables at the very end.

"How many girls are here?" She pointed at the doors on her left and right.

"Can be up to twenty at any point."

"Sex slaves?"

"That is not your concern."

"Am I going to be raped?"

Miguel felt any honor the alcohol gave him drain away. He sat her down at a table, pointing at the pizza. "Help yourself."

She opened the box, lifting a slice to her mouth. She seemed aware of her every action as well as her environment. This one had a strong spirit. Miguel put out his cigarette in consideration.

"Do you know my stepfather?" Lily took a bite of the pizza.

He gestured at nothing. "I don't know your stepfather. But, I know the type of man he is. I hope he comes through for you." He brushed her hair back.

The distant echo of metal caught Miguel's attention. He peered behind him, down the hall to see Dudko approaching. The boss had disabled the perimeter alarms remotely, and Ivan let him pass without proper protocol. *The fool.* Miguel put his hand over Lily's eyes just in time, spinning her out of the chair. "She almost saw you." His voice echoed down the hall. Miguel directed a blinded Lily towards her room. "Are you nuts?"

Dudko waved his hand at Miguel as if he had no credibility, and strolled into the office. Miguel belched up alcohol as he reached into his shirt pocket and turned on the recorder. He dragged Lily down the hall and into her room. "We'll continue our conversation another time."

"Who is that?" Lily stumbled into the room, but turned and rushed for the door as it slammed. She pounded and yelled.

Miguel clenched his fists. After hearing Lily fall against the door, he trotted to his office where Dudko took residence in his chair.

"You're early," Miguel scolded. "And what if Lily saw you?"

"Big deal."

"I thought she was a bargaining chip. You plan to kill her no matter what Doucet does."

Dudko smiled. "Of course. Sharpe has to die, no matter. It doesn't look like Doucet will come through. I did enjoy seeing him squirm. I'll have Razor on the roof of the Emerson Building to take Sharpe out when he passes the grandstands in his float. Stupid American, all he had to do was let me place a few men on his precious board. Too bad for him his replacement is on board."

Miguel's voice deepened. "You kill Doucet's daughter, and he won't rest until he kills you."

"He'll forget that notion once the men use him for target practice."

"Does Federov know?" Miguel turned the trashcan upside down in order to sit on it.

"Are you drunk?" Dudko said like a father would.

"I've had a little beer. I'm okay."

They both turned when a knock sounded on the door. Yaz walked in and leaned against the wall with his arms folded. "I had to kill the cop."

Miguel pointed. "Oh, yeah. I forgot to mention that."

Dudko stood abruptly. "What? I said to get rid of her, not *get rid of her*."

"She wouldn't leave. She was ready to force her way up here."

"You fool. Is she still here?" Dudko crowded him.

"In my trunk. I already dumped her car a mile away. I'm going to take her so far into the bayou that they'll never find her."

Miguel folded his arms. "What if she told someone she was coming here?"

"She didn't." Yaz stood defiant.

Dudko backed off. "He's right. She didn't."

Miguel tried not to slur. "How do you know?"

"Several reasons. The Feds forbid them from interfering. She would be disobeying department orders, so she certainly didn't tell her superiors. She came here two hours ago after punching Doucet in the face."

"She punched him in the face?" Miguel asked.

Dudko nodded. "Doucet is losing it. If she was supposed to check in with someone, they'd be here by now... Especially Doucet. I'm sure she left him to come here on her own."

"He's right. She panicked when I threatened to call her boss."

"Still, this should make you nervous," Miguel added.

"That is why I am in charge."

Yaz said, "Her car's GPS will lead them to Lakeview. If you don't need me for a few hours, I'll go dump her now."

"Wait until the early morning hours when the city isn't buzzing with cops and tourists. Right now, you need to take a truck and go pick up Five."

"He wants a girl again... Tonight?"

Miguel shook his head. "He's just going to kill whatever girl you give him."

"Screw Five. Shouldn't we keep him away from the building for a while?" Yaz clenched his jaw.

"Just do it. Doesn't matter if kills another one at this point. They're meant to be expendable, right?"

Miguel kept his cool. It was all on tape now. "Federov know all this is going down?"

Dudko closed his eyes and inhaled. "Since I'm here, I'd like you to set me up in the *suite* with that girl from Florida and the Canadian. Make sure the sheets are clean and shower them up good. Clean everywhere, huh?"

"Yeah, all right." Miguel got up, happy to set up the very last lay Dudko would ever have.

CHAPTER THIRTY-EIGHT

The clock ticked in the back of my brain. Every minute that swept by gave a stabbing pain in my chest. Vile thoughts of what Lily might be experiencing turned my stomach, but I had to remember that surely she was being treated fine. She *was* all right. Still, a sour retching feeling came up my throat.

I vomited. I rehydrated. Water tasted rotten.

The lights in my house were all on. I kept the heat off, but stayed drenched anyway. Headlights flashed across my curtains like a surreal hallucination. I looked out the window to see my brother emerging from a different car - a Porsche, a nice dark sports car like the one described by the motel employee. His body looked like an Under Armor mannequin, with solid muscles filling out a gripping Saints sweatshirt. I opened the door as he trotted in from the chilly weather.

"Back for more?"

"I'm sorry about that. Bone cold out here." He shivered to prove it, stepping inside.

"Maybe you should wear a coat."

"Jesus, you're heat broken?" He rubbed at his arms.

I backed away to the hallway to adjust the thermostat. "Not a good time, Dylan."

"I feel horrible about hitting you, so I swung past. I saw your lights on. I thought maybe you couldn't sleep either and wanted to talk?" Dylan cut right to the chase, and didn't bother getting comfortable.

"Actually, I'm glad you're here. First, I have to ask you something." I took a seat at the dining room table.

He followed. "Shoot."

"Were you fucking Lily?"

He had a blank expression, like he didn't hear me. "What?"

"Were you?"

He leaned forward. "God, no. Jesus. That's sick." He slammed the table. "How the hell can you ask me that?"

"It's not like it would be incest."

"But, it would be pedophilia." His words were slow and measured. "I have never touched Lily in an inappropriate way. *Especially on that beanbag chair.* Yeah, I know that's when things really past the point of no return."

All my life, I watched Dylan spin the truth, make up stories, and lie. He pulled that shit with my parents, his friends – with me. I picked up on earnest brightness in his eyes, and didn't think he was lying this time. "I wanted the question to shock you to get your reaction. She was seeing someone in secret – at motels, but I don't know who."

"You sure? Maybe it's a misunderstanding."

"I'm about to tell you something about Lily's kidnapping that no one else knows. And I'm going to ask for your help, but it could put you in danger."

"What kind of danger?"

"If things go south – life and death danger."

"If it will help get Lily back. I'm in. Whatever it is, I'm in."

I paused a moment so that he would feel the weight of the moment. "They're blackmailing me…"

* * *

I had explained to my brother about Barry-Boy and the chance that he could have been the one sending me those videos of Lily. After Dylan left with his mission to stake out Barry-Boy's residence, I sat at the kitchen table in the silence. My mind drifted from my own childhood to Lily's. My fingers drummed on the table while thinking of her interest in sailing. When she joined the sailing club, I thought it wouldn't last, but I stood corrected. She had learned many survival skills needed while on the open lake. She was strong, and smart. There were ways to communicate with other boats when crippled, adrift, and alone. My fingers drummed on the table… And then it clicked.

Jesus Christ, did she tell where she was in those videos?

CHAPTER THIRTY-NINE

Miguel's face tingled with numbness. His stomach flip-flopped. The recorder glowed on the desk, the most important item in his life – a fifty-dollar piece of technology that held a file worth four million dollars. He had listened to it three different times. A sense of triumph welled up in him.

He attempted to belch, but tasted a trickle of vomit instead. He washed the aftertaste down with more Jack, and then ventured into the hall to let his skin cool. For four years, he had roamed the third and fourth floor, showing the deviant power mongers to their rooms. That chapter was coming to an end.

A slight dainty cough echoed. He stopped at Lily's door and ran his hand over the cool metal, pressing his body against it like a magnet on a refrigerator. He fell backwards and caught himself, looking down at his feet. He didn't want this to go down, not to her. Somewhere out there was the boy she loved and he was waiting for her return.

Aware of the bad taste in his mouth and the swishing in his gut, he felt pangs for the leftover pizza. He staggered halfway down the hall when the buzzer sounded indicating someone bypassed the alarm. *Shit.* Yaz was coming in with Client Five. They sure had great timing.

Miguel made a return trip to the surveillance monitor to see Yaz driving the truck into the bay. It parked and Yaz opened the back. A man wearing glasses and a baseball cap stepped onto the bumper, and then jumped to the ground. Another monitor showed Client Five being escorted by Yaz to the staircase. Minutes later, the screen next to that one displayed Client Five entering the dungeon isolated on the fourth floor. Miguel turned away from the monitor and got up to eat the rest of the pizza in the cafeteria room at the end of the hall. He didn't want to know which unfortunate girl would meet her fate.

CHAPTER FORTY

"Knock, knock. You up?" The door swung open and a man she had never seen before stood at the entrance. Lily rolled over in the shadow of his silhouette. Was today the day they would kill her?

"I'm up. Who are you?" Her voice held strength.

"I'm not Miguel. That's all you need to know," He said, "Get up. You're coming with me."

"Are you taking me to my mom?"

"No."

"Are you going to rape me?"

"C'mon, get up."

Lily stood. "You're a pimp."

"Pimp. Funny American word."

"Remi's going to find me and kill all of you."

He smirked with a giggle. "Half the cops in the city are paid for. Hell, we probably could have gotten a cop to bring you here. No one is looking for you, except your father."

"Where are we going?" Tears dripped down her face as she entered the hall.

"Just to another room." He motioned for her to move forward.

She thought about a counter-attack, but she felt like a mosquito that would be swatted under his hand. Unsteadily, she walked down the hall with the man behind her, like a ghost.

"Miguel blindfolds the others. I won't do that to you."

The man escorted her upstairs to an ominous looking room on the fourth floor. He unlocked the door and pushed her forward, causing her to stumble onto a bed with a relatively clean mattress. It was then that she noticed the man sitting on a chair. A man she knew all too well.

"Dylan? Is that really you?" She ran into his arms.

The metal door shut. Her boyfriend didn't look surprised at all.

Her embrace loosened. "What's going on here? Do you know that man?"

Dylan shoved her onto the bed. He wiped his face hard, and then took the chair and threw it against the wall, cursing under his breath. She had never seen him like this. He looked like a man she didn't know at all.

"Dylan, you're not a part of this, are you?" She almost retched when she noticed the shackles on the wall and the tray of tools for God knows what.

"He told me you weren't here. Jesus, how could I be so stupid." He smacked his forehead.

"*What is happening?*"

"He knows about us. Jesus Christ, how did he find out?" He rubbed at his temples like he had a migraine. He just stood there, staring. He collapsed to the bed where he reached out to lower her hands to her lap. He looked deep into her eyes as if about to propose and stroked her cheek. It felt so familiar, and yet so depraved.

"Lily, I'm in so deep," he began, but stopped. His expression might have been that of hope.

A wave of disappointment washed through her body as if she had been bled out. "Oh, God. You're involved in forced prostitution?"

"I can't save you. Dudko expects me to... Shit."

"But, we love each other."

"Yes."

"What has the past year of sneaking around meant to you?"

"Everything. Everything."

"No. How could I have been so blind? You've manipulated me since I was thirteen. The special attention. I see that, now."

"I love you."

"You're sick. I gave myself to you. I hid our love from the world. And – and you're nothing but a rapist." Her body shook as if naked in a winter's snow.

"I would never hurt you. Never." His open face and moist eyes waited for an answer.

"Liar! Was our relationship some sick way to get back with your brother?" She spit at him, slapping him across his cheek.

He wiped off the saliva and became stone. "This is much bigger than the both of us." He straightened his shirt and fixed his hair.

As he primped, she slapped his face again from both sides and then pulled away, but he grabbed her wrists and squeezed. She didn't try to escape. When he released his grip, she lunged at him, scratching his face with her fingernails. "My mother's dead, isn't she?"

"Yes." He said sternly.

She wouldn't give him the satisfaction of a breakdown. "Who killed my mom? Who's to blame?"

He closed his eyes. "You are."

"Me?" she screeched, "What did I have to do with it?"

"When you and I were spotted together at the motel, Victor Dudko's men thought you were Fiona - your mother. He has plans for me to run for Congress. He knew if the story of my having an affair with my brother's wife got out, I'd be destroyed. It was to protect my political career."

"Then, why not just shoot her on the street? Why was I taken?"

"Victor Dudko has been waiting to get revenge on your father for all these years for killing someone close to him. This was his chance. I let them believe that I was having an affair with your mother to protect you. He would have killed you instead. Don't you see?"

"But, he knows about us now. He's going to kill me anyway." Lily jumped at him, but he punched her across the top of her head and she fell back on the mattress.

"I won't let him kill you." He fought off her attack, until she gave up in frustration. He continued, "Remember when we first got together? You were so into it, rebellious against your mom's new boyfriend. This doesn't have to change things. I can still save you."

Lily sobbed and the tension all drained away, leaving her without any fight.

"You're shivering," he said as he clumsily rubbed her arms. "Open your eyes. Look at me. Look at me."

Out of nowhere, Lily wailed. Her cries were only silenced by intermittent sniffles. The sound was soul wrenching and ghoulish to her own ears, trailing off like the muted moan of a haunted house. She went silent, as she couldn't breath anymore.

"What have I done?" Dylan sprung to his feet, holding his ears. "I'm a monster."

Lily saw her opportunity. "It's not too late."

His eyes quickly found hers. "I'm sorry. I'm so sorry." He reached for the shackles on the blood-stained wall to hold himself upright. After a minute, his eyes widened.

"What are you doing?" she hissed.

"I have to show him I don't care about you. It's the only way." He leaned on his shoulder while moving one metal cuff to the side and letting it fall flat again. "This is to save both of us."

Lily hugged herself. She watched him through tear-filled slits. This man she has known for years was out of his mind and this could be her only shot to save her life. "Sweetheart?"

"Dudko expects me to… Get up here," he commanded. He made a broad step and grabbed her arm. "Get up here, now." His voiced cracked as he pinned her against the wall, pulling her arm up to one chain, but his resolve faded.

"Get your arm up here −" he cried. His face looked sunburned and sweating. His head and shoulders bobbed. He slammed his palm against the bricks and grabbed her other wrist. "Do − as I say."

She stood her ground. "No."

He whispered into her ear. "If I don't treat you like the others, he'll kill you."

"The others?"

Before he could respond, her hand slipped free of his grasp and she fell to her knees, spinning around to see what was to come next. However, his whole body slumped in a heavy sob. Ten seconds passed before he started banging his head against the wall.

"I need Miguel to get me out of here," he sniveled. As if possessed, his body flew across the room and bounced off the door like a fly trying to escape a window. He pushed at a button with his fingers and then his palm, slapping at it. His breathing finally slowed, and he carefully pulled open a small panel set flush with the wall and punched a code into a keypad. The door shifted open.

Lily launched herself like a missile at Dylan, but he side-stepped her, sending her head first into the wall. All went black.

CHAPTER FORTY-ONE

The video of Lily played on the burner phone while comparing it to a Morse Code legend on my laptop. It impressed me to no end that she had learned it. My right-handed stepdaughter's index finger tapped at her knee. Her finger touched down once, for a long second, then bounced three distinct times. That was a 'B' according to the chart.

Her fingers moved rapidly, and seemed hard to control through her nerves, but after a half hour, I figured out enough to know her message. *Best Friend Movers* was eventually scribbled on a piece of paper. My heart jumped, and my chest hurt like someone punched my cracked rib. However, I didn't want to rush into the building without knowing Lily's full message. I tried Gracie's cell, but had to leave a voice mail.

After two hours, all she communicated was Best Friend Movers, over and over. I tried to call Gracie again, but to no avail. Suddenly, I was worried about that, too. Did I want to get the cops involved? The Feds? I rose and paced, sweating. Any attempted siege on that place could mean Lily's death. But, under the cover of night, I could go in alone. From my closet, I retrieved my Glock and silencer. In my trunk was the bolt cutters I stole from the raid.

It took every ounce of will power not to blow through red lights on my way to Best Friend Movers. Both my hands white-knuckled the steering wheel, drag racing between lights, barely stopping when required. Even in this early morning hour, an occasional car crossed my path. A headache gained momentum behind my left eyeball, enough to blur my vision. I was unbelievably close to finding my stepdaughter, perhaps just minutes. The digital clock read four a.m.

I parked around the corner from Best Friend Movers. Not a soul was on this stretch of industrial businesses, meaning this wasn't a tourist area. And considering the weather, I wouldn't expect any wanderers. Under the cover of a cloudy night sky, I used the bolt cutters to unlock the cage covering the front entrance. With the same tool, I busted the Plexiglas door away from its metal frame, sliding under it like it was a curtain.

My flashlight illuminated the rental office, which held no interest. The darkened bay contained some parked trucks and a few cars – one of them had an open trunk and what looked like an oil leak, but was otherwise empty. I saw no alarm panel, but in case I tripped any, I wasted no time in running to a chained up door in the rear. It was no match for the bolt cutter. Peeking inside, down the dim hallway, a man sat on chair, his head dipped in slumber next to an open pizza box and several empty beer cans. A light flashed above his head indicating I had tripped an alarm, but he was out.

My hand stayed on the door until it gently closed behind me with a demure click. I lightly crept up to the bald man, noticing a plethora of tattoos like the arsonist's swirling on his skin. He could be an innocent security guard, but there was too much evidence to the contrary. A loud voice came over his walkie and the man's eyes suddenly sprung open. He fumbled for his holstered gun with a gaping mouth. Before he could make a sound, I put a bullet in his chest with the aid of my silencer. While the man bled out on the tile, I realized another guard was trying to get his attention on his radio. I looked in each room on the first floor, but it was only used as storage.

The stairs leading to the second floor were vacant, but through a narrow windowpane in the exit door, I witnessed a figure pass by on his radio. I waited a few moments, and the same man leaned into frame, taking angrily into the radio. My Glock tapped on the door, then I sprinted down a few steps and aimed my weapon.

The door opened. "Ira? Is that you? Why aren't you answering me?" The man searched the darkness, eventually moving closer to me, letting the door shut.

"Da," I whispered. With that, two shots silently landed in his torso.

I stepped over him and stuck my head through the door, looking left and right – all clear. The second floor offices were littered with mattresses, racks of clothes, and dark rubber things, leather suits, and chains. Chills ran up my spine. I should have called in back up. Without resistance, I continued on to the third floor, which had no guards. Each door down the hallway was solid metal without locks.

The first room I examined had a girl lying on a mattress, sleeping. My heart beat hard enough to make my shirt vibrate. My flashlight hit her face. It wasn't Lily. I checked the inside of the door, but there was no handle. If I entered the room, I'd be locked in with her. Besides, was I going to rescue each girl one by one?

"I'll be back," I promised.

Moving on to the next door, my legs halted when I saw a figure in a room at the end of the hall. His head rested on a table like a kid that fell asleep at his desk in high school. In my peripheral, staggered rooms lined the hallway. Lily was behind one of these doors. I had to hurry. I swallowed my panic.

I softly, but deliberately turned the handle of the next door with my gun aimed at the slumbering guard. I waited, but the man never stirred. The next room was empty. I found that only a few of the rooms contained an occupant, but I knew there was a fourth floor. Ever vigilant, on my way to the staircase, I called for help.

"9-1-1, what's your emergency?"

With a hush, I spoke, "Yes, this is Detective Remi Doucet. I need to report a 108. Send units and ambulances to Best Friend Movers."

"Have you been shot?"

"No. I have to hang up. Sorry."

The first room I checked on this floor was different than the others. This door wasn't closed by hydraulics. It hung open a crack. Peeking in, the room appeared straight out of a horror movie, with blood-coated, cinderblock walls, shackles and a large, horrible mattress on the floor. I immediately knelt next to the girl lying on her stomach.

It was Lily.

CHAPTER FORTY-TWO

Yaz settled into his fourth floor office and turned on the monitor with the video feed to the dungeon. He fixed himself a drink, wondering why Dudko would want to put the pair in a room together and not tell Miguel.

After Egor Baskov had been killed, Yaz thought that he and Dudko would eventually become equal partners. Federov explained in a rare phone conversation with Yaz that he was too young and impetuous. Yaz threw a tantrum, proving Federov's point. He had since learned that an extreme impression, whether good or bad, makes a lasting one.

Kind of pathetic, he thought, *to just be a player in someone else's show.* He wanted to be top dog, but he was also realistic. He wouldn't have come this far without Federov and Federov trusted Dudko. Yaz would do his job and his opportunity would present itself. But he understood that some people were meant to stand in the background, supporting others. Being second string had its benefits: less responsibility, more free time, less worrying.

Yaz felt his stomach bubbling and ran to the bathroom just as the screen came to life. He usually blamed the rich food for his occasional bowel issues, but he knew it was nerves. He didn't really have time to watch Five anyway, as that detective was still in his trunk.

After fifteen minutes in the bathroom, he traveled back into the hallway to see the alarm light flashing at the end of the hall. It was curious more than anything else. He pressed the button his radio. "Ira, anyone there?" He waited. "Answer me, anyone there?"

He ran to his office to see what Five and the girl was up to. He couldn't believe it when he saw an empty room and an open door. He shot out of his office and sprinted down the stairs to the third floor. The first thing he noticed stepping into the hallway was Miguel hunched over in the cafeteria.

"Oh, shit." While shouting profanities, he sprinted to Miguel's office to see the two dead guards on the monitors. Panic finally set in. He bolted to Miguel's side, yelling in his ear. "Miguel!"

The Cuban slowly raised his head. "What? What?"

"The dungeon is empty. Ira and Peter are dead."

"What? Where's Five?" Miguel had been laying in drool. He wiped his mouth and focused down the hall. He almost fell forward, but caught the doorjamb.

"Help me check the rooms." Yaz started for the first door, which was Lily's.

"Fuck." Miguel exclaimed, stumbling to Yaz's side where he again repeated his four-letter sentiment.

"How did this happen, Miguel? Two of our men are dead, the girl is gone. Could Five have done this?"

"I don't know. Maybe it was the brother. What if he followed you when you picked up Five?"

"No. This is your fault."

Miguel lost his color, his eyes sobered. "The building has been compromised. We got to get out."

Yaz had sweat dripping down his face as he ran with Miguel to his office. "You were drinking. Careless!"

Miguel threw him against the wall and put his elbow into his throat. "Shut up about it. We need to work together."

Yaz nodded, understanding that he pushed a bit too much. He rubbed his neck and then took the time to check if any other doors were open until he reached the end. He began to feel pressure in his chest.

"What now?" Miguel asked, knowing full well that once he left the building, he was on his own.

"We need to get out like you said, and contact Dudko," Yaz countered.

CHAPTER FORTY-THREE

Miguel realized that depending on how things turned out with the cop's daughter, he might have to forget his plan and flee with his life. Because Dudko would be doing the same.

"All right, you ready?" Yaz asked Miguel, as a glaze coated his forehead.

"Yeah, I just gotta get my gun."

"Well, do it. We don't have time to waste. Luckily with Mardi Gras, it will take a while to dispatch police to this location at this hour."

Miguel sprinted back to his office. He stepped in and noticed his desk in disarray. Yaz materialized at the door. His handsome face that had been so difficult to take seriously was now hard and intimidating. Miguel pulled out his key and unlocked the drawer to get his gun and snatched the recorder before Yaz saw it.

"Yeah, I'm coming," he said, and left the drawer open.

"We don't have time to get the girls out. We need to get to the St. Charles office and I still have that cop in my trunk. Take your car and I'll meet you there."

The chilly air in the bay helped sober Miguel as he jumped in his light blue Subaru hatchback parked in the opposite corner from the trucks. He checked on Yaz in his rear view mirror as the man kicked at the car with it's trunk open. Miguel stopped and rolled down the window. "What are you doing?"

"My dead cop is missing."

"What?"

"She's not in my trunk!" Yaz looked close at the ground where they both spotted droplets of blood leading to the exit. "It really doesn't matter much, now, does it? Go! I'm right behind you."

Miguel sped onto the street, figuring he could still salvage the plan if he altered it just a bit. But, he had to make sure Yaz didn't follow. And just like that, in one night, it all came crashing down.

CHAPTER FORTY-FOUR

Gracie had lost a lot of blood and wondered why Yaz hadn't just shot her instead of knocking her out and putting her in his trunk. She dragged her feet on abandoned streets through the Warehouse District, praying that friendly eyes would spot her. She needed a main thruway, but couldn't focus on which direction to go. She almost laughed, imagining white tourists helping a Mexican woman staggering down a dark, barren street with a bleeding head wound. But locals would help if they saw the blood-drenched clothes, right? They had to see that she was a victim.

What did Yaz hit her with that caused this kind of wound? Her head felt numb, but something else drove her legs to move – maybe the will of God. She would die if she dared to rest, knowing the next few minutes were critical. Her feet scraped along, stumbling like a sleepwalker towards the headlights.

After a couple of yards, or blocks, or miles, moaning in determination, she saw something familiar: the remaining pedestal from where a statue of General Lee once stood, guiding her as a beacon. That man had fought for a war that supported slavery and now it was gone.

Her random thoughts took her to the history of slavery in New Orleans and how, once freed, some of these discarded people lived with the Indians on the outskirts of the city. She admired their struggle in the early to mid-1900's with the civil rights movement in a racist city that would eventually become eighty percent black, not counting Metairie and Kenner. Why was she thinking this? Blood loss. She needed to keep her mind going and her body would follow.

She staggered forward as if the reward of eternal life waited.

Once on the banks of Lee Circle, stunned civilians pointed and she let herself fall on the inclined hill of grass, relieved that she had been seen. When the blue and red lights reflected off the gas station across the street, she knew God was good.

CHAPTER FORTY-FIVE

There is absolutely no way he would ever work for Dudko again, Miguel thought.

Since Yaz hadn't tailed him out of the garage, Miguel was able to park on the outskirts of the Quarter. He strutted across Canal Street, then over to Bourbon where he stopped at the first bar he saw to get a Coke. *Fuckin' Yaz,* he thought. *I'll kill you, too, if I ever get the chance.*

He rattled the ice after draining the Coke and dropped back onto Bourbon. The crowd was still formidable, but thinning as a few of the bars had closed. He arrived at the entrance of Booty Call, and nodded at the bouncer who knew him well. Miguel entered this establishment for the last time, waving to employees as if saying goodbye.

Cherry Treasure danced for two leering men at the end of a well-worn stage. He sat at the other end and waited. When she noticed him while writhing on her back, her smile brightened. He called her over with a flip of his fingers.

She slinked toward him on all fours like a stealthy feline, until her nose touched his. He pulled at her earlobe with his lips. "It's time."

CHAPTER FORTY-SIX

The cold air filled my aching lungs as I carried Lily to my car. I gently propped her up with one arm, while opening the passenger side door. She folded into the seat without a problem. With a deep breath, I started the engine, calling Gracie at the same time. When Gracie's number went to voicemail yet again, I tried Trout.

He answered, "Remi, I got units on the way to Best Friend Movers. Are you there?"

"Not anymore." My vision blurred. Lily moaned.

"Where are you? Tell me what happened. The team needs intel before they raid the place."

"There are trafficked girls there. Two dead guards, one I left alive. Don't know if there's more. Tell the team leader to be careful."

"You need to be there to brief him. Give him the lay of the building."

"Can't. Can't explain right now."

"Are you in trouble?"

"No. Where's Gracie?"

Trout hesitated. "I haven't heard from Detective Castillo since yesterday. She never came back to end her watch and she's not answering her phone. Her car was abandoned, but no sign of foul play yet. We're checking hospitals."

"We need to find her. Call Agents Joiner and Foster. Get them to Best Friend Movers. I'll call back soon."

I hung up, forcing my eyes open and shut to stay in focus. Tulane Medical appeared in the distance, yet it seemed like a mirage. Tears fell over my grinning lips and I even laughed a couple of times, palming my daughter's – yes, *daughter's* head and squeezing her thigh. That growing migraine had miraculously disappeared.

CHAPTER FORTY-SEVEN

Dudko took the empty W Hotel elevator in this early morning hour. He bit at his manicured nails like he had in the Russian prison. Yaz informed him over the phone that the Best Friend Movers building had been compromised. A contact on the NOPD confirmed. The operation was now a total loss. *Federov won't like to hear his precious Cuban screwed them, but such is life.*

Miguel was long overdue to check in, which meant something happened to him. Perhaps he was waiting back at the Corporate Square offices. Dudko's hair stuck out in different directions and his golf shirt was wrinkled, the collar warped. His appearance didn't matter at this point. He needed to figure out the optimal course of action.

He exited the elevator on the top floor and nodded at Jason, one of Sharpe's security team, sitting outside his door. "Good morning."

Jason's bulky Marine physique stood. "Mr. Dudko? It's past three in the morning. Is the governor expecting you?"

"Oh, he'll want to see me."

Jason seemed unsure, but knocked on the door while staring at him. After a few seconds, he knocked harder. "Governor, Mr. Dudko is here to see you."

The door opened. Sharpe stuck his head out the door with his hand half-covering his eyes. His hair was unruly. "Victor, what in God's name are you doing here at this hour?"

"We need to talk… About our situation."

"Nothing has changed. I want your resignation. If you'll excuse me."

Dudko spoke in a soft tone. "Something has changed. I have an offer you can't possibly pass up. Perhaps, you can give me the opportunity to change your mind?"

Sharpe put his forehead against the doorframe. He sighed. "Alright, come in."

The beautiful suite was dimly lit and uncluttered, proving Sharpe was alone. *Too good to even cheat on his wife while he has the chance.* Dudko sat on the ornate sofa, throwing one leg over the other. He waited for the governor to slip on his robe and sit opposite him.

"I don't know what you could possibly say." He squinted with a yawn.

"I will be honest. I originally planned to support a candidate that would challenge you in the upcoming election. You take me out, I take you out – theoretically speaking, of course."

"You see the polls?" He laughed. "No one can beat me."

Dudko agreed with a slight nod. "Yes, so I am backing a congressional candidate. But, I want to show you how much this board position means to me. Show how much it could mean to you."

"How?"

Dudko handed him a cell phone with a picture on the screen. "What's this?"

"Look closely."

"It's money. Stacks of money."

"It's my money. One million dollars." Dudko held his stare. "One million to keep me on the board and to let me appoint seven men."

"You're bribing me? Are you serious?"

Dudko matted down his hair and pulled down on his shirt. "I

could have it delivered anywhere you want in an hour. I'll wire a transfer if you'd like."

The governor stood. "Get out of my hotel room."

He walked to the door. "Think about it."

"Don't hold your breath."

Dudko opened the door, but turned back. "If I don't hear from you by the time Rex starts…" He lowered his voice. "…I hope you have a really good ride."

CHAPTER FORTY-EIGHT

Just moments away from pulling up to the emergency room at Tulane, my cell phone vibrated. "Yeah, Doucet."

"Remi, it's Harrison over at Headquarters. I just received word from dispatch; Gracie's been shot and taken to Tulane Medical. She's asking for you."

"Damn. How bad is it?" I parked off to the side, near the emergency room entrance, with my police credentials on the dash. I stared at Lily who was gaining her senses back.

Harrison explained, "Head wound, but she's conscious, which is good. It's all I know. I just got off the phone with Captain Trout. He's there already."

"He's not at Headquarters?" I held my stepdaughter's hand. A spark lit in her eyes. She smiled.

"No, I called him just before you. Weird thing is, he actually said *not* to call you."

"He did?"

"Something about wanting to talk to Gracie before you do. I thought, screw that. Castillo's your partner and I've known you too long. That Yank needs to learn how we do things here."

"Thanks, buddy." I hung up just as Lily leaned in toward me. "Lily, I'm so sorry, your mom…"

"I know." She put her hand over her mouth and I reached out to her.

We hugged and cried and shared an immense grief that aged both of us. This could have been such a different outcome, but despite being safe for the moment, this would haunt our lives forever.

She wiped at her eyes. "I have to tell you something."

"What?"

She hesitated, as if searching for the right words. "I saw your brother at the building."

"Dylan?"

She nodded and swallowed hard. "He's a part of it."

CHAPTER FORTY-NINE

Miguel entered Cherry Treasure's apartment with his weapon held against his chest, looking around the room for any of Dudko's men to spring out from the 1980's style furniture.

"You're scaring me," Cherry chirped from behind.

He glanced at her incredulously, storming to the back bedroom. He returned to the tiny living room, put his gun down, and took his lady by the hands. "We need to be very careful. Everything has changed."

"We're doing it?" Cherry bit her bottom lip.

"Yes." His expression slowly morphed into a grin.

She kissed him. "I want to get out of these clothes… For the last time ever."

Cherry eased into the back bedroom. Miguel put on the television to catch any breaking news and relaxed on the couch, but his mind would not allow it. He heard Cherry slip into the kitchen. A pot slapped onto the stove and cabinets were opened. Fifteen minutes later the aroma of breakfast filled his nostrils. He glanced at her little kitchen table as she placed two plates of eggs and grits down just below her bare breasts. She wore only a pair of panties.

"You been cooking like that this whole time?" He rose from the couch, and felt at his crotch.

She sat, taking a dainty bite. "I did good?"

"You did good, Cherry-baby."

He had heard the story of her name on the first night they slept together. She stopped introducing herself as Terri Piper after starting a new life in New Orleans at seventeen, just seven years ago. The hicks that had apathetically raised her in Leesville were now a fantasy that her mind created. Still, she was her momma's girl and took to the pole all too well. She had told him the name Cherry Treasure sounded cute, and it had become a part of her.

Instead of sitting, he pressed his lips against her neck and she stopped to enjoy the warm sensation. His hand traveled down her arm, then to her chest. He dipped his finger into the grits and wiped it on her nipple so he could lick it off. His arousal was well received. She made short work of his pants, then took control of his erection. Miguel knew he had gained her love and loyalty after a string of abusive boyfriends. She would risk her life for him.

"Let's go over the plan again," he whispered as his fingers found that special spot inside her panties. "You've been dead-lifting the 45 pound plates at the gym, right?"

"Yes."

He tested her tight biceps. "Good, because that is very important. If you can remember the plan while I do this – *and this*, then I know you're ready."

Cherry moaned as his fingers worked, and she recited the plan word for breathless word. "First, I wait in the truck..."

CHAPTER FIFTY

L aPlace and its subsidiaries occupied the top three stories in one of the most prominent downtown buildings. New Orleans was no New York or Chicago, but there was still prime real estate in the CBD. Victor Dudko had planned to buy the whole building, then the whole block. He remained embedded in his top floor office on St. Charles Avenue, overlooking his city as dawn approached. The brothel building was lost, but so be it. He refused to let panic set in, like when he had gotten his *lowered down* tattoos. How Could Sharpe turn down a million dollars in cash? *Oh, well, a bullet will be much cheaper.*

After calming himself, he heard Yaz's voice from beyond his door. "Victor, you in there?"

Dudko ran his hand over his mouth to calm himself. "Come in."

Yaz entered looking ten years older, unshaven and with a cap and glasses. His loyal understudy stared back at the door as it slowly closed on its own. He stepped forward in short, staccato movements, conveying to Dudko there was bad news. Yaz had his gun sticking out from his pants.

"Nice disguise."

"We have a bigger problem."

"The *hard-headed* cop?"

Yaz clinched both his fists like a dramatic actor. "You know. Of course, you know."

Dudko placed his gun on the desk, then turned on a clock radio that sat between them. "Careful what you say in here," he whispered. The exterminator hasn't been here in a while."

Yaz pointed at the side of his own head. "Deflection."

"And where is she?"

"No idea."

Dudko was dead-pan. "She is one of two loose ends."

"Emergency cases go to Tulane. I can go there and…"

"No, you won't. She's already named you. Thankfully, you have no address."

"So, I need to disappear."

Dudko gave a nod. "But, not yet. Five is the other loose end. We thought it was the wife, but it was the stepdaughter."

"Five is a sick bastard. Why did you have me put them together?"

"The man needed to be controlled. If you hadn't fucked it up, we wouldn't be in this mess."

"Five won't talk and she knows nothing."

"Are you going soft? We need to find Five. And father and stepdaughter…?" He gave a thumbs down like a Roman emperor.

CHAPTER FIFTY-ONE

A gray-haired Asian doctor at Tulane Medical examined Lily behind a curtain in the emergency room. I watched him check her beautiful eyes, inside her mouth, and her ears. We refused the rape kit. She promised me in a calm, adamant voice that she hadn't been violated, and I believed her.

She seemed okay for the most part, but lapsed into a daze every now and then. I feared it might not be over for her, psychologically as well as physically. I needed to get her to a safe location that no one would know about. I needed Doc Margie to see her.

Like the bust at the Baton Rouge port, Dudko was probably so far removed from both the brothel and Gracie's kidnapping that he would come out clean. Convicting the key players under his web of corruption seemed impossible.

Personal justice was still an option.

Against the doctor's better judgment, we left the emergency room without admitting Lily. She had answered questions from a concussion protocol, and passed, so I figured not to leave her exposed in a hospital bed. The desk nurse gave me Gracie's room number, and I took the elevator with Lily at my side. We embraced all over again.

My cell rang as the elevator rose. I gripped my daughter's hand, then put my finger on my lips, asking her to stay quiet. "Hey, Dylan. I have Lily. She's safe."

"You do?" There was a long pause. "She's okay?"

Lily sucked in her lips and teared up, but I focused on the call. "No, we haven't spoken at length yet. She's kind of out of it. She might have a concussion. Are you okay? You sound stressed."

"You're going to hear some things, little brother. Just know… Just know I'm sorry."

"For what?" I acted oblivious.

"You need to go see Barry-Boy. He has information about Miguel that you need."

"Miguel? Wait. How do you know about him?" *Confess Dylan.*

His voice sounded weak. "I just wanted to say I'm sorry. I'm so sorry." The call ended.

Curious, I looked at Lily. "Miguel?"

She started crying. "He's a part of it, too. But, he treated me nice – didn't let anyone near me."

I smiled, and squeezed her hands. I couldn't tell her that I was still going to kill him.

We walked past the nurse's station. I saw two uniformed officers having coffee and a conversation near Gracie's door. Nearing the entrance, I half-expected a crew of doctors and nurses throwing the paddles on her chest in an effort to revive her, but things looked quiet.

As I peeked inside, a large man hovered over the bed wearing a LSU hoodie with his hands on Gracie's shoulders.

"Hey. What are you doing?"

The man turned to reveal himself as Trout. "Thank God. You have Lily. They found the girls – and two dead captors. Good work."

"What are you doing?" I kept Lily behind me.

Gracie spoke. "I was telling him how I got shot by Yazmovich."

"You need to kick those cops out there in the ass. They're barely paying attention to the door."

"I'll talk to them." Trout moved past me to look out the door.

I jumped to Gracie's side, Lily stayed close. "You okay?"

"Fine. It deflected." Gracie raised her hand to her ear. "Didn't even know I was shot until the ambulance came."

"Couldn't penetrate that skull, huh?"

The bandage wrapped around her head was clear of blood making her look like a swami. She stuck her tongue out at me with life in her eyes, then smiled at Lily with a wave. My daughter's bruised face darkened.

I squeezed her hand. "There is nothing between her and me, Lily. I swear it to you."

Gracie's mouth dropped. "What?"

"Dylan told me. Where did you get that idea?"

Lily focused on her shoes. "You were always doing stuff with her. You're a man, she's a woman." Her inflection revealed her thoughts. "Everytime she called or you went to see her, it just made me so angry."

I almost laughed. "All of this was from an assumption? Gracie is my closest friend."

"Mom's supposed to be your closest friend."

We hugged. "Oh, honey. She was. But, everyone needs that one close friend. You have Madison, don't you?"

"Yeah."

"Just happens that mine is a woman."

Gracie broke in. "I just don't find him sexually attractive."

Despite the situation, we laughed. I reigned it in, then looked at Trout. "You weren't wearing that sweatshirt back at the station."

"I slipped it on. It's cold outside." He stepped closer.

"You're a devote Bears and Northwestern fan. You don't own anything LSU."

"Remi," Gracie moaned. "Trout had fifteen minutes to kill me and escape. Don't go there."

Trout fell into a chair. "You're a damn good detective… too good. This was a gag gift from the guys when I came on board. I kept it in my office."

"You told me to go to the station while you were here. Why didn't you tell me to come straight here?"

"Look, you call 9-1-1 about Best Friend Movers, then leave the location and refuse to tell me why or what you were doing." He eyed Lily who stared forward in a chair. "I wanted the facts before informing you of Gracie's situation. You held back info from me this entire time, so you of all people should understand."

Gracie spoke with more volume. "How'd you figure it out?"

I squeezed Lily's shoulders. "I realized she was tapping Morse Code with her fingers in the video."

"Seriously? You go, girl."

"The Feds are all over that building." Trout checked his cell phone.

Gracie squeezed my hand. "Today's Mardi Gras Day. If Dudko wants Sharpe dead, he's going to get it done during the parade."

Trout's jaw dropped. "Wait. What?"

"More info I kept to myself. Dudko was blackmailing me to kill the governor. Dylan just told me something... Something he shouldn't know."

"Your brother is involved?" Trout huffed. "What the hell, Remi? I need to know these things."

I looked at Lily, who stared at the floor. My stomach turned when I thought of her motel charges on the credit card. It suddenly clicked that she had been seeing my brother. I spoke while trying to wrap my head around it. "He's involved, but, I'm not sure how deep. I need to know Lily and Gracie are protected."

Trout nodded. "We have the guards, and I'm not going anywhere."

Satisfied, I kissed Lily on her forehead and high-tailed it out of the room. If Dylan had any connection to my wife's murder, then that would be a category of pain all its own.

CHAPTER FIFTY-TWO

The white two-story home birthed six large columns in the front, built on land that had been raised two feet above street level. Its front yard ran flat as it extended towards the street, and then declined dramatically toward the gate along the sidewalk. Two magnolia trees stood guard halfway between the house and the sidewalk.

Dylan Doucet wandered through his empty Uptown home. Just hours ago, he had driven with numb tranquility through the security gate and parked around the back of his grand Colonial-style home in the well-to-do section of Prytania Street. He regretted ever attending that party where he learned of the exclusive *building*.

A cleaning lady came during the day and a chef bought his groceries and cooked meals for a week at a time. He merely slept there and entertained there. He had never *lived* there. Without a wife or serious girlfriend, he found it lonely to have so much space.

He laughed, wiping his mouth. His eyes itched with wetness. He sighed. He laughed again, building to where he couldn't catch his breath in a hoarse roar. He felt as if he lost time, years even. Like being so tired that you weren't sure if you shampooed. Or leaving the house in such a rush that you didn't remember dressing.

Lily had found her way out, or Remi saved her. Either way, a Russian hit man would be on his doorstep, or possibly Dudko himself. Everything he'd worked for, everything he'd sold his soul for, would be flushed down the toilet. But, none of that really mattered. Not anymore.

His plush furnishings offered no comfort, feeling more like a museum. He took a few steps, but didn't move far. He just stood, looking around. His desk called out for him to sit with nothing but the lamp illuminating the room. The stacks of research on political campaigns and Congress would lead one to believe that he had important work to finish.

How did things go so far, he asked himself. He had rationalized that his perversions made him sick and *the building* offered the medicine that would allow his normal life to continue. The attacking voices in his nightmares were merely the side effect. But today, something had sparked. God suddenly decided to pay attention. *No*, he thought, *it was more like Satan had finally decided to collect, but his soul needed to be tortured first.* What sane man could live with so much guilt?

An enormous calm took hold, and his muscles relaxed for the first time in what felt like ten years. His eyelids closed and a non-existent breeze cooled his skin. He smiled and finally walked to the kitchen and got a beer from the refrigerator and a gun from his safe. Also from the safe, he pulled out a copy of a DVD. This would fill him with the disgust and confidence needed.

He watched as the screen came on. If there were a God, Dylan would never meet him. Who was he kidding? He would never meet *her*, because God had to be a female. God was about creation and birth, not destruction. The hair on his neck rose. Two figures appeared in the wide entryway, and he instinctively slid his gun under a throw pillow. The video started playing, illuminating the Russian visitors.

"Dylan, my friend. You don't mind if Yaz and I sit and watch with you? What you got there? Oh, you having fun with one of the girls. Memories."

They both wore gloves. Yaz held a gun, and a bored expression.

"Lily got out," Dylan stated.

"Your brother got Lily out the building like some kind of pulp fiction hero, if you believe that."

"Good." His voice sounded pathetic. "Remi won't stop until you're dead."

Dudko shrugged. "Dylan... things have changed."

"You're going to kill me?" he laughed at the irony.

"It's a shame, too. I was so looking forward to having a Congressman in my pocket. I will eventually get the operation back on track and then I will pick a new wannabe, one with a stomach for politics. "

Dylan slowly moved his hand toward the sofa cushion. "You'll fail again." His fingers disappeared under the pillow.

"What do you have there?" Dudko inquired. He nudged Yaz.

Dylan pulled the gun out pointed to nothing in particular. Yaz immediately snapped into a firing position.

"I see what's going on here," Dudko scoffed, "I suppose you have incriminating evidence of me at the ready for when they find you. Well, it's a good thing we stopped by."

"All right. Kill me. Just fucking kill me."

"What do you have planned? I will slowly torture the fuck out of you first, I swear."

Dylan swung the gun at Dudko and fired a wild shot, causing Yaz to unload three rounds into his chest. The gun fell to the floor and the sound of the girl screaming on the laptop went mute. He couldn't move while struggling to breath, waiting for a final shot.

Dudko grew fuzzy in his vision as the man checked for wounds, but he was unharmed. "Why didn't you shoot his kneecap or something? We needed to find out if he told anyone anything."

"You're welcome."

"Let's search this dump for anything pertaining to our operation." Dudko retrieved Dylan's gun. "Take the laptop and any computers or devices upstairs."

Dylan's dimming vision saw Yaz step up to his shoulder. "Live and learn."

He heard the final shot, but never felt a thing.

CHAPTER FIFTY-THREE

Miguel wiped his fingers clean. He dialed the number while chewing on the last bite of his beignet.

"Yes," Dudko answered.

"Me. The usual place," Miguel's voice commanded. He sipped his coffee.

"Where have you been? Client Five is no longer with us. We have about eight hours until Sharpe is taken care of. Things have changed. Come to the office."

"You no longer give me orders. Meet me in the usual place if you don't want your entire world destroyed." Miguel insisted.

"What is this?"

"Your ruination if you don't cooperate."

"I expected this day would come, Cuban. Going against Federov will bring your demise." Three seconds passed. "I'll meet you. Give me fifteen minutes."

Miguel and Dudko had worked out a code to follow just in case of unauthorized listeners. *'The usual place'* meant the Moonwalk along the River. Miguel tapped the soles of his newly purchased boots on the Moonwalk bricks. He would break them in like a true soldier. He watched the barges floating under the Crescent City

Connection. The Riverboat Natchez was docked just to the right. Its gigantic red paddlewheel was the definitive icon of life on the Mississippi. Miguel barely noticed the frigid air welcoming a new dawn.

The river had always been an afterthought, detached like the scenic view of a mountain. Now he found himself on its banks, watching the brown water flow past his feet and feeling its power coursing by. He likened it to a giant vein pumping life into the land, awesome and humbling.

He held a copy of the audio he had duplicated to a flashdrive, occasionally flipping it in the air, imagining a stupid sitcom event where it flies into the water. He was no longer a mercenary for hire. He felt like a man fighting for his freedom, for his soul, and the life he imagined when he had once been loved.

Dudko arrived a couple of minutes late. He took a position next to Miguel. Except for a couple of beggars and hand-holding lovers, the Moonwalk was empty, but wouldn't be for long. Distant laughter proved that.

"Threats, Miguel?" Dudko pulled the bill of his cap down and nudged his sunglasses. "We lose the building, our candidate, and now you want a mutiny?"

"I want out," Miguel blurted.

"What?" Dudko laughed, "Out? There's no 'out' here."

"You're going to give me the cash in that vault." The river's aroma made it hard for Miguel to breathe, to focus. He blamed it on the constricting cold in his lungs.

Dudko laughed again, "You're looking to extort money from me? Federov told me where to find you the first time."

"I allowed myself to be found."

Dudko crossed his leg and rolled back his pants leg to reveal a holstered gun. Miguel looked into Dudko's eyes then glanced at a covered-up figure standing by a light pole about ten yards away. The woman flashed a large piece.

"Don't even think about it," Miguel said confidently.

"Why would you do this? Why not just disappear if you want out?"

"My retirement fund." Miguel held up the drive. "It's the Fed's Holy Grail. It's a little conversation that gives the cops everything they need. If you don't cooperate, the press gets it and the FBI gets it. They'll close the borders so fast, you'll never get out."

Dudko reached out to take the flashdrive. "How can I trust you?"

"Take the chance." Miguel leaned back. "And if something happens to me, my friend over there is instructed to deliver a copy to the cops along with a little letter I wrote. I get four million and you get my disappearance."

"Cherry Treasure? Really? There will be no place to hide, for either of you. Federov and I will hunt you down." Dudko let his pants leg fall over the gun.

Miguel's head rotated, paranoid. "I'll be in touch with how I want the drop."

"Why not just give me an offshore account number?"

"There are ways to trace those accounts and to put a freeze on them. We do this the old- fashioned way."

Dudko took one last look to the woman who still appeared to be pointing something from within her jacket. He got up and walked away, leaving Miguel with his final words. "You'll never get to spend it."

Miguel motioned for Cherry to hold still until Dudko was out of sight. When he was sure, he waved for her to come over where Miguel took her hands and smiled. The city was definitely beautiful; it was shame he'd never see it again.

CHAPTER FIFTY-FOUR

Dudko's office monitor was tied into the building's security feed. He watched as the six employees that he used as legitimate movers, minus the two dead guards, arrived at the office on St. Charles, detouring around the police barricades on the sidewalk. The building happened to be on one of the most crowded parts of the parade route, but the streets were still fairly clear at this point.

Hard-faced Razor and the five other intense men usually answered to Yaz, but not today as Dudko would call the shots. He paid Razor well to keep this team at the ready. He and the men stayed in the country on legal work-visas, living within four blocks of each other in houses owned by one of Federov's European businesses. Anytime, day or night, they might get a call for a hit, a drug drop, a well-deserved beating, or to even move furniture.

Dudko switched the video to inside the lobby as the men carried thick, canvass bags with them. For this mission, each was promised more money than they had ever been paid to date. He stressed the urgency in this mission and promised horrible retribution if any one of them spoke out about their orders.

Razor led them to the freight elevator, riding to the top floor.

The team streamed through the empty cubicles, gathering just outside Dudko's office. He switched off the monitor.

"Wait here," Razor commanded from just outside their boss' door.

Razor entered the office and nodded at him with a curious gaze, the disheveled man behind the desk. Dudko didn't comment. He proceeded to the vault in the back room. Dudko got up and followed the thick soldier. Razor pulled a piece of paper from his pocket and punched in the key-code for the door. The light turned green and the locking mechanism spun until the door clicked open. With his gun at the ready, Razor called back to his men. "Vlad. Mike."

They appeared instantly. Vladimir threw two gym bags next to the money stacked on the pallet. The two men bent down as Razor watched with his arms folded. They grabbed bundles of money, punching them into one of the bags.

Dudko paced near the wall. "Don't get any ideas yourselves."

Mike smiled with an ignorant expression. "Dead men can't spend money, right?"

Razor passed a look to Dudko and patted at the gun at his side. "I have enough bullets for every one of you."

Vlad and Mike finished stuffing roughly two million into each of their bags at about the same time. Vlad lifted it with one arm. "That's about 50 pounds."

"Out of the vault, both of you." Razor waited for them to leave before presenting the tracking devices to Dudko. He placed one in each bag.

CHAPTER FIFTY-FIVE

The sun rose on a very clear and beautiful Fat Tuesday. According to Miguel's weather app, temperatures were to top out at sixty degrees. After speaking to Barry-Boy, Miguel and Cherry abandoned her apartment for a hotel room that Barry-Boy kept with a standing reservation every year for friends and relatives visiting for Mardi Gras. This year, his parents couldn't make it in from California, so it was empty.

Miguel suffered through a restless nap, fearing that Barry-Boy betrayed him and that Dudko would come crashing through the door at the Place de Armes. Cherry massaged his neck and shoulders, but failed to work out the knots. He thought back to when he was young, invincible, and had nerves of iron. His muscles weren't as impressive as they once were, but he couldn't control the aging process.

Like it or not, he worried about having a permanent home and a payoff that he could retire on. Jumping locations was for the young. He took a deep breath and made the call to Dudko's private line.

"Yes," he answered.

"Do you have it?"

"Yes. Two bags as you requested. I hope you have a means of transport, because you'll be very conspicuous."

"Are you actually worried about me or fishing?" Miguel blew smoke in the air.

"There better not be copies. I will not be blackmailed twice."

"This act may not be honorable, but my word has always been. Honor amongst thieves as you always tell me."

"Federov has the resources to find you no matter where you end up."

"I have resources too, Dudko. My greatest skill is becoming invisible. I'm only going to say this once... take the two bags and..." Miguel continued until he had said all Dudko needed to know.

CHAPTER FIFTY-SIX

I parked down the block from Dylan's impressive home, waited for the neighborhood-watch squad car to pass, and then pressed on to his front gate. The morning sun piercing the tree leaves drew my attention to the immaculate lawn and garden that preceded the entrance. The windows were dark except for his living room. Without Gracie, it felt like an arm was missing, but I was in it alone from here on out.

The gate chilled my forehead as I leaned against it, feeling the weight of my fatigue. I promised myself I'd give him the chance to explain before beating the life out of him. I had about a half hour before the patrol made rounds again. A car passed every now and then, but there was nothing suspicious.

Motion lights flickered to life as I climbed over the gate, but the daylight made them ineffective. I had only been in his house twice, out of obligation, but I remembered being impressed.

Dylan didn't answer the doorbell or my banging, so I scraped past prickly bushes to the partially open rear entrance. A Porsche was parked at a slight angle next another sports car, but still pristine and undamaged. His level of involvement had me perplexed. Was he a boss, a player, or a pawn? At exactly what age did the sex start with Lily? Did it matter? Dudko had something on him. Maybe the only reason I stayed alive all these years was because of Dylan.

The open door triggered an alarm in my head. I drew my gun and entered, crouching, smelling the remnants of a discharged firearm. I took broad leaps to positions of cover, invisible until I came to the den. Dylan's bullet-riddled body lay on the floor like a broken doll. The morning sun created a bright box of light over his torso.

I dropped beside him to feel for a pulse, glancing around the room. By the looks of the couch and floor, he didn't have any blood left in his body. For whatever reason, Dylan messed up his role in Dudko's scheme. My brother led a secret life – one that might've involved my wife's murder.

My eyes filled as I patted him down. Would I find a reason why this ex-professional football player got chained to an international criminal in his pockets? Our childhood and adolescence passed before my eyes. I'd like to think he died trying to be a hero. Somehow, I think I'd be disappointed.

If this could happen to Dylan, then my daughter was still a target. I choked down the feeling of helplessness and stood. *Be a detective*, I thought over all other emotions. My legs gained the strength to move forward, and I checked each room, but they had all been ransacked. The killers did their own search.

When I reached the master bedroom, each drawer from his dresser had been pulled out and dumped. On top of some clothes was an open metal lockbox. It had been pried open. The killer left some pictures sitting out. On closer inspection, I saw it was photos of Lily, a few nude, dating back to when she was about fourteen. One of the more recent was taken outside one of the doors at the Orleans Motel. I quickly put the pictures down before vomiting on the carpet.

I secured the pictures on my person before finishing my inspection. His office safe was already open. There were insurance forms, contracts and other legal documents. Nothing I could use. The rest of the house was clear. Sweat dripped from my face as I got back to the crime scene. It dawned on me that I had absolutely no family left, except Lily.

I whispered, "Dylan, if you weren't already dead… Lord… what were you into?" The laptop playing a torture video caught my attention. I watched the screen until he sliced her face, then I collapsed at his side. Tears streamed down my face as I grabbed him by the shirt and shook his dead body. "How could you?"

With a guttural roar, I threw a right cross at his dead face. The room spun. It was too much, way too much. I buckled on all fours, trying to catch my breath, trying to figure out what to do next. Dylan had been in this up to his eyeballs, and he had paid the price.

Natural light grew stronger through the blinds. I assumed any staff had been given the day off for Mardi Gras, but he would have obligations today. Someone could come looking for him. Barry-Boy was the next piece to this puzzle. Miguel had visited him for a reason and Dylan told me to check him out. I ran to the sink and washed the blood off of my hands and forearms, not caring that I left prints – or vomit for that matter - all over his house.

CHAPTER FIFTY-SEVEN

A quick call to Trout confirmed that everything was quiet at the hospital. A gurney had been brought into the room and Lily was being allowed to sleep, under a doctor's care. I parked outside of Barry-Boy's porn shop, one of the few places Dudko wouldn't expect. The lights were off and the windows caged, but I remembered the side alley entrance to his apartment. With my gun drawn, I edged between the buildings and eased up the stairs. When no one answered, I tapped louder until I heard a voice on the other side.

"I got a shot-gun aimed right at your ass."

"It's Remi. Open up."

"Remi? What are you doin' here?" Barry-Boy opened the door with the shotgun resting on his shoulder. He was freshly showered with wet hair, smelling of Old Spice. He wore boxers and an under-shirt with a cloud of hair poking out the top.

"Going somewhere this morning?" I asked.

"You kiddin' me, right? It's Fat Tuesday."

"I need to talk to you. Let me in."

He reluctantly moved aside. "Sounds important."

I walked into a cramped cliché of a bachelor's pad. Besides the

Saint's memorabilia, the couch and chairs were encased in leather and the coffee table had been built with a few cinderblocks and a door. Instead of looking trendy, it just appeared sad. I saw the spiral staircase that led into his store. "I need some information and I need it straight from you, right now. I have no time for a deal."

Barry-Boy looked up at the round, prison-like clock on the wall and then sat down at his kitchen table. "Shoot."

I took the chair next to him and looked him straight in the eye. "What do you know about Dudko running a forced prostitution ring?

"Victor Dudko? The strip club owner? Sorry, Remi. Can't help you."

I swallowed hard. "You're just a distributor; someone on the outside. You're not important to him and you don't need to protect him. Tell me what you know."

"Remi, what can I say? I know nothing. Wait, is that why you been hanging around the shop?"

I threw my weight onto Barry-boy's leg with the barrel of my gun pointed at his temple. The silence was broken by piss dripping off his chair onto the floor.

"I have you on video paying off Yaz, his right hand man. You still want to lie? My daughter's life is in danger." Spit flew into his face.

He spoke in a short clip. "Best Friend Movers."

"Good start." My knee drove into his thigh as the barrel of my gun dented his temple.

"That's where he keeps the girls when they get moved through," he stressed.

"Not anymore. Who's Yaz?"

"His right-hand man. Manages Booty Call when Dudko's in Baton Rouge."

"Who's the Cuban?"

"Miguel-something. He told me he quit." Barry-Boy's eyes closed as he waited for the shot that never came. "I pissed myself, Remi."

"Common reaction. Don't feel bad." Trout was right about

Barry-Boy caving under torture. "Why would he tell you of all people he quit?"

"He wanted money."

"From you? Why did Miguel defect?"

"They had a falling out. That's all I know."

"You're really testing me." I pulled the gun away from Barry-Boy's head, sliding my weight further into his lap. I grabbed his hand, pushing it to the table and pressed the barrel against his pinky. "Tell me why Miguel was really here. I count to three and you lose the pinky. I count to three again and you lose the index finger. Got me?"

"If I tell you, I'm dead anyway. I'm DEAD."

"One…" I tightened my grip.

"Two…" I was practically sitting on him. His body trembled, but my bluff wasn't working.

"Three." Barry-Boy flinched causing enough pressure on my trigger to fire. Half of his pinky separated while his knee kicked up hitting the table. His finger rolled onto the floor. Blood squirted from his stub like he was a human super-soaker. He jerked from my grasp, but I regained control with my gun in his face.

With my amped-up adrenaline, I grabbed his hand and twisted it, but he fell to the floor, smearing the blood with his knees. Jumping on top of him like an MMA fighter, I managed to grab his hand and pointed the barrel at his index finger. "One–two–"

"Miguel's blackmailing Dudko. I'm helping transfer the money. He's going to give me a cut. It's my ticket outta here."

"Where and when?" I knelt on his neck as he lay on his side, twisting in a clockwise direction.

"In the French Market early this morning. Oh, God. I'm dead for sure."

I used his body to push myself up and walked to the sink to find a towel for him. He gingerly wrapped it around his hand. He was on the verge of crying while my insides were about to come out of my mouth. I just shot the man's pinky off in an interrogation and his bleeding seemed out of control. Panting like a dog, I turned on one of his electric burners full blast.

"What are you doing?" He asked with sweat dripping. "More torture?"

"We have to stop the bleeding with this metal coil." I found a nice, big wooden spoon.

"Ah, crap."

"Bite down on this." I put the spoon in his mouth and then picked him up by his armpits. "We have to do it or you'll bleed to death or at the very least, be too woozy to go collect your money.

He stared at me in disbelief, but resigned himself. "*Laissez les bons temps rouler*," he managed with the spoon in his mouth.

"Now, stand flat-footed and prepare yourself."

"Wait. Wait." He shuffled to the other side of his kitchen and pulled out a sealed container that looked like flour. He dumped a load onto the counter and then stuck his stub into it and rolled it around as if he was breading shrimp for the deep fryer.

"Enough with that already, Jesus." I pulled his wrist over the burner and counted to three slow and deliberately. Then, I forced his pinky stub on the glowing metal. There was a sizzle and a sweet, but nauseating smell of flesh and blood burning. Barry-boy wailed and stomped his feet, but didn't pull away. He took it like a tough guy. I felt as if I was doing human soldering.

Satisfied, I pulled his arm away from the burner as tears ran down his face. He stumbled to the kitchen chair and put his face in the bend of his arm, holding his injured hand upright. The bleeding had stopped. "The room is spinning," He mumbled into his arm, then looked at me with a sad, pale face.

"You should have just come clean when I first asked." I sat back down to Barry-Boy's relief. "The deal's going to happen as planned. My daughter's safety is my top priority here. I don't care what you do with the money. I want Miguel, Yaz, and Dudko. You can run naked through the street, for all I care. Do you get what I'm saying?"

He looked into my blood-shot, yet intense eyes. "You're saying to go along with the pick-up, take all of the money."

"All the money you can carry. Now, where are you meeting Miguel?"

"He won't tell me the specific place in the Market until he contacts me." He inspected his raw pinky stub.

"All right. You have pain pills for that?" I pointed.

"I got Hydrocodone." He carefully made his way to a drawer in his kitchen.

"Good, take two only. You're going to tell me the entire plan up to what you don't know. You're going to lead me to the pick up and you can keep the money. Can your nine and a half fingers live with that?"

CHAPTER FIFTY-EIGHT

The cold permeated every part of the bed on which Miguel slept. Cherry had opened the hotel room window fifteen minutes earlier, forcing Miguel into the fetal position under the comforter. It didn't relieve his goose bumps.

"Damn, girl. Can you get it any colder in here?"

Her nipples poked against her *Coon Ass For Life* shirt. "You told me you wanted to get an hour or so."

"The least you could have done was got in bed to keep me warm."

"I'm too nervous."

Miguel sat up on the edge of the cheap, antique-looking bed staring at the phrase on her shirt. "What is a Coon Ass, anyway?"

"Just like a Cajun or bayou born. New Orleans red neck."

"You people find pride in anything."

She crossed her arms "We have to."

"Close the damn window." Miguel thought for a moment. "Don't be nervous. The plan could fail. Money or no, you and I will always be."

"I just want you and I to get out of this city as millionaires. I don't care if we have to run for the rest of our lives. That's quite romantic, actually." Cherry giggled.

"You like money. Is that why you got with me? Because I gave you big tips?"

"Partly. Partly 'cause you were always nice to me."

Miguel shuffled to the bathroom, leaving the door open while he pissed. He scratched his belly and let out a fart, and Cherry pretended to be disgusted.

"You got some kind of snack in your purse?" Miguel asked.

"I was hoping you'd take me to Camilia Grill." She cast her gaze around the room as if to emphasize its sparseness. There was nothing to eat.

"We can't go out in public. Dudko has people everywhere. It's too risky. Go down and get us something from the continental breakfast to go."

"Fine. This will be the last breakfast I retrieve." *Good-bye city that care forgot*, she thought to herself.

CHAPTER FIFTY-NINE

Dudko ruminated at his desk in his plush corner office on the top floor as dawn came and went. He had taken a shower and dressed in spare clothes he kept in his office for emergencies. He managed to nap, but his office sofa wasn't that comfortable.

Two Nike bags containing the money and GPS chips were on the floor by his desk. He would get the cash back, but for now he had to prove his intentions to Miguel so that his men could get close enough to kill him. But all Dudko knew of the plan was that the money had to be dropped off in an empty box on the side of a purse stand in the French Market. After that, it was up to Yaz and his men to kill Miguel and whoever might be helping him.

Yaz entered Dudko's office and sat down in his spacious, suede chair facing the desk. He was sweating and sucking air.

"Take the stairs?" Dudko said, amused.

"Had to walk through the crowd. Give me a break. I should have just double-parked and let them tow it."

Dudko took a serious tone. "Is everything set?"

"Yeah. I drop off the money and get lost in the French Market. One of our men will take out Miguel when he picks up the bags."

"Yes, but it's not that simple. Miguel must be figuring that's *our* plan. There could be someone we don't know about. Hell, expect a drone to come down from the sky – anything. He's not just going to walk up and get the money. There's a plan in place that he believes will work."

"Maybe."

"Maybe?"

"He's operating on the assumption that if anything happens to him, that recording goes public. He might just think he can walk up and take the money."

Dudko nodded. "I trust you are loyal to Federov, but I have to protect my interests. I'm going to have you followed by Vlad. He has orders to take care of you if you detour from the plan."

He threw his foot onto his knee. "No offense taken."

"Now, getting back to Miguel. Who would he have working with him that he could trust?"

"That stripper girlfriend of his."

"Amateur. She'll just make it easier for us to find him. Could Barry-Boy be involved?"

"He sucks from the most powerful teat, which is yours. He doesn't have the balls."

Dudko had to agree. "Miguel might have some means of transport that we don't expect. Just be on the lookout for something funny."

Yaz nodded. "Funny – got it."

"Okay, get going. You got 45 minutes to get there and about another mile to walk."

Yaz hoisted the bags with a huff, and then swung each one over an opposite shoulder. He wiped the sweat off his forehead and headed out of the office. Dudko leaned back and closed his burning eyes. Years of building his empire came down to this day. His quest to be a mob boss would have to be put on hold.

CHAPTER SIXTY

Yaz didn't acknowledge Razor and the men as they waited for Dudko's orders to disperse. Once in the elevator alone, Yaz opened one of the bulky bags and suppressed a grin, quickly shutting his mouth. The elevator had cameras.

It was the most money he ever had in his possession. With his back to the elevator camera, he closed his eyes, imagining the perfectly stacked bills in his hands, smelling the good life and he even allowed himself a pre-victory dance in his head. Yaz had never entertained the thought of stealing money, but figured Miguel's plan, whether a success or not, would shine a harsh light on Dudko in Federov's eyes. This was Yaz's opportunity to prove his worth.

Once outside the front door, he spotted Vlad in the crowd just twenty feet away. Sure enough, he was being tailed, and despite his limited mental capacity, he knew Vlad to be a very good shot. Yaz nodded to his associate and put on his glittered, flowery mask for the journey.

The bags of money weighed down Yaz's accommodating shoulders, especially since he had to dodge tourists every few feet. He imagined gunning down a path, but then he'd have to exert more energy by stepping over them. He shifted the dead weight several times, but had to relieve the aching joints every five or ten minutes. Damn Miguel for making him carry it alone. At least it was chilly and he wouldn't sweat too much.

He could take Vlad out with a single shot, but that would cause a scene. Or approach Vlad to tell him Dudko had a change of plan and he was to go somewhere else, but what if that failed? Federov couldn't know Yaz sabotaged the plan. Somehow, when the time was right, he would make his move. He reminded himself to be patient.

A man pulling an ice chest in a Radio Flyer wagon walked by and Yaz stepped in front of him. "I'll give you one hundred dollars for that wagon."

The man stopped cold. "Serious? This is my boy's wagon. Plus, how am I going to carry all this shit?"

Yaz pulled two bills from his wallet. "Two hundred. Fresh and crisp."

The enthusiastic man pulled the ice chest off of the wagon with a huff and set it on the sidewalk. "All yours."

"Thank you." Yaz loaded the bags onto the wagon and swore to himself that'd he'd toast Miguel with a beer once he was in charge of the New Orleans operation.

Yaz's burning feet eventually reached the inviting archway of the French Market. The clothing, jewelry and trinket vendors set up their shops, cramming all the merchandise they could into tiny spaces, sure to have a huge sales day. Yaz skirted the outside of the Market with his wagon in tow, fearing a surprise attack within a pack of people. When he approached the designated purse stand, he searched for Vlad or the other men. Either they weren't there, or they were very good at hiding.

He dropped the bags in the only empty box between the purse table and the street, abandoned the wagon, and attempted to disappear into the Market. He caught a glimpse of Vlad with his own mask wandering nearby. People paid the large box no mind, looking to belong to one of the vendors. Yaz wished he could see Dudko's face when he realized that the tracking chips in the bags had been removed. Miguel would be killed, Yaz would get the money and the business, and Dudko would be exiled by Federov. Today would be a good day.

CHAPTER SIXTY-ONE

I had a different view of Mardi Gras as a cop from when I enjoyed it as a civilian. Granted, some policemen were douche-bags to anyone who didn't give them a *yes sir*, or *no ma'am*. And then some cops loved to dance in the streets with the marching bands. For myself, I liked to believe people made mistakes while having fun, and I could offer them a second chance at not going to lock-up.

Some locals didn't enjoy Mardi Gras as much as others, but the diehards prepared beyond expectation. Every year, they packed food and alcohol, tables, lawn chairs, blankets and ladders and start as early as 5 a.m. to stake out their territory on the parade route, if not the night before. Once the plot of land was inhabited, breakfast was served: usually donuts or king cake. Soon after, the first drink was consumed and the party started. Once set up on the parade route, there was always lots of time for football, frisbee, people watching or just walking the streets.

Zulu was the first Uptown parade, starting at 10 a.m. Depending on where one stood, it might be hours before the parade passed, but waiting was foreplay. The parades eventually made it into the CBD, where grandstands had been constructed for viewing. Driving nearby was ill advised, unless one liked deadlock and dead ends. The city became a ghost town, except for the parade routes. Every cop was on the job to keep order. Anything that happened in the chaos would have to be sorted out after midnight.

I'd shot off his pinky like a mobster, still in disbelief. In my line of work, pressure needed to be applied to get answers or better yet, a confession, but that had been blatant torture. The general public might not agree with such practices, but a murderer or rapist won't confess because someone brought them a Happy Meal, Coke and a pretty-please. Barry-Boy wasn't about to file a complaint.

He came out of the front entrance of his porn store with his bandaged hand raised to his chest. I trailed him on foot while holding an empty can of Budweiser, wearing a feathered mask over my eyes and a jester hat on my head. The streets in this part of the Quarter only had a few people out at this time of the morning. They were either on the parade routes already or didn't want to start drinking until lunch. Every now and then, Barry-Boy took a peek back.

When we finally reached the French Market, Barry-Boy stopped at one of the fruit stands and stole an apple from a vendor who had his back turned. He winced every time he moved his bum hand. His journey started at the far end of the Market where the fruits and vegetables were stacked high in boxes, but he had a ways to go. He walked across the Market's width to the one-way street that ran next to the river. He looked to his right, nodded at something in the distance, then walked toward a purse stand.

From between boxes of stacked fruits and vegetables I could see a sliver of Barry-Boy walking toward a large box. There was not a uniformed cop in sight. He progressed as if paranoid, his eyes darting. There would be virtually no traffic directly inside the Quarter, except for a cop or government official with special permissions, but this was the corner edge of the Quarter where cars were free to travel just a block over. If you moved a barricade, you could get in for a short distance before being caught.

An older model light blue Ford truck crept along behind Barry-Boy about thirty yards away. Several people were loosely scattered about the street, however it inched toward Barry-Boy, like a cougar anticipating the attack of a gazelle. He stopped near the box, bent over to wipe something from his shoe, but that was just for show.

The truck veered directed at him. Panic surged in my chest. *It was a double-cross.*

Barry-Boy sprung up with a fat man's reflexes and threw his good hand into the box, heaving out a bag with an exaggerated jerk. A woman with a hat and glasses driving the light blue Ford stopped on the side of him. With a huff, he spun close to 360 degrees as he threw the bag into the bed of the truck, and then repeated his action with a second bag.

I closed the distance on the truck while scanning the sparse crowd. Three men converged toward the same spot. Barry-Boy attempted to climb into the bed of the truck, but his bum hand slowed him down. One of the men was close, but the truck peeled off. Barry-Boy fell to the ground, rolling along with the other man. His mask slipped, and he thrust it back into place as fast as he could. I had seen the distinctive features. It was Yaz.

The truck's horn blew as it narrowly missing pedestrians that dove onto the sidewalks. The two other men were running behind the truck, firing guns. The truck's back window shattered. The early-bird shoppers parted in terror. People bumped into each other, some of them yelping, as there was nowhere immediate to run. The French Market patrons looked like the men running away from charging bulls in Pamplona. The truck smashed a barricade, sending it flying into a tree. It disappeared, along with the two men that had been chasing it on foot.

Yaz appeared confused in the street; the real transaction had been completed. Barry-Boy was supposed to lead me to a motor-cycle he had stashed, but his real plan had been to escape in the bed of the truck. Being preoccupied with the distant shootings, no one had spotted me. I sprinted toward Barry-Boy as he hobbled toward Esplanade Avenue.

"What the fuck is he doing?" I mumbled, throwing my legs into full gear.

However, Yaz surprised me by grabbing Barry-Boy first. "You're involved in this, you little fuck?"

"Yaz?" he squealed. Then the masked Russian saw me slow to a jog.

"Doucet. I should have known." Yaz ignored me and hit Barry-Boy in his face, letting him fall to the sidewalk. "You signed your death certificate."

Barry-Boy laid on his back cradling his bandaged hand. "Remi! He's going to kill me."

Yaz reached under his sweatshirt as I rushed him, ramming my knee into his solar plexus and pushing him down on the road. He rolled to his knees and I could hear him wheezing.

"What the fuck are you trying to pull?" I yelled at Barry-Boy while kicking Yaz's firearm out of reach. Yaz stayed on his side, sucking air.

"I led you to the drop off. Here's Yaz, one of the guys you want."

I grabbed Barry-Boy. "Is there even a motorcycle?" I let go with one hand and drew my gun on Yaz as he tried to get to his feet. "Don't move, asshole. I'd like nothing better than to put a bullet through your pretty face."

A few brave pedestrians on our side of the Market were glued to our little drama. Yaz ignored me and stood up anyway. "Calm down, Doucet. I'm not goin' anywhere."

"Stay where you are Yaz," I commanded. "You're right, Barry-Boy. This is better than following that truck."

Yaz smiled under his mask. "I'm better than the four million getting away?"

A small crowd and various venders watched behind tables and beams. I didn't want to take the chance of being recognized, but it was now or never. I placed the end of the barrel on Yaz's mask.

"Where is Dudko? I have no problem shooting you."

Barry-Boy held up his hand. "He will."

"You won't shoot me because you are an officer of the law. There are people everywhere. Do you really want to end up in prison when you just got your whore of a daughter back. She was fucking your brother. Did you know that?"

He was baiting me, but it still made me furious. Barry-Boy looked to have lost his balance and eased onto his butt. I focused on Yaz. "One last time, tell me where he is, or I blow your face off."

Yaz smiled and scratched his ear, almost causing me to squeeze the trigger.

"Don't flinch, Remi."

I lowered my gun and shot him in his foot. Screams erupted in the crowd. Spectator's heads disappeared again. Yaz raised his leg in agony, then fell. I expected a slue of cops to surround us, but not one appeared.

"You son-of-a-bitch," He howled from a sitting position.

I stepped up to Yaz and placed the hot barrel an inch from his nostrils. "Your nose is next."

"You wouldn't." Yaz pulled his head away and attempted to stand. He swung his arm up at the gun, but missed by several inches.

I fired.

An echo rang through the Market. The remaining stupid onlookers with their cells held high disappeared like roaches. Yaz's mask had a small entry hole as he lay still on the sidewalk in a red and gray mess sprayed across the sidewalk.

I still felt the reverberation against my palm. "One down."

Barry-Boy tooled down the street with an odd run, holding his hand against his chest. I had no other choice but to give chase. Within moments, I was on Esplanade where Barry-boy attempted to climb on a Suzuki motorcycle. The truck was probably supposed to drop him off here. How he planned on driving with one hand, I didn't know. I threw him to the ground and climbed on the bike.

"Where is Miguel?" I asked, pointing my gun at him. I fired between his legs.

"That was his girl, Cherry, in the truck. She's going to the bridge and I was supposed to follow on the bike to help her get the money to Miguel. That's all I know."

I burned rubber towards the Crescent City Connection. Mardi Gras traffic would slow her down. If I knew my traffic reports, the bridge would be at a standstill, and this motorcycle slid between cars easily.

CHAPTER SIXTY-TWO

Cherry had pinched several red marks into her thigh to stay focused. From an aerial view she had seen on the news, Mardi Gras can appear as mass confusion. The interstate that ran through the heart of the city looked like a knotted shoestring of traffic. A clogged mass led to the Crescent City Connection over the Mississippi causing Cherry to creep along at about five miles per hour, looking in the rear view mirror every couple of seconds. They had Barry-Boy. She was on her own. It set her imagination ablaze that four million dollars was in the bed behind her.

As the traffic inched forward, Cherry crossed over St. Charles Avenue where thousands of people were waiting for the floats. The exit for St. Charles had been sufficiently barricaded to deny traffic on the route. She blasted Mardi Gras songs on the radio as she waited fifteen minutes to finally make it onto the bridge. Miguel had given her instructions to stay in the right lane and drive to the peak of the CCC, then to turn on the hazards and call him on his cell phone when parked.

She was near faint at the thought of a mistake, much like the very first time she stripped. Miguel had never struck her, but his rough exterior and past violence frightened her, as well as turned her on. She had been involved with guys like that before, ones that just snapped when things didn't go right. Luck and slutty good looks had always been on her side. Now she had to use her brains. Could Miguel be using her until the money was in his hands, only to cast her aside like so many other had? Should she have thought of a plan B?

Cherry reached the top of the bridge, despite the bumper to bumper. She estimated to be hundreds of feet above the Mississippi when she put the Ford in park, much to the dismay of those behind her. The truck was still now, hazards flashing, the gap in front growing wide. She dialed while waving her hand out the window for the aggravated motorists to pass.

"Miguel, it's me. I'm on the bridge. Are you down there?"

"I'm directly under you, love."

"Barry-Boy isn't with me. He got caught by men that were waiting for us. What now?"

"That's okay, Cherry. He was expendable insurance. You can do this. We talked about what to do if something happened to Barry-Boy. It's plan B time."

"Plan B? I don't know."

"It will be dangerous, but it's the only way now. You're strong enough. Just hurry up." Miguel hung up.

Cherry took a deep breath as if meditating and jumped in the rusting bed. She took one of the two thick ropes that had been neatly rolled to avoid entanglement. Both ends of the rope had been secured to lock-clamps big enough to fit around the top portion of the bridge's metal railing. Cherry had to hook each bag to one of the clamps. Each bag had its own rope.

Honey, Miguel had said, *I've seen you do things on a pole that most gymnasts can't do. If you can't climb down that rope, well, I guess I just have to spend all this money myself.* Miguel had smiled and slapped her ass in confidence.

The people stuck behind her honked as they merged into the left lane. All she needed was for one chivalrous drunk to get out of their car to help or a maniac to smash her windshield with a tire iron.

Luckily, on this day, no one wanted to waste any time, even it was an attractive damsel in distress.

She had asked why not just get away in a car on land, but Miguel said the mobsters would be expecting that. He said they had to do the unexpected. None of Dudko's men or corrupt cops would have access to the river. From the drop-off point, they would be able to tie up at any dock, north or south, for an easy escape.

Cherry yelled out and waved her apologies to the passing cars as she clamped the rope to the first bag's straps. In the distance, she heard the odd sound of a lawn mower. Barry-Boy? She glanced up to see a fast-moving object weaving in and out of traffic. It was no lawn mower - it was a motorcycle – and that wasn't Barry-Boy. For no other reason other than instinct, she quickened her pace. That same stink of failure rose in her nostrils. This was just another one of God's jokes, teasing her with a carrot at the end of a stick.

No, the cycle of doomed dreams would break here. Cherry soldiered on, sliding the bag straps through the clamp and its hinge snapped closed. From there, she dumped it over the truck bed and onto the road where the long rope followed behind it like a snake. She grabbed the other end of the rope, jumped from the truck and clamped it to the side railing; a perfect fit. Then she dragged the bag over the walkway where, looking down, she saw Miguel in his boat staring back at her as it fought the current.

The motorcycle roared louder, almost upon her.

She lifted the money-filled bag past her waistline, struggling with all of her might to push the bag over the railing until it fell of its own accord. It weighed about fifty pounds as Miguel had said. Her boyfriend had calculated the length of the rope with the height of the bridge and the level of the river on this particular day. He was so smart. She rushed back to the truck and repeated the entire routine with the second bag. Behind her, the man skidded to a halt, jumping off the bike into a full run toward Cherry as the second bag began its decent. *Yes*! She straddled the railing and peered down to Miguel, who had positioned his boat in front of the first bag. Then, she felt hands on her body.

CHAPTER SIXTY-THREE

I felt lucky to have caught up with the truck. The girl had thrown the bags of money over the bridge and appeared to want to jump to her death. The rope continued whipping against the railing as she clambered over. I lunged and pulled her off the railing onto the ground. In that same second, I caught a stationary portion of the rope, just before it snapped upwards to follow the path down to the river. The velocity pulled me forward and I instantly let it go before the rope skinned my palms. When I saw the clamp on the other end, I understood.

Directly below, a boat kept position in front of the second bag of money. The first bag had already been cut off. The man I suspected to be Miguel masterfully steered with one hand against the current while cutting the second taut rope with an extraordinarily sharp knife, allowing the bag of money to fall in the passenger seat at his side.

Miguel yelled something I couldn't hear.

I fired a couple of shots, but at best, I might've killed a fish. Suddenly, I felt a blow to my back. The girl struck me with surprising strength.

"I need to get down there. Move out of the way," she insisted.

I pushed her to the narrow walkway, where she flopped with her hands over her face. Looking at the rope dangling over Miguel's boat, I decided to climb over the railing myself. Miguel was waiting to see if the woman would descend. Or maybe he knew it would be me.

The woman stared with disbelief as I hung on the outside railing, appearing to want to follow me down on the other rope. However, the two lines were so close, if she fell, she could take me down with her. With my legs and arms wrapped around the rope, I let my grip loosen and started a faster descent. Halfway down, pops rang out from below and a quick decision needed to be made. I let go and began a free-fall, curling into a ball about fifty feet above the water. I landed with a shocking smack into the river.

My layered shirts and jacket took the brunt of the impact. My skin stung like a giant jellyfish got a hold of me. I opened my eyes to see which way the bubbles were rising and turned toward the brightening surface. Upon reaching the frigid air, Miguel was only ten yards away, coaxing the woman to slide down the rope, but she hadn't left the safety of the rail.

I caught hold of the boat near the motor, but Miguel didn't seem worried. Within minutes, the water would render my muscles useless. "Where's Dudko?"

His gun was trained on my forehead. "Is that all you want?"

I didn't attempt to climb on board. "That's all I want."

He leaned to me with his forearm on his bent knee like we were buddies. "He's probably at the grandstands on St. Charles to watch his sniper take out Sharpe – from the roof of the Emerson building if you're interested."

The water smacked up at my face. "Take me to shore."

He howled with laughter, then put his foot on my shoulder to push me off. "For a smart detective, you're not using your head. He won't stop until you and your daughter are dead. And he can make that order from any country in the world."

Miguel's eyes flashed up to the woman one last time before pushing the boat to full throttle, leaving me in it's wake. My skin burned and my muscles stiffened while swimming toward the shore.

As my clothes started to pull me under, a loud buzzing registered above me. I rolled onto my back to see a blue and red news helicopter hovering. I was being filmed.

I waved my hands for them to get closer. At twenty feet, the co-pilot opened the side door and released a ladder that rolled down to touch the water. I latched on with a thumbs up. The bird rose slowly as I climbed a few rungs, letting water drain from my clothes.

Hanging about thirty feet under the bird, I stuck out my badge and pointed it at Miguel's boat. The pilot stuck his head out his window to get a look at me. I recognized this guy from the traffic reports. He used to be a combat pilot in the Gulf War and I'm sure he retro-fitted the ladder in the news chopper because he imagined a scenario like this one. Although he couldn't hear, I yelled, "Get me to that boat, now!" My serious expression and jerky arm thrusting forward got my point across.

CHAPTER SIXTY-FOUR

oments earlier…

M "Where is Yaz?" Dudko questioned over the phone.

"Yaz is… No longer with us," Razor answered, "The cops have the Market surrounded on horseback and with squad cars. The packages are gone. They got away."

Dudko shouted, "You idiot. What happened?"

"Barry-Boy was in on it. He threw the bags into a truck that was driven by Cherry and Yaz tried to jump in the back, but couldn't. We put some holes in the truck, but it got away."

"It seems my tracking chips are stationary right at your location. Who killed Yaz?"

"Doucet shot him in the face, then took off after Barry-Boy."

Dudko rolled his eyes. "What happened to the car we had planted? Why aren't you following that truck?"

"All the tires were slashed."

"Slashed?"

"All four. We think Miguel knew about it." Razor's voice lost strength. "We couldn't do anything."

"Why didn't you tell me about this earlier?"

"There wasn't time. I was trying to find another vehicle to break into."

"Find Barry-Boy and see what he knows. Kill him, then call me immediately."

"There's a shitload of cops here and they're not letting anyone leave. They're questioning everyone."

"Which way did she head?"

"Up Esplanade."

"Don't say anything. I'll handle it."

He hung up and rubbed his bloodshot eyes. *Up Esplanade.* Could she be circling around to cross the Crescent City Connection? Miguel used to brag about boating and docking at little ports up river. That bitch is going to dump the bags into the river from the bridge. Did he trust Miguel to honor his end of the deal?

He picked up his cell phone and dialed. "It's me. Get that helicopter here, now. I'll be waiting on the roof."

CHAPTER SIXTY-FIVE

The Army vet looked to the boat, then back down at me. His eyes either asked if I was sure, or if I was crazy. I threw my index at the boat with force. The ice-cold air cut through me. He winked at me with a laugh I couldn't hear, then turned to his co-pilot. We tilted forward toward the target. In just seconds my feet were dangling about twenty feet above the Cuban.

Tiny shots echoed in the distance. Someone other than Miguel had fired at us. I glanced down to see him still driving the boat. In a sudden maneuver, the helicopter dipped, then circled around to allow me to see a second bird closing in. More shots whizzed by.

Dudko had his own helicopter.

My body flailed on the ladder as we turned sideways, climbing and dropping. The courageous pilot had me practically skimming the water, catching up to Miguel, knowing my intention was to be dropped into his boat. The next shot hit the helicopter's tail. That was enough danger for the pilot as I felt myself rising. I let go of the ladder, landing on the rear seat of the boat, nearly breaking my back.

While continuing to steer, Miguel tried to get a bead on me as my body regained feeling, but he couldn't stop or Dudko would have him dead to rights. He kept me off balance by cutting right, then left, and he succeeded. I smashed against the insides of the boat while gunshots rang out in the air.

"Miguel," I yelled in a guttural voice that forced him to turn his head. "Straighten up, and I'll take out Dudko." His back faced me as if considering it. The boat took a hard right as the helicopter almost touched.

"How can I trust you?" He yelled.

"Lily said you were nice to her. You're not the one I want to kill."

The boat settled on a fixed path. I propped myself up onto the seat, feeling like I had been in an industrial-sized washing machine. My shaking hands retrieved the gun from my ankle holster. Dudko's pilot nosed the helicopter up to the boat's rear. It veered to the right, exposing the bird's open door on the left side. Dudko was hiding in the cabin, but a large man aimed his weapon at me while hanging out the side. More shots came.

"Do something, Doucet," Miguel commanded, as river water sprayed his face.

I flung my arm over the side of the boat and fired, but aiming was futile. With one deft maneuver, the pilot crossed over the top of the boat, crushing Miguel against the boat's console with its landing skids. It snagged the windshield, cracking it, and at that point, the helicopter needed to recover. Miguel crumpled with a bloody, concave chest, and the boat immediately circled as the current pulled us.

I believed my Glock to have one more bullet. I had to save it. My head popped up to see the pilot making his way around. However, the boat would eventually circle itself into a barge in the distance. I tripped on a red jug of gasoline while diving for the shifter, pushing it to full. As I regained control of the craft, Dudko's helicopter pulled on my side.

Lily might know how many knots I was traveling, but I'd have to guess about forty miles per hour. That news helicopter followed our movements from a safe distance. I swerved around the barge, leaving Dudko to catch up from the other side. When they pulled close, just about ten feet away, I saw Dudko had replaced the gunman, aiming his weapon directly at me. I let go of the wheel, snagged the five-gallon container of gas and tossed it straight up at the propellers with every ounce of strength. Dudko looked up in time to see the entire front of the bird catch fire. When he turned to me, I already had my gun aimed. My bullet hit him right in the chest.

I watched as the propellers chopped into the water first, whipping the tail in after, stopping its momentum cold. But, something was wrong. The gasoline had sprayed into the boat and set it ablaze, also. With the boat beginning to circle again, I jumped in the Mississippi.

Thankful to be out of the burning death craft, I waded. Just fifty feet away, I watched Dudko slowly sink below the surface. As the fiery boat circled toward me, another helicopter descended. This time, it was the unmistakable orange markings of the Coast Guard.

I squinted as the water rippled around me. A Coast Guard member was lowered from a rope, strapped in tight to a harness. He entered the water next to me, asking me if I was okay. Without much chatter, he wrapped a buoyant strap around my back and under my arms. Immediately after, we ascended, attached to one another.

CHAPTER SIXTY-SIX

"You have to get us to the Emerson building now," I yelled, just as our feet planted solid on the cabin floor.

The male pilot and female co-pilot glanced back at us as a young, clean-cut guardsman unhooked me from his harness, then helped me to a seat. They were all dressed in matching orange jumpsuits. He grabbed a blanket and threw it around my back. "I think we should get you medical attention first."

He paid me no mind as he stowed his rescue equipment. I clutched his sleeve and screamed so he could hear me through his helmet. "Lieutenant, there's a sniper on the roof of the Emerson building and he's going to kill the governor."

His eyes snapped to me. "I know you. You're that detective."

I nudged forward. "You'll have to go through ten people before they can contact the closest policemen. Tell your pilot to do a fly-by. We can at least see if he's there."

"There's protocol…"

My voice grew hoarse. "You know who I am. You know I'm not a nut. You want Steve Sharpe's blood on your hands?"

He considered it a moment. His hand cupped the mouthpiece

of his headset and looked to his pilot. "Johnny, I need you to buzz the rooftop of the Emerson building on St. Charles."

The pilot's mouth moved, but it was impossible to hear. However, I heard my rescuer speaking to him just fine. "Possible sniper attack on the governor. Yeah, I know. There's no time. Tell Emily to call 9-1-1."

The bird tilted dramatically. My stomach dropped as the chopper rose, cruising parallel to the parade route, which was thankfully very close to our location. The guardsman secured an M16 rifle, sat next to me, then lock and loaded a magazine.

"There's Rex! His float is a few blocks away." I shivered under the blanket as the parades were in full swing. Crowds were lining the route, catching beads, doubloons, cups and other throws. Between the floats, marching bands danced and dipped to horns and drums we couldn't hear.

He opened the cabin door, creating a vortex of frigid wind. He pressed binoculars to his eyes. The pilot's flight plan took us directly over the building, high enough not be a concern. Slowly, we descended so that we could see clearly with the naked eye.

"There's someone on that roof. Take us close, Johnny." The guardsman took a prone position with his M16 snuggled to his cheek.

The crowd glanced up as we hovered way closer than any helicopter should, just above the roofs of the St. Charles businesses and power lines. We were on the other side of the street; the open side of the cabin facing the front of the Emerson building, a five story, industrial looking structure. Trash and debris blew in the windstorm. The parade halted, waiting to see what we would do.

The man on the roof had noticed our approach and packed up his gear in retreat. I thought he would get away, but then a stream of uniformed police officers shot out of the roof entrance, weapons aimed. The assassin put his bag down and raised his hands.

I patted the guardsman on his shoulder. For the first time, a wave of relief filled my body. "Can you land this baby on the helipad of Tulane Medical?"

He glanced at me and smiled. "There's protocol…"

EPILOGUE

My eyes searched Gracie's hospital room until I found my stepdaughter sitting on a gurney. She leapt off and we embraced like we never had before. She pressed her face into my neck with tears in her eyes. Trout was on the other side of Gracie's bed.

"We heard." Trout smiled. "Good going. I want to hear the whole thing."

"So does every law enforcement agency in the state, including Joiner and Foster. Let me tell you, it's a hell of a tale. But, the Feds are waiting for me so they can find the rest of the players and wrap up their investigation. I can't stay long."

"Finally, that cancer is out of our lives." Gracie reached out with her hand. Her color had returned and her eyes were alert.

With my arm around my daughter's waist, I entwined my fingers with Gracie's. "You think it's over?"

"Federov?" Gracie asked.

I shrugged. "I'll see what Foster and Joiner have to say." I took Lily's pinky in mine and led her out the room. "We need to talk."

Once in the hallway without anyone around, I looked at my

stepdaughter and stroked her hair. "I'm so sorry about your mother."

"They killed her because they thought she was me... with Dylan." She broke down crying. "I'm so sorry, Remi."

"It's okay, sweetie. Dylan was a good-looking, rich celebrity. You were thirteen. He manipulated you. How about going out with boys your own age from now on?"

"You don't have to worry about me dating for a long time."

I held her tight. "You are my daughter, you know that?"

Her head nodded while pressed against my chest.

"Hey, did I ever tell you how your mom and I met?"

"Yes." She sniffed and wiped her eyes. "Tell me again."

ACKNOWLEDGMENTS

This book has been on and off the shelf more than any I've written. It's been edited to where it doesn't look anything like its original draft, so much so, I've had my doubts about putting it out there. But, I owe it to the story.

I'd like to thank Detective Bruce Brueggeman for answering my random questions, Alicia Franklin for her enthusiastic reading, and Addie Dean for being an inspiring cheerleader. I'd also like to thank the Internet for helping with endless research.

Andy Fitz – It's about time.

And thank you New Orleans.

ABOUT THE AUTHOR

E.J. Findorff was born and raised in New Orleans, but currently lives in Chicago. He graduated from the University of New Orleans and served six years in the Louisiana National Guard. He is a member of the International Thriller Writers Association.

Website – www.ejfindorff.com
   Twitter - @ej_findorff

ALSO BY E.J. FINDORFF

UNHINGED

KINGS OF DELUSION

WHERE THE DEVIL WON'T GO

A FRENCH QUARTER VIOLET

ONE HUNDRED BULLETS

Lightning Source UK Ltd.
Milton Keynes UK
UKHW022216051120
372880UK00003B/309